PIECE OF FAE

HARET CHRONICLES QILIN: BOOK FOUR

LAUREL CHASE

Cover design by

Christian Bentulan

ISBN: 9781090823465

DEDICATION

This series is for all the girls who like sex and sugar.

So, that's everyone, right?

Carry on.

CHAPTER ONE

CARLYLE

Time was impossible to measure in the silver-walled cage the Council had trapped me in. Every breath felt like it dragged on for an hour. I'd tried counting the seconds, but that excitement wore off at a few thousand.

Just as my stomach had given up rumbling for any kind of meal and I'd begun to yawn more than chew my fingernails, the lights above me dimmed to a bare minimum.

"Fucking nighttime, I guess," I grumbled, stretching out on my bed.

Sure, I was tired, but I couldn't calm down enough to actually sleep. The Ringmaster had given me the barest glance of my guys when he'd opened the window, but since I couldn't feel my magic, I couldn't feel any of my mating bonds, either.

I was beyond worried that something would happen to one of them, and I wouldn't even know.

I tossed on the bed, smacking my fists against the cool sheets. It wasn't uncomfortable here - in fact, it was a nicer bed than I'd had many nights in my life. It was the fact that I was trapped that was keeping my nerves on edge. Anyone would hate this, but my Qilin nature made it a thousand times worse.

At some point, I must have drifted off, though, because when I woke, everything was different.

The room was black - or maybe it was my eyes. My lashes struggled to open, crushing against something covering my face. I tried to move my hands to claw it away, but they were bound to my sides. I felt thick straps at my wrists and ankles. Even my hips were locked down with something.

I opened my mouth to scream, but soft lips covered them, pressing my lips against my teeth.

A tongue dipped in my mouth, tasting, and a moan rumbled against my lips.

"Donna struggle," a voice said. My brain pinged the voice as familiar but somehow wrong. "Be still, Qilin, and I'll remove your mask."

My breath was coming too fast, and I knew I was moments away from full panic. I forced myself to be still, locking my muscles down one by one. I needed this mask off, and more.

Strong fingers pushed the black fabric up to my forehead, and my pupils constricted painfully at the sudden light. As I blinked my eyes into focus, I saw a handsome redhead staring down at me.

He looked like Killian.

He wasn't, though. I studied him, not certain how I knew this person wasn't my fae.

"Ya need my power," he said, his voice again giving me the distinct impression of almost-not-quite right. He bent over me again, pressing his mouth to mine and kissing me more firmly. A hand brushed across my nipples, then slid down to the band at my hips, running along the inside edge, against my bare skin.

I squirmed against the intrusion, trying to twist my face from his kiss.

His other hand snaked into my hair, though, and he yanked my head back to center. "Be still," he growled at me.

That was it - this wasn't my fucking fae, and he'd officially worn out his welcome. I went pliant in his grip and widened my mouth, waiting. As soon as his tongue swept back inside, I chomped as hard as I could, grinning like mad when I tasted blood.

He shouted and jumped back, shoving my head hard to the side when he moved. It hurt, but I knew I'd hurt this traitor worse.

"Who the fuck are you?" I asked, lifting my head as much as possible to look around the room.

It wasn't my room - I was in something that looked more like a hospital ward. Ah, fuck. My stomach rolled as I realized I was probably here for the Council's brand of testing.

And if this asshole was my first test, had I passed or failed?

Heavy footsteps approached my bed from somewhere

behind my head, and I tried to twist my neck around to see. A shadow fell over me, but I still couldn't see a face.

"Somebody tell this douchebag that consent is a thing these days," I said, keeping my voice cold and calm. "You can't go around kissing unconscious girls anymore, Prince Asshole."

A snort came from the figure behind my head, followed by a cough that I guess was meant to cover the indiscretion.

"She knows I'm not him," the redhead said, looking straight over my head.

"Indeed," a new voice said. "I'll drop the glamor and see if our little Qilin is any more amenable to your kisses then."

I almost gagged as the illusion of Killian's face and hair dissolved like sand being brushed away, leaving long white hair and lavender eyes. Fucking *Aleron*.

He leered at me, sliding his gaze down my bound body. "How did you know I wasn't the fae?" he asked. "You're not mated to him."

"I know what shit tastes like," I shot back. "And you've been licking someone's asshole to get here."

His face darkened, and he started toward me, only to be shoved back by some unseen force. I gloated a bit that he'd been reprimanded, but I didn't know who was handing out the punishment. It was probably someone even worse.

"Who are you mated with, Qilin?" the voice asked. The shadow lengthened as the person finally came around the side of my bed to stare down at me.

I'd never seen him before, and I already didn't like him.

He was obviously fae, as he wasn't wearing any glamor.

His skin was deep reddish-brown, almost burned in appearance. His eyes glowed with a deeper orange than Killian's ever had, and his ears were so pointed they almost looked craggy. He was dressed sort of like a doctor, except his lab coat was black instead of pristine white.

"I'm here to test your powers, so you may as well tell me where to start. I can certainly figure it out my way, but I assure you, it will be much more unpleasant."

I glared up at him, swallowing down about a thousand insults and curses.

"Well?" he prompted, reaching into the pocket of his lab coat and pulling out a vial. I eyed it, remembering the awful potions I'd already been dosed with here in the Council.

"Dragon, lion, mage," I ground out.

He smiled in approval, except it was more like his lips just stretched horizontally over his teeth. "And your magic?"

"Fire, strength, and spells." I hated giving up intel, but I assumed they had plenty of less straightforward ways of getting the same information. From the corner, Aleron grunted.

"She doesn't shift yet, though," he said, skirting around the bed to my other side.

"Could you taste her power?" the fae asked, still staring at me.

"No. It's still blocked," Aleron answered, giving the fae doctor a pointed look.

The fae's eyes narrowed, and his lips turned up on one side. "Not by me, it isn't."

"Impossible," the other Qilin scoffed, bending lower to peer in my eyes. "She wouldn't know how to do that."

"I know I don't want your fucking tongue in my throat," I hissed at him. "And I don't have to be mated to Killian to recognize him. That glamor was shit," I said, turning back to the fae.

His eyebrows shot up. "My glamor is impeccable. Even the young fae's uncle didn't know the difference when he saw him."

"Well, I could tell. Try again, if you're so cocksure."

"You would test *me*?" he growled, his eyes glowing, like embers. I steeled myself, pouring everything I had into not looking scared. This was one crazy fae, though.

Something in his manner told me he'd killed before and wouldn't have a second damn thought about doing it again.

I wondered if he was one of the ones responsible for making the other Qilin go *boom*.

"It would be interesting, though," Aleron said.

"Ask Jantzen to play those games, then, Qilin. I have other things to test," the fae snapped. He unsnapped a buckle from one of my hands and placed a rubber ball in my palm. "Squeeze this," he commanded.

"Well, that's a little simpler than I expected," I replied, wrapping my fingers around the ball.

"Harder. I'm testing your strength, girl."

Sighing, I debated what would be better - showing off or keeping secrets.

"That's likely all she has," Aleron said, leaning against the far wall. "Her lion is barely more than a pussy cat."

Anger coursed through me, and my fingers bounced against the soft surface of the ball, testing it. It was hooked to some sort of digital recording machine, and I saw the graph waver as I played.

"Better?" I asked the fae, pressing until the reading was about three-fourths of the way to the top.

He shrugged and tapped a few notes into a nearby laptop. While he was distracted, I sneaked a look at Aleron. Catching his eye, I moved like lightning and hurled the ball at him. It embedded itself several inches deep in the wall behind him, only a few inches from his shocked eyes.

Ripped wires dangled from the mangled skin of the ball, and belatedly, the machine toppled to the floor as it lost the battle for balance.

"How was that, doc?" I asked, keeping my eyes on Aleron.

"You missed," the Qilin scoffed, but I could tell he was shaken. Fucking good.

"Can I have another ball, then? I didn't realize I was testing my aim, too." I looked back at the fae, who was examining me with a lot more interest now. I'd probably just fucked myself over giving him that much info, but it had been worth it.

CHAPTER TWO

CARLYLE

The fae walked around to the opposite side of my bed and unstrapped my other hand. I immediately pushed myself up, keeping my eyes trained on Aleron. He seemed like a revenge sort of guy.

"So, all my magic should work in here?" I asked, trying to sound casual. The fae snorted, though.

"Only as I allow it. No need to start plotting your escape, because it's not happening on my watch."

I shrugged. "I usually just wing it, anyway. Do you have a name?"

"Not one that concerns you," he said, turning away to rummage in a cabinet.

"I'll just call you Dr. F, then," I said, starting to run my mouth. It was usually a good way to get people talking. "You know, F for Fae. Or Fuckface. Or Fantastic. We'll just have to see how our relationship develops."

Aleron pushed off the wall and swaggered nearer. He evidently had the world's shortest memory. "You're a lot more attractive with your mouth shut," he said, combing his long white-blond hair back with a delicate motion.

"Yeah? I bet you're pretty hot with a hole in your head."

"How's your shoulder?"

"How's your ex-boyfriend?"

"Such children," the fae snapped. "All shifters are the same - beasts."

Aleron glowered at him, but I just grinned. "You need this beast, though. So, sorry to tell you, but I'm your new favorite burden."

"Are you all spark and no flame? Or can you spit fire as well as you spit insults?" the fae asked, grasping a bar on the back of my bed and wheeling me toward a door in the room. Aleron kicked it open, and we moved into a bare room lined completely in stone.

He left the bed in the middle of the room, and then they both stepped back out, leaving me alone.

A noise crackled above me, and the fae's voice came over an intercom.

"Whenever you're ready," he said dryly.

I sighed. It had been a while since I'd used any of Jack's magic. I'd really only done it when I was really angry - practically murderous. Then again, thinking about Aleron playing sleeping beauty was making me hot in all the unsexy ways. I thought I should downplay my power this time, though.

9

The good doctor didn't need to know everything.

I closed my eyes and focused on the magic inside me. Now that it wasn't blocked, I was both surprised and enchanted by how much there really was. Not to mention how beautiful the colors were as they swirled together in an almost-rainbow. A couple of the colors were missing - namely, Toro's bright blue and Jai's indigo.

Dair's was the brightest, since it had only been a couple of days since we mated, but the rest were there.

I was becoming quite the full little vessel.

Pulling up some of Jack's fiery red magic, I felt the heat in the room increasing. Parting my lips, I breathed just the slightest current of sparks into the air, blowing hard enough to push them beyond my bed. I opened my eyes and watched them drift and settle on the stone floor.

"I sense more than that in you, Qilin," the fae's voice said, hissing over the intercom. "Do not waste my time."

Rolling my eyes, I sent a bit more power through my intentions, coaxing the sparks on the floor into hundreds of tiny flames. I raised them higher and higher, until I was adrift in a sea of red and orange fire.

Okay, so evidently, I was going to be a show-off.

"Now, dampen them," the fae commanded.

Grumbling to myself, I started pulling the magic back inside me. I took my time, knowing he'd just give me another task when this one was done. None of these tests were hurting me, but I had a feeling that logging my powers was just the beginning for this guy.

Once all the flames had been sucked away, the door behind me opened, and my bed was pulled back into the hospital room.

Heat trailed behind us, and I smirked when I saw

Aleron wipe a bead of sweat from his forehead.

"So, Eagle. What powers did your mates give you, besides some ugly brown wings?"

"I'm not the specimen on display, here," he snapped. I grinned wider, thinking probably he didn't have anything as cool as I did. My enjoyment died a little, though, as I remembered his horn and the way he'd been able to tap into my mind. How he'd been able to shut down Jack completely and take over Toro's actions.

I was being too hasty in judging him. I didn't need to let my pride shove me into a fall.

"And the spells," the fae said, ignoring us completely.

"How about you let me siphon out of here. We can play hide-and-seek."

"You won't be going anywhere. I only wish to see a procurement spell."

"How do you know I can do those?" I asked. "Maybe I got some potions power or mind control, instead."

"Alisdair's powers have been thoroughly cataloged, as he is an employee of ours. Unless you have been intimate with another mage, it is impossible for you to channel that sort of magic." He gestured to the ball, still embedded in the wall. "Procure that."

Pursing my lips, I did as he asked. He pointed to a few other things around the room, each larger than the last, and I did each of them without fighting. At least the room didn't have any plants or other living things.

I didn't know exactly how rare ability that was, but Dair had been shocked when I'd once procured a flower. I was still hoping to leave this room with a few secrets.

"You have good control and range. How about something from your room? A pillow, perhaps?" the fae requested.

I sighed, closing my eyes to imagine the cell I'd been trapped in. A second later, I was holding the thin white pillow, and he was approaching the closest thing to a smile I'd seen yet.

"You have a very useful skill set," he said, his fingers typing rapidly across the keyboard. Finishing, he snapped the laptop closed and fixed me in his gaze. "Yet none of these abilities explain how you were able to discern Aleron was not Killian."

I shrugged. I suspected it had to do with the very nice bit of action I'd shared with Killian, Sol, and Jack, just hours before being kidnapped here.

But I wasn't about to share that with either of the men in this room.

"Neither does it explain why you cannot shift. Even unmated Qilin can learn to shift - that magic is yours. Not channeled."

I blinked at him, surprised for the first time. "I don't need my guys for that?"

Aleron chuckled. "So innocent. Did they lure you into bed with the promise of pure unicorn beauty? Sparkles and glitter?"

"Ah, fuck. You really don't know me, do you?" I flopped back onto the hospital bed.

"You were raised human?" the fae questioned, and I nodded. "Then perhaps disbelief is blocking your natural abilities. You were taught magic doesn't exist, and bodies are static. Shifters in Haret are taught the opposite, and most learn the fluidity of their form as early as humans learn to walk."

"Wow," I whispered, imagining how cool that would

be. Damn, I hoped Haret was as interesting as I'd been building it up in my head.

The fae pushed a button on the wall and spoke into a small intercom. "Bring me the serum I requested."

"What? What are you going to do to me?" I began struggling against my remaining bindings, but the fae quickly pushed me flat on my back with his magic. It felt a lot like a heated version of Killian's air currents, though I'd never been on the blunt end of such force. It pinned me despite my lion's strength, and it was a matter of seconds before my wrists were bound again.

I continued to writhe in the bindings, but my magic had been closed off again, as soon as I'd been brought back in this room. Whatever physical strength I retained from Sol's mating bond was no match for the straps around me. They tingled against my skin - the more I struggled, the more those pricks sharpened.

"They're equipped with iron needles, Qilin," Aleron gloated, watching me fight. "Everything here has been laced with iron," he added, his face darkening just enough to tip me off that he was no stranger to their methods.

I wasn't sure if that made me feel better or worse. I was glad he'd been tested - satisfied he'd been put through this same disrespect, not to mention that they knew the specifics of his magic. Yet it was pretty telling of the organization that they didn't trust anyone they were working with.

A second door opened, and a mage in one of those odd silver knight uniforms entered, carrying a white box. The fae snatched it from him and shooed him away. He set the box on the counter and opened it, pulling out a syringe.

I stopped struggling - I wasn't getting out of this one,

and it would only hurt more if he had to ram it in my skin. "What does that do?"

"It should tempt your Qilin out of hiding, and hopefully pull her to the surface." The fae leaned over me with the needle poised at my neck. Ah, fuck, I was going to hate this. "I should warn you, this will prick a bit."

He sank the needle deep in my skin, just as Aleron started laughing. A white-hot pain radiated through me immediately, and I lost all control over myself. A scream ripped from my throat as my body tried to reject the serum's hold on its muscles and bones.

Pain stabbed into my mind like shards of broken glass, slicing into my carefully-made mental barriers.

I felt something stirring deep in my chest, and I knew it was my Qilin form.

She was awake, and she was pissed.

CHAPTER THREE

CARLYLE

The more the serum tore through my body's defenses, the more my Qilin fought it. I was nothing more than the battleground. My insides felt pockmarked with holes from artillery shells, and I crumbled like an exploding building.

I caught bits of conversation from the fae doctor and Aleron, but mostly I felt locked in an unending nightmare of pain and fear. The fear came mostly from my Qilin form, like she was a whole other consciousness inside me. She was terrified of being pulled out, and this put me into hyper-protective mode.

"I've never seen someone fight this so much. She is very strong," the fae said, his face a blur above mine.

I imagined the Qilin with physical form, like I used to

with the emotions I'd pulled from people in LuAnn's booth. I tried to calm and contain her, the way I could cordon off the depression I sucked from customers. But she wasn't having any of it.

"She's not that strong," Aleron grumbled, and my Qilin screamed at the idea in rage.

That's right, I thought to her in my mind. *He's an asshole, and not the sexy kind. We're going to beat him, but we have to do it together.*

She still shuffled and shied away from me, hiding in the dark corners of my mind like a memory I couldn't quite retrieve - like when you see someone you should know, but their name simply won't come to you.

"I'll have to end this, or we won't have a subject left. Her mind could disintegrate," the fae said, sounding annoyed at the idea.

I struggled to surface and tell him off, but there was another prick in my neck, and darkness crept in. My Qilin retreated so deep that I couldn't find her at all, and my mind shut down as I drifted away.

When I woke again, I was back in my cell, with a raging headache.

The worst fucking migraine in the world, times two. Plus I had to pee, I was hungry, and I couldn't remember the last time I'd had coffee or sugar.

Groaning, I rolled off the bed and dragged myself to the silver toilet. While I sat there, my eyes adjusted, and I realized I wasn't alone.

I hurried to dress myself, skittering back from the redheaded fae form slumped on my floor. Was it actually Killian this time? If this was fucking Aleron again, I was going to feed him his nuts for breakfast.

The lights began to brighten, evidently signaling daytime. I realized the redhead wasn't the only addition to my room. There was a tray of food - toast, fruit, and eggs - and a large pitcher of water with a single glass.

I grabbed the pitcher and guzzled directly from it, draining nearly half before my belly protested.

Kneeling down next to the man, I risked touching his bare arm. I didn't feel anything, really. No power or magic. I couldn't feel glamor or see it.

Still, something in my heart recognized this person as Killian. I couldn't have explained it if forced to, but that didn't erase the gut feeling. I smiled to myself. Evidently, the Ringmaster had some pull after all. I'd asked for the fae, and I'd finally gotten the fae.

I checked his pulse and breathing. He seemed to be sleeping. Knowing this place, he was most likely drugged.

Maybe - if I worked with the Ringmaster's requests - I could bargain for more. I could begin playing the game again rather than just being a pawn.

If Turin returned, I'd bargain with him, too. I'd play all the angles and see which deal was best for me and my team.

Deciding I'd let Killian sleep off whatever it was, I turned my attention to the food. I tried to save more, but I was starving, and there really wasn't enough for two people.

The more time passed, the angrier I got at our situation. I'd play the game all right, but I shouldn't even have to.

All I'd done was exist. All my team had done was complete their mission as instructed. Sure, they hadn't come in as quickly as asked, but we'd been planning on it.

Now, we were all locked up in cells, subjected to the sort of treatment a criminal might get.

Or a prisoner of war, in my case.

I wasn't sure where my guys had gotten the idea that I was going to be treated like a Queen, because it sure as shit didn't seem to be the Council's plan. I guessed it was just more of the same bullshit any government spews to get citizens on board for difficult times and tasks.

Fuck, I just wanted out - out of this cell, but also out of the whole game in general. I'd be happy to help the Underbelly kids, and maybe open the Path so people who'd been trapped on Earth could go home.

I just didn't want to be a pawn, caught in a power play between the mages and the fae.

I didn't want to be a weapon.

Folding my arms over my chest, I started to steel myself for whatever the hell was coming our way. If I had to fight, I wanted to wield my own power and pick my own battles. I needed to be strong enough to defend and protect, too - mind, body, and magic.

A big part of that meant I needed my Qilin.

Closing my eyes, I began rifling through my mind, trying to find the part of me that had stayed secret and hidden for twenty-one years.

CHAPTER FOUR

KILLIAN

"Wha' the fuck happened?" I peeled my face off the cold-ass floor where I'd just woken. My brain was fuzzy, and I couldn't remember where I was or why.

"Welcome to my throne room, fae."

I blinked my eyes groggily at the hazy figure before me. The voice was Carlyle's, but I'd never heard her sound so hard - bitter, even.

I rolled to my back and heaved up into a sitting position. As I took in the narrow, gray-walled room, my awareness of our situation returned with a rush.

"Goddamn Council," I growled. We were being held in cells by our own people. Looked like Jai had been more right than we even knew about the corruption here.

"Yep, fuck them. And your asshole uncle. Fucking Ringmaster, too. And Aleron. Looks like all the party invitations went out," Carlyle drawled.

Holy fuck, we'd made a deep list of enemies just for doing our job. I pushed my way slowly up the wall, testing my stomach. Those potions were murder on your system, and the last thing I wanted was to be hurling up my guts in front of Carlyle.

I eyed her through half-closed lids. She looked a little haggard, but unharmed. Thank fuck she was safe, at least. For now.

I wanted nothing more than to rush at the bed and crush her close to me, but I didn't deserve it. None of us deserved the comfort her arms might bring - we'd dragged her into this mess. Some rescue team we'd turned out to be.

Besides, I didn't know who might be watching us - these Council rooms were heavily monitored. I didn't know a lot about their methods, but I knew that much.

I needed to play my cards close, like I'd always done around my family. Life had taught me that lesson well enough.

Turin would use her against me - against all of us if he needed to. It was better not to show him how much I needed this savage little creature curled in the corner of her mattress.

I scrubbed my hands over my face and tugged at my hair, looking over at her. She finally smiled at me, but it was one of those smile-through-the-shit looks.

It made me want to hug her and punch someone all at once.

"How long have I been in here? In this cell?" I asked.

There were huge gaps in my memory - blank spaces where I felt like time had passed, but I had no distinct events or people to make the minutes concrete. "The last big thing I remember is being thrown in a cell like this one."

"I can't tell for sure, but if they dim the lights on the sun's schedule, then just a night. I got one meal when they dumped you in here. I saved you a little, but there wasn't much to begin with. I was trying to let you sleep off the drugs, but I was starting to worry," she added, her voice dropping to nearly a whisper.

I could feel her remaining fear, and it ripped my goddamn heart out.

I had no right to call this girl mine, but knowing she'd feared for *me*? Fuck. I needed to get it together, for her sake.

"Wonder why they put us together now, when they didn't at first," I said. If I could figure out their motives, maybe I could figure out a weakness.

"I was told to pick one of you. They took their fucking time bringing you, though," she said, glowering at the blank wall across from her bed. I studied her, wanting to ask why she'd requested me over any of the others, but not trusting my voice to be steady. It was crazy how much I yearned for this girl - it scared the hell out of me. Nothing good had ever come of me wanting something so much.

For someone like me, it was better not to want.

"Seriously, though. What the fuck?" She gestured around at the four blank walls and the toilet with a grimace that bordered on desperation. I cracked a smile, but it was probably as bad as hers.

I'd seen these cells before - from the outside. I'd never heard of anyone escaping them.

None of us did well locked up, but it had to be a million times worse on her Qilin nature.

"Are ya okay?" I asked, massaging my temples. I felt like six kinds of shit, and I was starving on top of it all. Noticing half a piece of toast and a few bites of eggs on a tray, I grimaced. I didn't want to take that last bit of food from her, either. Hopefully, my stomach would stay quiet.

I leaned down to touch my toes, stretching my spine, then straightened, rolling my stiff shoulders.

"I'm fine," she said with a shrug, patting the bed beside her in invitation. "So, the Ringmaster's here," she started, and I slammed my fist into the wall. Of course, that did nothing but crack my knuckles and rip a few more curses from my lips.

"What does that fucker want?" I asked. I joined her on the narrow bed, and she immediately leaned into my shoulder.

It startled me a bit - she did shit like that to Sol and Jack all the time, but not me. All awkward and shit, I slung an arm around her small body and tugged her close.

"He wants what he's always wanted - for me to open the Path. He's the one who told me to pick one of you guys and learn how to shift," she said, ending on a sigh. "Which is going to be fucking impossible if my magic is blocked."

"Yours, too, huh?" I'd hoped maybe her cipher nature would slip through the Council's holding rooms, but they'd been ready. Probably on account of that other fucker, Aleron. They likely knew all they needed about Qilin from him - not to mention their experiments. I wouldn't be surprised if they came for her one of these days, to run tests.

I'd fight them off if I were here, but I knew enough to know I'd probably lose.

"So, I asked for you, because I'm guessing it's my lack of glamor skills," Carlyle continued. "Otherwise, I would have figured out to shift from Sol or Jack, I think."

At least she had a logical reason for asking for me - I wasn't sure I could hold it together if it had been something sappy. But fuck if this wasn't a good idea wrapped in a bad one. "Your Qilin form is what they all want. If ya shift, you're handin' it to them on a platter."

She pushed herself off the bed and began to pace the narrow room. With every turn, she glanced at the blank wall across from me, her eyes searching for something I couldn't see, either. "I know. But if I don't shift, I may never make it through this. I have the best chance of surviving this and saving you if I'm at my strongest."

"Donna worry about saving me, Savage. Or any of the others."

"Fuck you." She narrowed those lavender eyes at me, and I knew she'd be doing her own thing, just like always.

I smirked. Her attitude was one of the best things about her. "Aye, that's wha' we'll do when we get out of here."

"Then shut the fuck up about me saving you and teach me to shift."

"I have none o' my magic in here," I reminded her, gritting my teeth.

"You must have some glamor still, because I can't see your cute little pointy ears yet." She grinned at me, and I felt my face heat. My fae ears were about as fucking sensitive as my cock, and I wasn't interested in hearing either of them called cute or little.

Trying to distract myself from how her words made me want to fuck her senseless to prove something, I focused on the intel instead. I'd grown so accustomed to keeping my glamor in place over the years on Earth that it felt almost more natural to appear human. Staring down at my hands, though, I focused enough to see the pale, inked skin layered over my own fae blue.

She was right - my glamor was still in place. "I donna feel my power, though. An' I have no control over the air." I tested a few things, to make sure. I couldn't glamor anything else, and the air was unresponsive to my call.

"Well, how does the glamor work? I've only seen your true form once - that time on the beach."

Her cheeks flushed just a little, and I cursed under my breath. Intel, goddamn it. I had to focus on the intel.

"Did you see Turin's form?" I asked.

She shook her head. "He looks a little like you, but he passes for human, too."

"Then maybe the Council's not stripped us of our inner magic. Jus' the outer."

"Yeah, I don't know what that means," she said, shrugging and plopping back onto the bed.

"Inner magic is stuff that only affects ourselves. Toro should be able to shift if that's true, and Sol. Probably Jack, although bein' a dragon, they likely did somethin' else to keep him down."

She nodded, her eyes far away in thought. "They must be keeping that open so I can shift," she muttered. "Toro's shifted," she continued, glancing again to the opposite wall. "The first night in here, the Ringmaster did something to this wall, so I could see through it like a window. Everyone is here together, just in different rooms."

I grinned. Knowing everyone's location was good. "That makes things easier. If shifting and glamor work, tha's a start."

"What about Jai's mind reading?"

I considered. "They must be blockin' him somehow, maybe with somethin' besides iron. They have potions mages that can do damn near anything."

"I thought you guys had been here before. Haven't you been through all this, like in training or something?"

I chuckled. "They train us like grunts. Physical, tactical, and digital human shit. How to track, how to protect. We donna get the inside scoop on their interrogation methods or the newest Haret tech and magical tech."

"Search and find," she murmured, fiddling with the edge of the coarse blanket.

"Pretty much," I affirmed, nodding when she glanced up at me. She gazed at me for a long moment, and I was reminded of the very first time I'd seen her. She'd given me the sexiest fucking challenge stare I'd ever seen, and I'd been hers from that moment on.

Turin would guess it soon enough, too - especially if they expected me to give her any magic. I wouldn't be able to hide it from him, and that would suck because then he'd know how to make me squirm.

It was enough that I had to deal with my family's drama here, too. We'd evidently added treason to our legacy. I hated it, but I wasn't exactly fucking surprised Turin was involved.

I wasn't taken aback by Aleron, either - the Council likely had something to bind him here. What I didn't get was why the fucking Ringmaster was here, and why he was working with the Council. As far as I'd known, they were rivals.

If the public race to the Path had joined forces with the private one, our little team was solid fucked.

CHAPTER FIVE

CARLYLE

"Here's what I don't get," I said, flopping back onto the bed. Killian raised an eyebrow when I paused too long. Honestly, there were a lot of things I didn't get.

"The Ringmaster siphoned into this room," I said. "He shouldn't be able to do that if the magic is blocked. Or am I missing something?"

Kills frowned. "It might be possible. I donna know enough about siphoning or potions. It's suspicious, though."

"Turin was glamored in here, and you are, too. Jai and I could do his mind-speak thing back in the other room, where we were in the iron chains."

His frown deepened, and he shook his head. "You're

right. Tha's not addin' up."

I didn't understand enough about the sources for any of the guys' magic to see any pattern that might exist - even Killian's theory about inner and outer magic didn't really match. Obviously, I knew nothing about what the Council was capable of.

All I knew was that Grunkeld had insisted *all* of our magic was blocked by these smooth, silver walls, and that had apparently been a damn lie. It made me wonder what else he was lying about.

"He doesn't know all my magic, though," I murmured, mostly to myself. I uncurled my legs from the bed and began walking the short length of the room again. "Nobody does, because I can mix it up. I can create something new that they've never seen before."

Killian made a shushing noise, discreetly pointing to his eyes and ears. Loudly, he said, "Ya could…if ya had magic."

Killian's reminder of the complexity of our situation killed the slight buzz of excitement that had been forming, and I sighed. Not only were we trapped with no significant magic, we were most likely under heavy surveillance. I had to keep my voice down. Leaning my forehead against the wall across from my bed, I tried to visualize my guys on the other side of it.

Jai? I called, closing my eyes to imagine projecting my voice beyond these walls and into the general direction of the cell I'd seen him in. There was nothing, though. Were they still there? Or had their safety been merely an illusion to keep me compliant?

"I'd feel their pain, though, wouldn't I? Through the mating bond?" I glanced backward at Killian.

He shrugged, folding his arms over his chest. "Never been mated."

Another sigh bubbled up from my chest, and even I was getting annoyed at myself. I wasn't one for self-pity. I was more the action type, or maybe the *distr*-action type.

"Maybe you should get a mate, then," I said on a whim, turning fully around and leaning on the wall to watch my fae. I'd pretty much made up my mind that I wanted all of these men - I just wasn't sure if Killian and I had progressed enough for it to be a real option.

"Yeah? An' where would I find one?" he asked, playing along as he pretended to search the room.

"Aleron might take you under his wing," I offered, and he grimaced, his eyes straying to the neck of my thin sweater. I'd stretched it out too far when I was taunting the Ringmaster, and now my odd hole of a scar was showing.

"I'll kill that fuckin' Qilin if you donna do it," Killian said, and I believed every syllable. His hands clenched into fists, twisting in my sheets.

"You'd kill to protect me, then?"

He slid his eyes to me warily. "Of course."

"Why?" I prompted. He didn't think I was serious about taking a new mate - I had a feeling a fight was coming if I wanted him now.

"Because it's my job," he growled, his neck reddening in anger. "I signed up to find and rescue a Qilin, an' ya still need fuckin' rescued."

"And that's all," I finished, nodding. My tone told him I didn't buy his bullshit, though. I kept my voice barely above a whisper, stalking closer to the bed. "So you fucked me on the beach. Why?"

"Ya needed my power."

"You let me suck you off while Sol's cock was deep in your throat. Why?"

"Felt good. An' ya *still* needed my power."

"You're going to let me climb on that bed now and ride you. Why?"

He startled, and I grinned, pressing myself against the bed now. He needed to be pushed, and I was in a pushy kinda mood. I barely got within arm's reach, though, when his hand pressed against my belly, holding me back.

"We canna," he whispered, his eyes sliding around the room like someone else might have slipped in.

"Are we on camera, then?"

He nodded. "Always."

I huffed. That added a layer of weird to it, but I wasn't a quitter. "So we'll just keep our fun under the blanket. They'll know, but they won't see anything."

"Carlyle, I said no." He rose and sidestepped me, and I got the distinct impression he wanted the fuck out of the room. That made me spitting mad in a split second.

"What is your goddamn problem?" I hissed. "I'm not blind, Kills. I see the way you look at me. My instincts are as good as they get with what people want, and *you* want *me*." I knew I was right. I'd scented his desire - and something deeper than sexual want - every time I'd laid hands on him.

It was woven deep into the fabric of his unique winter wind, cedar, and whiskey scent. He wanted me with the darkest, most locked-down parts of his mind. What was keeping those parts from taking over?

I moved toward him again, and he dodged me. My pride was taking a hit, but I ignored it. My gut was telling me to keep going, keep pushing him. I'd seen the way his cock responded when I used my strength to shove him around. Sol had explained that Killian needed to be dominated sometimes, to prove shit was real.

Jai revealed once how Killian thought he wasn't good enough - not for me, not for anything.

I needed to remind him how good he actually was.

"Get your ass on the bed, fae," I ordered, pulling my alpha tone from deep in my chest. He shuddered and backed into the corner, his eyes continuing to flick around the room. "I don't care who's watching. Let them get their rocks off. I want you and your fae cock."

"I canna give you my power," he warned, edging away. He was closer to the bed, though, so I kept closing in.

"I know. This isn't about power. This is about pleasure."

"That's all I am, then?" he whispered, looking shocked that the words had slipped from his mouth. I froze. This was sounding too similar to Dair's arguments, but there was a darker layer here that I needed to be very careful peeling back.

"Absolutely not," I said, still not moving an inch. I lowered my voice, though. "Having you is so much more than your glamor or your air magic, and so much more than how well you wreck my body."

I saw his chest rise with a deep breath, and he met my eyes. He opened his mouth, then closed it again, his face falling.

"Tell me I'm wrong," I challenged, still keeping my voice at a fierce whisper. "Tell me you don't want me, and I'll leave you alone. I'd never force someone into bed, let alone into a relationship that's supposed to last centuries.

31

Tell me," I repeated, letting my voice slide into something closer to pleading.

"You're na' fuckin' wrong, Qilin," he growled, the back of his thighs hitting the mattress. He glanced around again. "But if Turin sees me with ya, he'll be holdin' all the right cards."

"What does that mean?" I wanted to hear him say it.

He glared and turned away, looking straight at the opposite wall.

"Kills, they all know Qilin get their power from their mates. There's a reason the Ringmaster brought you in here, and it wasn't to keep me company with small talk."

"I know that," he grumbled, his shoulders slumping a bit.

"Then they'll expect us to try and transfer power," I pointed out. He didn't answer, and I bit down on a sigh. Goddamn difficult men. "Why are you afraid of Turin?" I whispered. I knew he was locked inside his memories now - I could sense the despair, but I didn't know what it stemmed from. "Tell me what happened?" I asked, never thinking he'd follow through.

He made a choking noise and braced his forearms on the wall in front of him, his back muscles flexing through his thin shirt as he tried to control his breathing.

Taking a risk, I darted around him and slipped between him and the wall, staring up at his golden eyes. Their color was dulled with self-hatred. I cupped his cheek with one hand, but he twisted his face away.

Closing his eyes, he whispered, "When you told us your story - how your powers locked you into actions you never wanted - it all sounded too fuckin' real."

"It *was* real. For years, it was my whole reality," I said, swallowing back the panic that still rose up when I thought of all the times my power over human emotions had created chaos in the people around me. All those years in foster care - all those people who were attracted to me. My body had soaked in their desire and bounced it back tenfold, regardless of what I really wanted.

My body said yes to their advances, even while my heart screamed no. I'd been trapped in a lie, with no way to break its hold.

"What happened, Killian?" I whispered again, fearing the answer but knowing we both needed it to be said.

"Ya know my parents promised me to Kana," he began, his arms sliding off the wall. He turned and leaned his back against it, standing next to me. His lips barely moved as he forced out the whispered words. "Well, tha' wasn't the first time. I was a prize - a beautiful gift they could give over an' over. An' they fuckin' *gave*." His voice was rough now, and his words sawed open my heart as I thought them through. I didn't need him to tell me specifics. I understood enough.

What kind of parents did this? What kind of society embraced it?

Again, unease flashed through my heart. I was working toward saving a world, but was it worth saving?

"Savage," Killian said, drawing me back with a hand on my wrist. "Haret is worth saving. It has dark places, but so much light, too."

I smiled, realizing I'd spoken aloud, and his answer had been fucking brilliant. "Then I guess, by that same logic, you're worth it, too."

His lips opened to retort but closed around a grumbled curse.

33

"Look, Kills. We don't need to work through our pasts in the next ten minutes. We have a lifetime to deal with that. Just think about what you *want* - not what you think you deserve. It's the only way I've ever found that let me move past all that shit. That first night you and Sol found me, I wanted *both* of you, and it worried the hell out of me. I thought I'd beaten that part of myself into submission." I shook my head, glancing up at him. "Fuck, the first time I saw you in that festival crowd by the river, I wanted you more than I'd like to admit."

"Yeah?" He glanced over at me, his expression a tiny bit more confident.

"Fuck, yeah. You were gorgeous and sexy and dangerous. I wasn't sure if you were a human or an Underbelly person, though, and I had a bad history of falling into bed with the wrong people. So I kept away, even though I didn't want to. Then when Sol started showing his interest in me, I fought myself so long."

"Savage, you fucked him in about three days," he reminded me, cracking a grin.

"Fuck off. That's a long time for me," I confessed. "Which is why it's so goddamn hard to wrap my brain around you and Jai."

"The vampire could kill ya with a twisted thought. He's scared shitless he'll screw up."

"Do you think he will?" I asked.

"Nah. He cares for ya too much."

"Do you think *you* will?" I prodded, giving him the side-eye. "You forgive and trust everyone but yourself, Kills. Believe me, I know way too well how that works. I also know it's a shitty way to live, and ever since I stopped being a human and started being a Qilin, my life has gotten a lot more fun."

"More dangerous, too," he said, gesturing around the room.

I shrugged. "Worth it."

"Still doesn't erase the danger. I canna let Turin see us together. He knows me too well."

I wanted to push him into admitting what he feared revealing to Turin, but I hesitated. We'd moved forward a lot already, and I didn't want him to feel badgered.

I'd take him damaged - I didn't need to fix him to love him.

I crossed the room to the tray of cold toast and eggs. I offered it to him, and he shook his head like I'd expected. I took a bite, then pressed the rest in his hand.

"Please," I said. "Who knows when we'll get anything else."

Finally, he took it, and I backed away, settling on the bed. This was going to be a long, awkward day if he was hell-bent on refusing any sexy times. If the Ringmaster thought I was squandering my time with Killian, he wouldn't be so willing to work with me.

I needed to test my theory about shifting with Killian's magic, which meant I needed to get him past this embarrassment and fear of his uncle.

CHAPTER SIX

CARLYLE

"We need to fight," I muttered, keeping my face down. Killian slid me a confused look. "They know I need your power, and they know we have to be physical to get it. Right?"

He hesitated but finally nodded.

Without waiting for further permission, I lunged off the bed toward him and shoved at his chest. He stumbled a bit, taken completely by surprise. "If you want to hide emotion from Turin, keep it just physical," I growled. Keeping my face angry, I flipped him the bird, and he finally seemed to get it.

I reached for his pants, where his cock was already growing tight against his jeans. He batted my hand away, rolling his eyes, but ending in a smirk. When I shoved at him again, he grabbed my wrists and held them above my head. Stepping even closer, I rolled my hips, pressing my breasts against him.

"I canna look at you. Turin will know," Killian repeated, sounding embarrassed.

"Then fuck me from behind," I ordered, rubbing myself against him again. If I looked like the initiator, and he was just doing his job to provide me with magic, surely that would keep his uncle in the dark a little bit.

"I donna wan' them to see," he hissed, his golden eyes flashing with something hotter than either anger or lust.

"Then cover my white ass with the blanket. Full of fucking excuses, aren't you?"

Growling again, he yanked my wrists apart and spun me toward the bed. Twisting my arms behind my back, he took both wrists in one hand again, using the leverage to bend me over the bed. I grabbed the sheet and threw it over my back as he wrestled down my leggings and panties.

To someone watching on camera, I hoped it would look like we were only after exchanging power, as if it were a chore. They didn't need to know I was already aching and wet - I wanted this as much as it probably looked like I didn't want it.

Killian's dominance was all the hotter for being an act. He unbuckled his jeans one-handed and nudged his hard cock against my pussy, his legs kicking my knees apart. I turned my face and snapped my teeth at him, and his eyes widened as I pressed back against him. His tip slid in, and his eyes widened when he felt how ready I was.

Suddenly, the dominance stopped being an act. My fae

flipped his asshole switch on, and I reveled in his rough touch as much as I loved his abrasive manners.

He let my wrists go but grabbed a handful of my hair, keeping his other hand firmly on my hip. He didn't pull to pain, but his grip kept me from getting too far away. I pressed my palms into the mattress for leverage, and the two of us slammed together.

"Ride that cock, Qilin," he growled. "Get your power and get me off."

Our charade grew harder to maintain as Killian hit a rhythm. His fingers strayed lower onto my clit, rubbing me in time with his fierce thrusting.

It was almost too soon when I came with a cry, pressing my face into the mattress to hide how much fun I was having. My back arched as I bucked against him. He let go of my hair and pressed me deeper into the bed while he continued to pump, finishing inside me moments later with a shout and a smack to my ass.

I hid my grin in the sheets as he pulled out of me and wiped himself off with a corner of the sheet. He refastened his jeans, then stretched his long form across the bed, giving me a self-satisfied smirk.

Remembering the way he'd been so thoughtful to clean the sand from me on the beach, I knew this was part of the act, too. I flipped him the finger again and dragged my hand through my pussy, making a show of wiping his cum all over the sheet. Just for good measure, I sat down on the toilet and wiped myself again.

He chuckled, stretching back with his hands behind his head as I rearranged my clothes. My heart warmed with the knowledge of our shared trickery - I was no expert on relationships, but I'd bet good money that stuff like this grew strength. We'd stuck it to each other while sticking it to the Council.

"We got off while throwing them off," I muttered with a snicker. I resisted joining him on the bed because that might undermine our tricks. Instead, I slid down the wall opposite him, resting my hands on my knees as I sat on the floor.

It was time to see if any of his magic had passed to me, despite the room's blocking action. I closed my eyes, imagining what he looked like without his glamor.

I'd only seen it for a few seconds that night on the beach, and the details were hazy. Still, I painted the picture in my mind as best I could, telling my brain the power to see it would be there.

When I opened my eyes, I gasped as his true fae form shimmered in front of me for a split second. The smooth, silver-blue skin that seemed to be glowing from within, and the sharper lines of his body and face. Not to mention those pointed ears I wanted to bite just to revel in his reaction.

"Anything?" he asked loudly. I glared and shook my head, keeping my expression frustrated. I'd learned to be a decent actress during my time with LuAnn, and it was coming in handy now.

Turning my gaze from Killian, I studied the room around me. I bit down on my excitement as I realized *something* really had worked. He hadn't been the only thing glamored.

The four walls seemed somehow less solid now, as though they were made of thick fog or smoke. Scooting around to lean against the bed, I stared at the wall that should contain a window. I unfocused my eyes and refocused, playing with my vision like I was trying to make sense of one of those hidden image pictures.

It was so fucking hard not to react when my eyes suddenly focused on the shimmer of glass, and I could see beyond the window for a split second. My heart surged as I saw the same six cells across a hallway. My eyes skipped across the cells, counting and assessing my guys anxiously.

Toro was floating listlessly in his tank, and Jack was shackled with iron bands surrounding his entire arms. His head hung low on his chest, and I couldn't tell if he was sleeping or nearly passed out.

Sol was stretched on his stomach on a bed like mine, and Dair was pacing, his shirt sleeves rolled to his forearms.

My joy was short-lived, though, as I realized Jai was nowhere to be seen - his cell was empty.

I pushed to my feet, going straight to the wall before I remembered I wasn't supposed to be able to see anything. I tried to cover it by swiveling and pacing, throwing my hands around like I was angry. In truth, my stomach was churning with worry. What were they doing with Jai?

My eyes slid over Killian, who had closed his eyes and was pretending to sleep. He looked mostly human again, and I was frustrated to realize my sight was already fading back to normal. A glance at the wall confirmed it - the power I'd gotten from Killian hadn't been enough to sustain more than a few minutes of magic.

The room wasn't completely blocking our magic, but it sure as shit was making it short-lived.

At this rate, I'd be fucking Killian once an hour. "Worth it," I mumbled to myself, biting down on my lips to keep from grinning.

"What's tha', Qilin?" Killian asked, cracking one eye. I huffed and shoved his legs over, making room for myself on the bed.

"This place is bullshit," I griped. I threw an arm over my face to block the light I couldn't turn off, trying to make sense out of what I'd learned.

There was definitely glamor at work here - both in what I could see and what I could do. The fact that I *could* access magic was huge. Whether or not they knew, was the next question. Surely, the Ringmaster knew, and that's why he allowed Killian in here.

Thinking of the Ringmaster and his circus made me realize how much this place was like a fun-house mirror maze at a carnival. Every time I thought I was seeing or understanding the real thing, another illusion was revealed.

The mirrors reflected everything except reality - like the glamor hid everything they wanted me to be able to see.

"It's the Ringmaster," I whispered to myself, knowing he was behind this. I wasn't sure how or why he had so much influence here at the Council, but I knew in my gut he was the one pulling the strings right now.

If that were true, what would he want with Jai?

And how the hell could I gather enough power to shatter these mirrors and find the exit of this shitty fun-house?

CHAPTER SEVEN

CARLYLE

I snuggled my face under the blanket, pretending to sleep. Killian rolled closer, feigning the same, and the two of us whispered to each other with closed eyes.

It was possible the Council had audio that could pick up our conversation, but I felt like we were being as discreet as we possibly could. I needed to talk through my theories. It didn't matter that we were at the Council - my gut told me the whole thing was just another of the Ringmaster's riddles.

"So, I feel like this whole room is like a big Chinese puzzle box. You know, those wooden games where you have to press just the right button or turn the dial a certain direction in order to snap open a hidden compartment."

Killian frowned, and I could tell his brain was working it over just like mine. There was something here that we were missing, and I didn't think it only had to do with me shifting into a Qilin. Sure, that was going to be important, but I felt like there was still a step missing.

There was something I had to do before I could get to that stage. I just didn't know what it was.

"Let's lay it out," I muttered, half to myself. "We know these rooms are supposed to block magic, but Turin still had his glamor on when he was in here, and so do you. I saw through some of it for a few seconds. Plus, the Ringmaster was able to siphon inside."

"The tech isn't anything special," Killian added. "These rooms have standard double-speak glass and touch-specific panels for entry."

"Ah, you lost me," I said, smiling although he couldn't see me. "I don't think that stuff is standard on Earth."

Killian ducked further under the blanket, and a bit of light brightened our hidden spot for a second. He grinned. "Probably not. Double-speak glass can look like one thing an' be another in reality."

"Like glamor? Should I be able to see through it with your magic, then?" I asked. Was it really just glass that *looked* like a solid wall?

Killian sighed. "No. Well, sort of. It's a natural thing in Haret, though. Like ya got marble or concrete here. We have double-speak, and some people have an easier time seeing through its true form. Without the iron blocking me, I'd be able to. But if I had to guess, I'd say it's you playin' Qilin mix-master."

That boggled my mind - I could be making new magic without even understanding how to do it. I knew way too fucking little about this world that I'd apparently been born in, not to mention my own powers. "Okay. So, what about the touch-specific panels? That sounds like a fingerprint scanner."

He shrugged. "It's jus' regular magic. The mages spell it to a specific person's touch."

"Can we trick it? Is there a counter spell?"

"No idea, Savage. If there is, Dair's your man." He sighed and glared.

"Hey, don't get discouraged. I asked for you, and we're gonna figure this shit out - the two of us." I lifted the corner of the blanket enough to let some light in again, so I could look straight into his bright golden eyes.

His guarded, golden eyes.

I bit down on a sigh. Killian and I understood each other, to a point. He was holding back, though, and now was so not the time.

He had a history, and I'd respect it like he'd respected mine. I'd gotten the sense from Sol that Killian didn't think much of himself, and I had my own instincts telling me his tough exterior was probably hiding a whole lot of soft uncertainty.

I'd been there before. Hell, sometimes I still visited.

But we didn't have time for self-doubt in this game.

"The thing with puzzle boxes is that one wrong move could lock us out forever, or worse," I whispered. Before he could respond, I leaned in and pressed a soft kiss to his lips. He startled against me, but he didn't pull away.

I closed my eyes, thinking of how we'd fucked in the sand the night we rescued Jack, and he'd taken me from behind not ten minutes ago, but we'd barely shared a kiss outside of that. For all I knew, he had the same fears as

Dair - that I only wanted him for his magic.

His lips moved slightly beneath mine, and his hands slid onto my hips under the blanket's disguise. His grip was harder than I'd expected, and I gasped into his mouth. That seemed to flick a switch in him, and his tongue plunged between my lips, delving deep into my mouth.

The kiss was far too short, though. Killian broke away before we really even got started, his scowl fierce.

"I canna," he grunted, nearly shoving me away as the blanket fell away from our faces, revealing us to whoever might be watching. "Turin will use it all against us," he whispered.

"Kills, I still don't care." I was aggravated and trying not to let it show. His uncle should want us to be getting busy if he hoped for me to find my Qilin form. The whole Council should be giving my guys champagne and roses and sending them in here, one by one. Or, you know, three by three would work, too.

"I mean, they know how my magic works." Obviously, they did - Aleron had tried to press his magic between my lips, but I wasn't about to tell Killian that.

Another thing about puzzle boxes is you shouldn't smash them in a jealous rage.

Killian bolted off the bed and stood facing the double-speak wall, staring straight at it as if he could see through it, though he'd told me he couldn't. "They know."

"Then what's the problem, fae?" My temper was flaring up even more. What the hell *else* was wrong, then?

"Jus' stop, Savage," he said, his voice almost too soft for me to catch. "Stop wantin' me to be somethin' I'm not."

I climbed out of bed and slipped between him and the

wall. Hands on my hips, I planted myself right in front of his face. "What exactly are you?"

"You need more than me," he said, avoiding my question.

"No shit," I snapped, and his face jerked to the side as if I'd slapped him. My heart sank as I realized how he'd taken my words. "Look at me," I demanded.

He didn't, though.

Too bad for his ass that there wasn't anywhere to run away in this tiny room.

I reached up and shoved at his chest, finding it way too easy to push Killian backward. My lion's strength from Sol was another thing that seemed to be working in this odd room, at least in part.

Killian stumbled as I kept shoving until he fell onto his back on the bed. His face was a twist of surprise and anger, but I didn't let up. I pushed him flat on the bed, and then I climbed up and straddled his chest. My fingernails pressed into his muscled chest, making deep crescents in his shirt.

Deciding to hell with keeping my voice down, I growled, "I need more than *you* because I was made that way. Not because you're lacking. It took me my whole life to be able to own up to that and admit that being insatiable is a blessing, and not a goddamn curse. I need all of you - all fucking six of you, if my gut is right. Haven't you been paying attention, fae? I'm not a one-man kinda girl."

The barest edge of a smirk pulled his lip up as I wound down from my tirade, and I breathed out in relief. "Now, I just had this same argument with the mage. Am I going to need to record it and just play the video for the vampire, too?"

This earned a snort. "Probably," he said, his lips parting even more. I wriggled my hips down over his jeans, rubbing myself against his growing erection.

"So, are you in or not, mate?" I whispered, keeping my face neutral and growing still. His eyes widened as he took in how serious I was. His hands strayed up to rest on my waist, his fingers warm even through my clothes.

Before he could answer, though, a popping noise echoed in the cell, and I was blown off his body by a blast of magic. I tumbled onto my back on the mattress, recovering a millisecond too slow to react.

The Ringmaster was there, and then he wasn't. And neither was Killian.

My jaw dropped as I blinked around the empty room. My fae was gone. I'd failed to get what I needed from him, and now he was gone.

Fuckity fuck.

Running to the double-speak wall, I shoved myself at it, trying to use my strength against it. Gritting out a scream of frustration, I struggled to see anything beyond the wall's flat silver surface. Nothing. All I succeeded in doing was exhausting what tiny magic I had left from Killian.

I pressed my palms to my temples, running through a dozen pointless ideas. I simply didn't have enough magic to do anything with. Everything was dampened just enough to be a tease.

I pushed to my feet and paced the narrow room, trying hard not to focus on how small it was or how trapped I felt. I could handle this. I could beat it.

Just as I swiveled around for another lap, the Ringmaster siphoned back in, nearly landing on top of me. I shouted some sort of garbled curse at him, but he merely stepped back and smiled, looking oddly sad as his lips twisted. His cane was braced before him, like a barrier, and his other hand was behind his back. I eyed him warily.

"It's so hard to find good wishers these days," he tutted. "You young people think you know what you want, but when you get it, you just squander your luck."

"I wasn't squandering anything! I need more time with him. My shift isn't even working with your mage potions - didn't Dr. F tell you?"

He looked confused for once, and I kinda liked it. "Who?"

"Ah, the fae doctor."

"His name is Marcel," the Ringmaster said, sounding oddly normal.

"Well, whatever. He gave me that serum, and I tried to shift. It didn't work, obviously."

"Hmmm. Well, I came here to give you another chance. This is your last wish, though. This isn't a fairy tale where you get three. I'm not a genie," he added, looking insulted.

"Nope, just weird," I muttered under my breath.

He drew his hand from behind his back. Gripped carefully between his thumb and forefinger was a dandelion - the kind with all the fluffy white seeds. I sighed.

"So, I'm supposed to blow the seeds and make another wish?" This was ridiculous, really. Why couldn't he just ask like a normal person?

He shrugged as if to say he couldn't give two shits what I did. Handing me the flower, he brandished his cane like a sword, backing away.

"On guard, Qilin! If wishes were fishes, we'd all swim

in riches. Choose well, or you'll drown your sorrows in blood and tears."

And of course, that was when he siphoned back out, because he was evidently goddamn incapable of having a normal conversation.

I held the dandelion up to the light, staring at its dozens of tiny seeds. Placing it carefully on the bed, I resumed pacing. I'd never thought about how often I took walks before being trapped in here. Even when I'd lived with LuAnn, I'd taken several walks a day, just to get out and feel the freedom beyond four walls.

Did he mean for me to choose Toro? I wasn't certain I needed the fish, although he could certainly help me figure out my shift. But if the shifting magic I had from Jack's and Sol's mating bonds weren't strong enough in here, I doubted Toro's magic would be, either.

I went back to my idea of the puzzle box. The Ringmaster certainly wasn't above dropping misleading clues. I shook my head. The fish wasn't the answer. Riches? Dair was wealthy, I knew that. So was Killian's family - but he had none of it.

I wasn't sure about the others, though they'd all dropped hints that they were from important families.

The blood and tears part just made me fucking nervous. That sounded like torture.

Blood, though. My mind latched onto the idea of having Jai in here. If I was trapped inside a riddle, he might know enough to help me puzzle it out. If I was locked into seeing something that wasn't really there, maybe it wasn't a physical glamor at all.

My steps grew quicker with excitement as a new idea formed.

Maybe the reason Killian's power hadn't been enough was because the glamor wasn't just on the surface of things. Maybe the glamor was actually *inside* my own head. *That* would be a problem for Jai's power.

And if I wanted the vampire in my mind, I knew it would hurt like fucking hell - I'd seen what it had done to Gina.

Making the decision, I grabbed the flower off the bed and brought it to my lips.

CHAPTER EIGHT

CARLYLE

Feeling goddamn ridiculous, I stared at the fluffy white flower. It trembled in my hands, and a few of the seeds floated toward my face as I took in a deep breath.

"Bring me the vampire," I ordered the empty room.

Tapping into my inner six-year-old who might have believed in this sort of thing, I blew the seeds as hard as I could. Swiveling the stem in my fingers, I made sure to blow every fucking seed off the stem.

The Ringmaster would be a stickler like that, for sure. I watched as the seeds floated gently to the floor - for some reason, that seemed like especially *bad* luck.

I'd always liked the idea of the seeds getting caught on the breeze and flying out into the world to find your wish.

Seeing them settle on the cold floor was a little depressing.

"Ringmaster," I shouted, after a few seconds passed with nothing else happening. "Bring me the vampire!"

There was nothing, so I shouted his name again. I knew someone was watching. Someone was listening. Maybe it was just my overactive imagination, but I could feel the artificial eyeballs and ears attuned to my every movement and conversation.

Eventually, someone would alert the mind mage with the cane, and so I kept shouting until my voice grew hoarse.

I sprawled back on my bed, chanting the words, then whispering them as the night grew long.

"Goddamn Ringmaster!" I yelled with the last of my voice, closing my eyes against the raw scrape of air across my throat.

In the following moment of silence, a distinct popping sound jerked me up. Sure enough, there was the fucking man of the hour. His coming and going had to be part of the game - asshole.

"Impatient, greedy girl," he said with a seething grin. I swear, if he'd had a mustache, he would have been twirling the thing. As it was, he was practically tap-dancing with that infernal cane. "How do you take your tea?"

"What?" I croaked, irritated that he could still surprise me with his dumbass remarks.

"Do you take your tea with cream and sugar? Just sugar? Perhaps a little blood?"

"Blood," I replied, shrugging. If he didn't have to make sense, neither did I. "Definitely blood. Now bring me the vampire so I can get some."

"Ah, yes. We could have tea with blood if we only had

blood. Or tea. And isn't tea magical?" He sighed, his eyes going all weird and dreamy.

I flopped back on the bed. "No wonder Aleron left your ass."

He was in my face in a flash, towering down over me with a glare.

"Too bad your mind mage power doesn't work on me, huh." I smirked at him. I could tell by his eyes that he'd be peeling the skin from my bones right now if he had the power to do it.

My heart was pounding in my chest, though, and I knew I couldn't keep up the brave face much longer. He couldn't hurt me, but he could definitely hurt my guys. I had a game to play, and I couldn't afford to lose.

"Look, I'm sure Aleron is shit in bed and you left him. Probably all take and no give, not to mention he never sucked you off, amiright?"

He startled backward, narrowing his eyes in such a telling way that I almost burst out laughing. Somehow, I kept my cool.

"I know what you want, and I can get it. I just need the vampire. And the fae back," I added on impulse. Maybe I could mix-master it up with both sides of the glamor - inside and out.

"Two? No, no. Greedy girl is two too greedy. I can't give you that much power." He pivoted on his heel and began to pace my room, getting about three steps in before the walls turned him back around.

"Then I can't give you the Path or the Portal. Or Aleron."

"*You* can't give me Aleron." He pointed his cane at me and sneered.

I resisted laying out my plan of giving him Aleron on a silver platter, cut into bite-sized pieces with his own fucking horn. Nope. That image wouldn't get me anywhere with this deranged ex-mate. Instead, I laid out the other truth I'd been betting on.

"Aleron acts like he wants me for his mate."

The Ringmaster interrupted me with a derisive snort, but I held up a hand to stop him.

"We both know he doesn't want *me* - he wants my power. He won't stop coming after me until the way to Haret is secure."

The man before me tapped his cane on the floor, considering. "Once the Path is open, it will be just us again," he said, his gaze growing thoughtful. "We'll have no need for you."

"Gee, thanks. But yeah. So are you gonna bring me the two men I need to open the Path, or should I just ask Turin the next time I see him?"

That got me a death glare. I had a hunch Turin wasn't aware of the Ringmaster's games. If the fae ever returned, I'd bargain with him, too. It would be one hell of a balancing act, but I could handle it.

"I need their power, mage. You know I do."

He sighed. "I'll see what I can do."

"Not good enough," I challenged. "You act like you have the power here. Like the Council listens to you. You act like Turin is just a grunt, but Dr. F and Aleron have been testing my power. I'm calling bullshit on your influence - the good doc will figure it out eventually, and you'll lose your shift. Bring me the vampire and the fae, or I'll start taking my bargaining chips elsewhere." Just for good measure, I pushed my hands under my breasts and licked my lips, hinting at what I might be willing to do for a bargain with Aleron.

It kinda made my skin crawl, but it had the desired effect. He made a muffled sort of scream and popped out of the room. Hopefully, he'd be back with Killian and Jai. I leaned back on the bed to wait, suddenly exhausted and just wanting to leave it all behind in sleep. It had been ages since I'd had sugar, too, and it was making me a sad, grumpy Qilin.

Maybe that was Aleron's problem, I wondered, smirking to myself. Either way, he was one messed-up dude. If the Ringmaster weren't so damn evil, I'd almost feel bad for him. He had it way too bad for that crazy Qilin.

But hey - all was fair in love and war. They were pulling my strings with my men, and they had to be crazy if they thought I wouldn't do the same.

I closed my eyes against the dull light in the room and allowed myself to slip into an exhausted, dreamless sleep.

The clatter of a tray yanked me awake, and my heart pounded with adrenaline as I blinked around the room. The door was just closing behind one of the Council workers, and I leaped out of bed toward it. It sealed itself just as my fingers brushed the edge, and I groaned, banging my fist on what was now just a wall again.

There was food, though, so there was that.

I fell to my knees, scooping the eggs and toast into my mouth. I probably looked like an animal, but who the hell cared. Shit, if they'd sent a cinnamon roll, I'd probably be rolling on the floor in orgasm as I licked the icing off my fingers.

I sighed, shaking the image away. "Ringmaster, bring

me the vampire," I yelled, intent on starting up my tirade again.

The air in the room constricted like the oxygen was being sucked out of it, and I staggered to my feet. I almost fell back over when the Ringmaster siphoned into my room, just inches from my face.

"Goddamn it," I cried, stumbling backward. "Ah, thank fuck," I whispered as I saw both Killian and Jai gripped in his hands. Neither looked conscious, but they were here. Tears pricked behind my eyes. They were really here.

The Ringmaster cackled and dropped their bodies on the floor. I scrambled to check them - they were breathing.

He bent down to look in my face, his hand darting out to grasp my chin. His face twisted into something lethal, and I shuddered. I'd taken to thinking of him as a lunatic, but sometimes I forgot just how calculating and ruthless he really was.

"Drink up, or your lungs will drink and drown," he hissed. "Get your shift together, Qilin, or the next wish is mine. And I don't collect men - I collect their magic."

The double-speak wall flickered, and I gasped as I saw a new scene beyond my window.

Crawling to the glass, I moaned as I took it in. My other guys were still in their cells, but now every one of them was spread-eagled and tied tight to a table. It looked like the opening scene of a horror movie, and my stomach churned.

"No," I whispered. "What are you doing to them?"

"I'm doing nothing. Turin and Marcel are growing impatient with your progress. They think a bit of pain will spur you. From experience, I simply have to agree. So, drink in your pleasure, pretty Qilin, or drown in their pain."

With that, he siphoned out of the room. The double-speak wall solidified immediately, and my heart pounded. Fuck, I had to figure this out.

"Jai?" I called, moving to shake his shoulder. "Killian! Wake up, boys. I need you."

They both began to groan and move stiffly, waking up slowly from whatever they'd been dosed with. Killian breathed out a solid stream of curses as he rolled to his back, massaging his temples.

"Fucking mages and their goddamn potions," he muttered, finally sitting up to look at me. "Hey, Savage," he whispered, his voice softer. I scooted to him, crawling into his lap. I gulped against the shaking sob that was threatening to break out of my chest. Killian's arms wrapped around me, and he made a shushing noise.

"Please donna fuckin' cry," he whispered. "I canna handle that."

"Such a guy thing," I choked out.

"You like my guy thing," he said, scooping me closer and nuzzling my neck. A shaky laugh made its way out of my mouth instead of the sob, and relief flooded me.

"Hey, vampire," I murmured, fixing my eyes on Jai, who was just waking up enough to understand where he was. I called to him in my mind, and his eyes widened.

I heard the barest whisper of reply inside my head, and I grinned.

"Get up. We have shit to do."

CHAPTER NINE

CARLYLE

It didn't take much to explain my problem to Jai and Killian. Jai's face darkened as I described what I'd just seen outside my cell.

"I expected as much, but I hoped it wouldn't come to this. You need my magic." The look he gave me ran a shiver up my back, then straight down again to my core, where heat exploded. My heart pounded as I understood he was really going to let me have him. "I'm nowhere near full strength thanks to these cells, but perhaps that's better," he added.

"Yeah, boss. Now you won' kill the Qilin," Killian joked. Jai didn't smile.

"Ah, we don't have a lot of time," I prompted, my

nerves singing as I stood. Well, this was awkward as fuck all over again.

Killian snickered. "Out loud, Savage."

I huffed. "It's true, though. I feel like a teenager playing a party game. Quit staring and kiss me so I can get in the mood or something."

Killian's gaze flipped to challenge, and he stalked toward me, backing me into the wall. I held my ground, and his strong arm wrapped behind my waist, sliding below my ass. Lifting me easily, he guided my legs around his waist.

Pinning me between the wall and his hips, he began to feather kisses along my jaw. The tension of our task quickly started to dissolve as I tuned into the sensation. I moaned into his mouth as his tongue licked across my lips, then swept into my mouth. I locked my ankles behind his back and rolled my body into his.

Slitting open my eyes, I stole a glance at Jai, who was still hanging back, watching. He didn't look nervous, though. He almost looked like he was enjoying watching me with Killian. I raised an eyebrow at him, but my eyes fluttered closed as Killian dipped his mouth between my breasts, finding a particularly sensitive spot.

"Bed, fae," I whispered, and Killian gripped my ass, turning us to the bed. He laid me down on my back and hovered over me, never stopping his kisses. I reveled in his strength, running my fingers over the corded muscles of his arms.

He tugged at my sweater, and I sat up enough for it to come off. Jai knelt on the bed, pressing his chest to my bare back and keeping me from lying back down. Killian adjusted, pulling my legs around so we all fit on the bed.

He kissed his way down my body, tracing his tongue around the full curves of my breasts.

Jai's hands were cool on my spine as he stroked up and down, supporting my weight but keeping a bit of distance still.

"Do you trust me?" Jai whispered, his breath mingling with my hair as he nuzzled against my neck.

I almost snapped at him, but I held it in until I could answer him in a calmer tone. "I think I trust you more than you trust yourself," I said finally, arching my neck to the side. His tongue slid up my sensitive skin, tracing and sucking at my veins. My breath stuttered, and Killian leaned back enough to see what was happening.

I caught the hunger in his eyes. He liked to watch, and he liked to participate.

"I need your magic," I whispered to my fae, holding his gaze. Challenging him the way I knew he needed. "Both of you. I'm in a prison cell, but I've been watching the wardens, and I know the secret. I have the key."

"What are you talking about, Savage?" Killian asked, shifting a little closer. Jai pressed in harder against my back, and Killian grasped my upper arms to steady me. Suddenly, I was the cream in the middle of the cookie.

It was a perfect place to test my theory.

"I think I'm in a mental prison, too. You're here - you're real. But everything else here is a glamor - I know you've felt it. I think the strongest glamor is in my head, though - I think Aleron or maybe even one of the Council mages added a blockage in my brain."

"Fucking brilliant," Jai said, his voice catching as he understood. "And lucky, too. These cells are blocking me just enough that I won't be too much for you."

I resisted rolling my eyes, leaning my head against his shoulder. I still thought I could handle him full-strength, but I kept quiet. I turned my face toward his and kissed him lightly on the cheek. "I need you to crack open my mind, and then I need Killian's magic to shred the glamor inside. Then maybe we can get the fuck out of here."

Killian's rough hands slid down to grasp my elbows, and he pulled me closer. "I'm in," he offered, and I caught the glint in his golden eyes.

"Not yet, you aren't," I shot back, lifting my head to glance pointedly down at his pants. His cock was growing long and heavy in his jeans, but that's not where I wanted him.

"Killian, on the bed, clothes off," Jai spoke up, a delicious note of alpha seeping into his voice. Killian responded immediately, and my core heated at the sight. "Ready yourself," my vampire added, and I wasn't certain which of us he was talking to.

"Yes, boss," I whispered, letting him know this was his mission to accomplish. If I was going to be opening myself wide and resisting my mind's natural inclination to fight back, I needed to submit my body to them, too.

"Fuck, baby, I hope I can do this without killing you," Jai murmured, almost too soft for me to hear.

"You can, and you will," I answered, working to drop my mental barriers as much as possible. I let him tug me off the bed and turn me to face it.

I gazed down at Killian, spread naked on the bed now. He was like a sculpture of manly perfection, with his pale skin and dark ink rippling over muscle after muscle.

"He wants your pussy," Jai said, his voice stronger this time. "Don't you, fae?"

61

"Aye," Killian said, staring straight into my eyes. From behind, Jai slipped his fingers beneath the waistband of my leggings and panties and began sliding them slowly down, his fingers like electric pricks against my bare skin. I shivered against the feeling, not sure whether it was too much or too little. Kneeling to guide the clothing down my legs, he paused to grasp my ass in both hands.

I gasped in anticipation, but he only stood and pressed against my bare skin from behind. His hands reached around and cupped my breasts.

Kneading them and rolling my nipples in his fingers, he pressed harder against my back, pinning me between the bed and his body.

I moaned against the icy tingles traveling across my skin. My nipples tightened as he rolled his body into mine, my back flush against his smooth, hard chest.

Killian cursed under his breath as his hand fisted his cock, and he began to stroke himself while he watched Jai and me.

Jai slid his hands to my wrists and lifted my arms above my head, trailing kisses up my arm as he nudged my hands back until they locked around his neck, and he buried his face in the soft skin at the base of my neck.

I gasped as he licked and sucked hard, as though he might suck the blood right through my skin.

I imagined him biting me, and he shuddered against my body as the image reached him through my lowered mental walls.

"Careful," he warned, moving his mouth back to my ear. "This is not the place for such pleasures."

His hands slid down the front of my body, stuttering over my ribs and squeezing the tops of my thighs. He pushed a knee between my legs, urging them wider. I rolled my pussy over his legs, needing the friction *now*.

Killian was breathing harder, both hands pumping his cock now. I was eager to take over the job, but when I started to climb on the bed, Jai grabbed my hips.

"He wants to taste you first. Don't you, fae?"

"Fuck yes," Killian answered, and Jai gave me a little push forward. I dipped my head to drag my tongue across Killian's tip, tasting the bit of pre-cum there, and he groaned. His hands flew to my hips and hauled me forward until my pussy was right over his mouth.

"Good," Jai said, moving to the side where I could see him. "Begin."

Killian's tongue plunged deep into my core, and I cried out, my fingers curling around his wrists as he held me tight against him.

My head fell back as Killian fucked me with his tongue, but out of the corner of my eye, I saw Jai begin to strip. His body was a different sort of perfection, but just as beautiful as my fae's. His muscles were tight and coiled beneath his smooth skin. Every movement was purposeful, and nothing was wasted.

He slunk toward me, lowering his mouth to my breast. Taking my nipple between his lips, he sucked as gently as Killian was sucking hard on my clit.

I released my hold on Killian's wrist to reach for Jai's cock, sliding my hand down its silky length for the first time. He made a sexy groan and his tongue sped up on my nipple. I felt the tiniest prick of his fangs against my skin, and his cock jumped in my hand as he tasted my blood.

I knew blood was a special sort of aphrodisiac for vampires, rather than the food source Hollywood had made it out to be.

I just didn't know how far the turn-on went, or how it might affect me if I started to take on Jai's power. All I knew was Jai feared himself under its influence the way a reformed alcoholic feared a single sip.

He released my nipple with a pop and leaned in enough to find my lips. His lips barely brushed mine as he teased, switching to demanding and back again so fast I couldn't keep up. His hands twisted my face toward his, and all of my senses were wide open. My fae and my vampire assaulted my body in the best way possible.

My thighs began to shake as Killian pushed me closer and closer to orgasm, and the wetness between my legs was so slick I didn't know how he was keeping his grip on my clit.

Thank fuck he was, though. One of his hands slid off my hip and under my thigh, where he pushed two fingers deep in my pussy. I was so blissed out from Jai's kissing that a few thrusts were enough to shatter my control, and I cried my release into my vampire's mouth, my body trembling to stay upright.

"Very good, fae." Jai pulled his lips away long enough to praise Killian, and he climbed on the bed. Kneeling next to us, he directed our next movements until I was poised to sink down on Killian's cock, and Jai was behind me, his fingers massaging my lower back.

"Not yet," Jai instructed as I pressed down on Killian's tip. "I need that."

"Need what?" I asked, ending on a gasp when his fingers slid lower, spreading my ass and trailing down to swirl through the wetness between my legs. He used one hand to push my chest down onto Killian's hot skin, opening me even more.

I didn't know if I could handle his mouth on my pussy, but as his fingers began to spread the moisture up and around my asshole, I realized that wasn't what he had in mind.

"Relax," he whispered as I swallowed hard. His slick fingers circled my asshole before dipping gently inside, stretching me wider and making me wetter with each pass. I moaned, pressing my face into Killian's abs. His cock twitched beneath me, and I realized he was in a perfect position between my breasts.

Raising myself up just enough, I squeezed my arms tight to my sides, pressing his cock between my breasts. He got the message instantly, and began moving his hips in slow thrusts, fucking my breasts while Jai continued massaging and stretching my asshole.

Fuck, my pussy was aching to be filled.

Killian grinned down at me, and Jai chuckled. "Patience, Qilin. All the pleasure will soon be yours."

Ah, right. It had been a while since I'd spoken out loud again, but couldn't a girl get some slack? These two men were driving me out of my mind.

"You want my cock in your pussy?" Jai whispered, leaning over my back and pressing his hips against my ass.

"Yes," I managed, my body thrilling at how close we were to what I'd wanted for so long. I'd build myself one of these goddamn silver rooms if it meant Jai would trust himself with me.

"Or do you want my cock in your ass?" Jai continued, moving his cock up and down between my two openings. I moaned, too far gone already to decide.

"You're the boss. Fuck me how you want," I

whispered.

He slid lower and pushed his cock deep into my pussy with a quick, powerful thrust. I cried out as he pumped hard, filling my core with those delicious pricks of icy sparks. My body rocked harder on Killian's cock, and the fae moaned, looking down at me a little desperately.

Jai pulled out of me, and I whimpered, needing so much more.

"Take your fae," he said, his hand sliding around my neck to pull me upright again. He didn't squeeze, but the thrill of having his strong fingers against my pulsing skin was everything. Killian reached forward to grasp my wrists, keeping me locked between them.

I felt both helpless and worshipped at the same time, and every nerve in my body was soaking up their touches and searching for their magic.

Jai and Killian worked together to line my pussy up with the fae's massive cock, and I groaned in bliss as I sank down inch by inch.

As my body stretched to fit him, Jai began to play with my asshole again, and I trembled with anticipation. Could my body handle what he wanted? All these times I'd told him I could - this was my moment of truth.

"Please, boss," I whispered, and he made a noise of appreciation. I felt his cock prod my tight hole, slick and wet now. He loosened his hold on my neck, allowing Killian to pull me forward a little more.

"It might hurt," Killian whispered, catching my eye. "But it's worth it." He grinned, and I felt a shot of heat as I pictured him and Sol together. I rocked myself forward on his cock, and his piercing rubbed me deep inside just as Jai breached my asshole.

Killian lifted his head to reach my lips, and he kissed me fiercely as Jai worked his way slowly inside. I squeezed my eyes shut at the sensation of being almost unbearably full. How could my body take them both?

Then the vampire began to move, and a whole new spot inside of me lit up like fireworks behind my eyes.

"Oh," I breathed, and Killian chuckled against my lips.

Jai's cock pressed my interior walls tight against Killian in a way I'd never felt before, and I growled with need as the pleasure started to hit me. Killian stopped laughing and groaned in my mouth.

"Fuck, tha' feels good," he gasped, and I grew even wetter as I imagined how his cock must feel, its length being rubbed by Jai's cock. I lifted my chest just a little so he could start moving, and my mouth dropped open in dizzy awe as they both began to thrust inside me.

Jai's arms banded around my shoulders and hips, locking me in, and Killian's hands squeezed my thighs, stroking my soft inner skin as he and Jai worked to drive me insane with pleasure.

"I'm in your body, now let me in your mind," Jai rasped, his body beginning to cool against mine. His icy magic swirled against my back and pulsed inside my body, smoothing over any twinges of pain and pricking awake every thought and memory I'd ever had.

It was like being fucked in a rainstorm of icy droplets, forced to suck down every cold drop and loving how it cooled my over-heated skin all the way down.

I calmed my mind as much as possible, letting their movements shatter my insecurities and disintegrate any regrets I had from my past.

Once, I'd feared my own desire, because I didn't

understand it. Now, I relished it, because I knew it would make me strong enough to protect these men I loved.

The room began to grow darker as I sunk into a sort of meditation trance, hypnotized by pleasure and rhythm. Jai's presence grew larger in my mind, filling all the cracks and sliding into every corner.

I cried out and whimpered as his power began to pry apart the secret places I'd locked away, but he didn't back down.

"Now, Kills," he cried, and through my haze, I felt Killian begin to rub at my clit. His thumb was slow at first, pulling my attention to that spot of pleasure like a magnet. As the pain in my mind intensified, though, he sped up his cock and his thumb. He worked to keep me locked into pleasure instead of the piercing ice in my head.

Finally, something in my mind shattered, and waves of bliss cascaded over my body. I came hard around the two of them, my body sucking what it wanted from Killian first, then Jai.

The room filled with our shouts and moans until I couldn't tell whose voice was whose, or which hands were where, or where my body ended and theirs began.

And finally, as I began to breathe again and come down from the heavens, I realized I couldn't tell where my mind ended and Jai's began, either.

He'd broken down every barrier and laid waste to the glamor that had been planted in my head. I could feel so much of his magic pulsing inside of me that I wondered how he had any left.

His muscles shaking, he pulled his cock from me with a groan and collapsed onto the bed. His eyes closed almost immediately, though his fingers reached for mine, interlocking tightly before he passed out completely.

I slumped down on Killian, completely spent. "Have you ever done that before?" I whispered.

He chuckled, throwing an arm over his eyes. "Na' like that. With Jai, never. Here I thought I'd seen all the fuckin' in the world, and you and the vampire have to show me I'm jus' a baby."

I giggled, pleased that I could still give my fae new experiences. So much of it was new for me - I loved being on the giving end, too.

"Did it work? The magic?" he asked, his hand sliding around my waist.

I nodded against his chest. "I can see everything they didn't want me to see, now." I was too exhausted to explore the ideas just yet, though. I let my eyes slide closed, reasoning that it would be even more suspicious to the Council if I started using new magic right away.

I wasn't sure how much they understood about what Aleron was calling alchemy - if they knew, I guessed they would have had all my guys with me, given us a huge bed and a bunch of porn to watch or something.

Smiling as I nestled closer to Killian, I thanked the moons of Haret that we still had some secrets to guard.

CHAPTER TEN

CARLYLE

It took me way too long to realize what was happening.

I was dreaming, but my mind was also wandering. Like, outside my body wandering. Or maybe, my body was with it. It was fucking hard to tell.

I could see my body as I moved, but it was all shadows and refracted light, like when I'd visited Jack in the circus through our dreams.

Even asleep, it was trippy as hell, and it made me a little nauseous wondering how exactly my magic had concocted this mix of power. It felt a bit like siphoning, only I wasn't taking my body with me. I was existing in a state of flux - similar to the middle part of the siphon - but I was able to direct my consciousness.

Another magic was at work, too, I realized, as I figured out how to direct where I was going. Killian's air magic was helping blow my form in the direction I wanted, and I was sure as hell hoping his glamor was going to keep me hidden. I didn't think I could fight back like this, because everything I tried to touch was like smoke.

I passed through walls and doors without touching them, seeking a tangible presence that I could feel like a change in the air before a storm.

Finally, I found the end of the trail of instinct I'd been following, and my gut twisted.

Aleron and the Ringmaster were huddled together in an office I'd just entered. I almost screamed when Aleron swiveled his face to look in my direction. His lavender eyes narrowed, scanning right over where I was hovering, and I held my breath like it would make a goddamn difference. If he could see me, I was done for, no matter how quiet I was.

He didn't see me, though. His eyes never focused on me, and even when the Ringmaster turned to follow his gaze, neither of them reacted in the slightest.

So, I was glamored to be invisible, and I was either traveling through walls on magical air currents or trapped in the siphoning stage of flux. What was the damn world coming to? Aleron would shit himself to have power like this. I grinned to myself and nearly laughed out loud before biting my lips closed.

I didn't know if my magic would take care of sound, too, and I had no idea how long this power would last. I might fizzle out in the middle of this office, barefoot and weaponless in front of my two worst enemies. Or two most annoying, anyway.

Giving myself a mental smack for fortitude, I drifted closer to listen in on their conversation.

"I just don't see how you expect me to trust you," Aleron said, leaning back in his chair. He had a glass of amber liquid in his hand, and he glowered at it before tossing it back.

"We want the same things, Aleron. Still."

"Power? Money? Revenge? Relationships are built on less, I suppose, aren't they, Jantzen?" Aleron eyed the Ringmaster like he was considering it, but for some reason I didn't buy it. I was also marveling at the fact that the Ringmaster had an actual name. All this time, I'd never heard it from anyone.

It seemed like I'd just learned a powerful secret, but I had no idea how to use it.

"I'm not going anywhere near that Path until the Council can guarantee I won't explode trying to open it. Let the girl try first."

"Indeed. Let Jill fall down and break the crown to show you how it's done."

"And how exactly are we supposed to get to Haret and claim that throne, if we're unlikely to succeed?" Aleron asked, his voice tight with irritation. I didn't blame him - it was frustrating as shit trying to talk to the Ringmaster.

"I have a plan for that," the Ringmaster - Jantzen - said. I shook my head. It was weird thinking of him with a real name.

"Show me. If you want to earn my trust, you need to spend large," Aleron said.

The Ringmaster hesitated, and Aleron scoffed, rising to leave. I shuffled myself away from the door, not willing to risk seeing if my magic allowed a person to pass through me, too.

"Oh, hasty pasty. I'll show you mine if you show me yours." The Ringmaster's grin was wolfish, and I got the sense this was an inside joke. Gross. I mean, totally something I'd say to one of my guys, but ew.

Aleron sauntered forward a few steps. "I don't need your cock anymore, Jantzen. I have three new mates - ones who treat me with the dignity I deserve."

"Servants - nothing more than slaves who behave," the Ringmaster spat. Aleron shrugged in agreement, and now my stomach was really upset.

How could you truly mate and exchange power without love? Dair and Sol had assured me that wasn't possible, but Aleron seemed to have managed it.

I cringed when I realized he would have done the same to me - and still would - if my guys weren't there to stop him.

"Still better than what little you have to offer," Aleron returned, holding up his finger and thumb in a measurement too small to be realistic. Hopefully, anyway. I mean, even evil people deserved more than two inches of cock, right?

"Insults and sneers - that's all you were ever good at. No true humor. No talent. Just the chosen one who chose wrong. The last Qilin King who stumbled and fell into the wishing well, while the hopes of two worlds came tumbling after." The Ringmaster was right back to his creepy self, and as he stood and brandished his cane, Aleron actually flinched.

That drew my attention more than any of their angry bedroom talk. What had the Ringmaster - Jantzen - what had he done with that cane? What magic did it truly hold?

I needed to get my hands on that thing.

Aleron scoffed, making a point of shrugging at the cane. "At least I'm better than a washed-up, dream-soaked carnie. You think having those circus camps of Haretian rejects gives you any respect with the Council? They don't want you back. They're hoping you decide to stay on Earth - they're betting on it, actually."

"Bet to win, bet to lose. Someone's heart breaks - at least I get to choose. You're nothing but a pawn."

"Fuck you," Aleron growled, and I smirked. How eloquent.

I still hated the Ringmaster, for sure. He was going to die, and I'd do it if nobody else did. But I had a bit of respect for him after this conversation. He was smart, in a crazy sort of way, and I respected smart.

"The house is no longer taking bets on that one, Qilin," Jantzen sneered. "You lost your chance. I still need your horn, though - it works better than your cock."

Aleron grumbled something under his breath and yanked open the door, but the Ringmaster shoved some magic at it, slamming it closed.

"I need your horn, Qilin. And I need hers. Dark and light together, remember? I have all the other pieces I need. Every. Last. Fucking. Piece."

Aleron turned slowly, his gaze disbelieving. "Every piece?" he repeated.

"Every piece but the Qilin. You're the only one I've told. So, pretty prince. What will be your first decree as King?"

Unease spread through me as I sensed a shift in Aleron's mood. He was getting excited by the Ringmaster's words, and I didn't just mean happy.

He was fucking turned on by the offer of power.

Not only was that twisted in its own way, it was hella bad news for me. It meant he'd do damn near anything to get my horn - whatever that meant.

I had a pretty good guess, though, as the Ringmaster began weaving a spell, conjuring an image between them. It was like he was opening a window, and we were staring through its hazy glass to the other side. The fog cleared, and I gasped, clapping a hand over my mouth.

Neither of them noticed, though, if my noise was even audible. They were too intent on the picture.

"The Portal," Jantzen announced, flourishing his fingers like a proper Ringmaster would do when introducing an act. "Nearly ready for my final show here on Earth," he added, as though he'd read my fucking mind.

"Is that..." Aleron's voice trailed away, and I gaped, hearing something I'd never heard from his mouth before.

Fear. Raw, panicked fear.

"Yes, Qilin. That is the Enforcer. He'll come for you, too, unless you have the right sort of protection. That means me, in case your memory is too short. So. I ask again. What will be your first decree, if I pick you up, dust you off, and fix your fucking crown?"

Aleron stared at the Ringmaster, and I felt like I was witnessing an historical moment. The come-uppance of the century. When the servant got served and the master got mastered.

When the-

"I'll do it," Aleron whispered. "Whatever it is. I'll do it."

"Excellent bet," the Ringmaster answered, the words

rolling off his tongue as he circled his arms around Aleron, drawing him in for a deep kiss. Aleron moaned into Jantzen's mouth, but I wasn't certain it was with pleasure.

Feeling shaky, I snuck closer. I needed to see that Portal. I needed to understand.

Austin had shown me a glimpse of the Enforcer, too, but it hadn't terrified me as much as it did Aleron. Maybe I just didn't know any better.

Peering into the window, I saw a large, round frame set with pieces of stone that looked like stained glass or a back-lit mosaic of glass. It was beautiful - the sort of doorway I might have dreamed up for a magical land such as Haret.

There were two gaps in it, though. Holes waiting to be filled.

Through those holes, I could sort of glimpse the Enforcer, in all his bull-headed minotaur glory. Panting and snuffing. Roaring and brandishing a fiery spear.

Seeing the Portal and the Enforcer together, I thought I finally understood Aleron's fear, and I crossed my arms across my chest and squeezed tight to keep my hands from shaking so much.

The Enforcer was stomping his hooves, waiting for his chance to collect me, the way the Ringmaster had collected all those poor kids. The way he'd collected all the beautiful, sparkling pieces of stone.

I knew what they were. Jack had told me once, and I'd glimpsed one with Kana's death before we saved her with Jack's scale.

I'd held Toro's bright blue one in my fingers after I'd pried the dark magic from it and saved his life.

Those stones were the *kardia* of all the Haretians the

Ringmaster had ever played his game of Life or Liberty with. The magical souls of every kid who'd never made it out of the Underbelly alive.

Burning with the need to destroy this Portal and all it stood for, I swiveled back to the Ringmaster and Aleron, intent on finding a way to make myself whole again and attack them with anything I could find.

The sight that greeted me, though, wiped away every other thought in an instant. It was like a train wreck - I didn't want to watch, but I couldn't tear my eyes away.

Aleron was on his knees before the Ringmaster, with Jantzen's cane pressed across his shoulders like a bar. His face was buried in the Ringmaster's crotch, and the Ringmaster was pinning him between his hips and the cane, thrusting hard. The sucking noises and moans were all the extra information I needed.

Honestly, I couldn't help but be a little proud of the Ringmaster. He was pretty good at being bad.

I was still going to wipe them both off the face of Earth and Haret, but I'd let him get his dick sucked first - the humiliation Aleron must be feeling was so epically worth it.

Grinning like mad, I turned my back on them and drifted down the hall, trying to figure out where the hell I was.

The magic that had propelled me forward was fizzling, and I had no idea what would happen if it ran dry while I was in this state.

If a mage got lost in the siphon, they would be lost forever. That possibility scared the shit out of me, so as soon as I recognized the hall leading to our cells, I sped up, feeling the extreme drain on my energy and magic.

Tumbling to my knees on the floor of my cell, I cried out. My body was whole again, and the floor was cold and hard against my skin. I had no idea how I'd traveled like that, but I determined right away I was going to figure out a repeat.

CHAPTER ELEVEN

CARLYLE

As I stumbled to my feet in the dimly-lit room, I realized it was too quiet.

When I'd fallen asleep, two men had been pressed against me. Now, their breathing was gone. I rushed to the bed, yanking back the covers. Gone. Goddamn it, both of them were gone.

A soft wail escaped my throat as I slumped onto the empty bed.

Fuck if I didn't feel more alone than before the Ringmaster had brought them to me.

Tears pricked behind my eyes, but I scrubbed furiously at my face. I would not let them get to me. It had to be the Council - the Ringmaster had been a little too busy to pull this off. That meant my games with Jantzen were over, and I'd be playing on a new board soon.

Fear tingled through me as I realized whoever had taken the guys would have also noticed my absence. I didn't even know how I'd left my cell, and I'd already been found out.

Sure enough, I heard the soft swish of the invisible door open behind me. The lights rose, and the good doctor fae entered my cell, towering over the room. His deep red skin glowed like an ember in the dim light.

"I hear you've had company," he said, his eyes skimming the room.

I didn't answer, my mind racing. Did *he* know what I'd just done, or was it Turin or Grunkeld?

"Where are they?" I asked, as soon as I could trust my voice. "I woke up, and they were gone."

He raised a delicate eyebrow, and my heart nearly pounded out of my chest. "They have been returned to their necessary places like the good toy soldiers they are."

My stomach lurched at that description. My men were so much more than mindless toy soldiers. They were kind and intelligent and-

"Save the speech, Qilin," the fae sneered, and I cursed to myself, realizing I'd been mumbling my thoughts aloud again.

"I need them back if you expect anything." I folded my arms over my chest. The fae clicked his tongue like a disappointed old woman.

"Where is your Qilin independence? Why are you so dependent on your mates? Is it because you were raised as a human female, and you know no better than subservience?"

"What the fuck?" I blurted, staring at him, wide-eyed. He did not just go there.

"Oh, surely you know what I mean. Humans love to subjugate one another, and their women are so much smaller. Fragile. Without magic, it was only natural for their men to learn to protect. But protection can sour quickly into dominance, and any strong being can learn to dominate a weaker one. Do you know what I speak of?"

I narrowed my eyes at him - he was asking me something else, hidden between the lines.

"Tell me, Qilin. Who is more dominant - you or your fae?"

I glared. "That's a little personal, doc."

He shrugged and looked pointedly at the bed. I grimaced, imagining him watching Killian and me. "I have seen him take you from behind, regardless of what modesty you played at. Yet, I think it was not his idea. He's weaker than you. That's why his family ruined him - nobody likes a weak-minded fae."

"His family ruined him because they were cruel, and you can fuck the hell off." It was a damn struggle to keep my voice down and my hands to myself. I really wanted to fly at that arrogant fire-skinned fae and pummel him.

"Tell the bedtime story however it lets you sleep. I know the truth. That fae isn't worthy of this institution. The vampire, though..." He trailed away, glancing at the double-speak wall. "His power is very interesting. I look forward to studying him."

This time I really did fly off the bed toward him. I never made contact, though, as he used his magic to send me sprawling hard on my tail bone. His magic was a little like Killian's air, but with the heat of fire. I'd been blown back by a blast of heat so strong my skin felt tight and dry.

Even as I groaned against the pain in my back, I wondered if I'd be able to replicate that with Jack's fire and Killian's air. I stashed the idea away. If I knew more about magic, I'd be doing a hell of a lot better mixing it.

"You have such incredible potential," Dr. F murmured, shocking me by reaching down and holding out his hand to help me stand. "I'd hate to see you bound to an idiot like Aleron."

"Well, there's something we agree on, at least," I muttered, pulling my hair over my shoulder and braiding it. "Why are you here, anyway?" If he was going to take me for more tests, I wanted to get it over with.

"I came to ask you how you managed to pass me in the hallway ten minutes ago when all of our security cameras placed you right here in bed."

"What?" His description rattled me. So, not only had I traveled out of the room in an invisible body, the fae and the cameras had both seen me at the same time?

"Your fae's glamor is not so powerful as that, and your vampire's mind control is not so precise. Tell, me, Qilin. Whose power were you accessing? Your day will go very poorly if I do not get an acceptable explanation."

"I have no fucking clue," I said, shaking my head and feeling a little helpless. "Bring it on, because no amount of torture could get me to tell you something I don't know."

His eyes narrowed on me, and I expected a wave of fire or pain, or at least a serum.

Instead, he waved his hands over the room, and I gasped as the air shimmered with unraveling glamor. Killian and Jai were still in the bed! Even the soft sound of their breathing greeted me, and I turned to the fae, wide-eyed.

"Impressive, no?" he boasted, and I realized he was showing off after I'd guessed his trick with Aleron. I *was* impressed, but I wasn't about to let on. "They won't wake, though. Not until I have need for them. Now, tell me everything you remember, so we can figure out your magic together."

I backed toward the bed, and he watched me patiently. My hands rested on my guys, one palm on each of them.

I marveled at how I hadn't even felt them before. They didn't stir, but feeling their solid warmth gave me some strength. The fae's comment about being dependent on them was rankling a bit - I was capable, all on my own.

It didn't make me weaker to have them around, did it?

"I take my magic from them," I began, mostly to myself. The fae just nodded. "Without them, I'm just a cipher."

"Ah, yes. Jantzen's crude term. Ciphers are not powerless, Qilin. They just experience magic differently than other Haretians."

"Are all Qilin ciphers?"

He nodded again. "All pure-bloods. Aleron is, if that's what you're asking."

I thought about the scene I'd just witnessed. The Ringmaster's cane was supposedly enormously powerful and deadly. I hadn't seen its magic in person, but I trusted Jack's stories. Yet, Aleron had borne it across his back - like a yoke on a beast, certainly. But not painful.

I tucked that idea away - if the cane didn't affect Aleron, hopefully, it wouldn't affect me, either.

"I keep the magic of my mates inside me. It's the strongest, and it doesn't seem to run out completely, though it's good to, ah, refill." I wasn't sure why I felt more comfortable talking to the fae doctor now - Marcel, if the Ringmaster was right.

Maybe it was just the first rational conversation I'd been able to hold about my powers, with someone who knew more than me or my guys.

"That is known, as well. Tell me something that isn't known. Tell me how your essence passed through the double-speak, leaving your body behind."

I gulped and shook my head. "I really don't know," I insisted. "Sometimes the colors get all mixed up and make new colors. New magic. I must have mixed it, whatever it was."

"I don't understand - colors and mixing?" His voice sounded impatient, like someone who was trying to learn, failing, and hating it.

"Each magic I gather has a different color to me. I don't know - it's just a thing I can sense. Like smells." I knew I wasn't making much sense, but my brain was trying to figure it out as I talked, plus I was trying to keep some of the information to myself still.

Marcel tapped his red chin thoughtfully. "You need more. I will wake them, and you will mate with them both."

"What? No." I balked, skittering away from his fingers as he reached toward the bed. I mean, yes, I planned to mate with both of these men, if they agreed. But not here. Not *now*, and not as an experiment. "Fucking no," I said again, raising my voice as the guys began to stir.

Killian blinked at me groggily, as though he couldn't quite figure out where he was or what had happened. He struggled to sit up, but his muscles seemed almost paralyzed.

"It's time for an experiment, young fae," Marcel said with a creeptastic grin. "Let's see just what Turin's nephew is made of."

I darted toward him, shoving at him to stop whatever he was about to begin. Killian groaned and sat up, now staring straight at Marcel in horror. Jai still hadn't opened his eyes, but he was stirring.

Just as Marcel reached into his jacket pocket and withdrew one of those infernal potion vials, the room vibrated with the pop of siphoning. I jerked back against the bed as the Ringmaster and Aleron appeared in the cell, making the space really fucking crowded.

Aleron and Jantzen exchanged a quick glance before Aleron shifted and charged the fae.

I jumped to my feet on the bed, trying to haul Killian and Jai into the corner with me. I screamed in reflex as Aleron's horn caught the fae's upper arm, gouging a deep channel in his flesh. The fae roared and sent a bolt of magic into the Qilin.

The Ringmaster popped around them and straight onto the bed, yanking my arm so hard I toppled right over.

"Now," he cried, and Aleron whirled on us, offering his large horse body as a shield from the fae's fire. He screamed a horrible whinny, but the Ringmaster locked his arm around the Qilin's neck, and his other hand was like a vise on my arm.

Just as he pulled us into a siphon, Jai woke, and his eyes connected with mine.

"Jai," I cried, my voice already fading as I was sucked away.

My last, haunting vision was my vampire, absolute

panic on his face as he scrambled up and reached for me, his fingers only inches from where they needed to be.

The roar from his lips split my soul in two as it reverberated against the cell, piercing into the siphon and following me all the way through the cosmos.

CHAPTER TWELVE

DAIR

I heard the roar, and I immediately knew what it was.

It was a rare occasion when our vampire leader lost his cool like that, and my heart sank with the implications.

I could also tell the noise was coming from the wrong direction. I'd seen the Council workers drag an unconscious Jai into the cell next to mine a few days ago, but my hearing pinpointed the sound as across the room, where they'd put Carlyle.

My heart pounded harder as the noise continued - if anything, it was growing louder. Jai was seriously out of control, and it was scaring the fuck out of me. What had happened? Was Carlyle hurt? Was Jai hurt? How had he gotten into her cell instead of his?

The questions spun through my mind as I struggled pointlessly against my bindings again - I'd tested every spell I could think of over the last few days, but my magic was too weakened here. I could still hardly believe the Council had gone this far with their treatment of us.

It was certainly a poor judgment on our part that we'd given them so much benefit - we should have run a long time ago. I would never again trust my people, and this knowledge weighed heavily on my chest.

If we were somehow successful in returning to Haret, that would only be the first of many battles. If the Council here on Earth had grown this corrupt, I had no doubts that its counterparts at home would be, as well.

The walls around me began to shake, and I fastened my eyes on the pane of double-speak glass, wishing I could access enough spell magic to make it disappear. It felt as though the entire building was on the brink of collapse, and as much as I wanted that to happen, I needed to be free of this damned table first.

I knew Jai's power was virtually untested - if this were truly all his doing, I feared it could be too late for our Qilin. I clung to the idea that, as her mate, I would have felt her pain. I'd felt it in brief bursts several days ago, but nothing at all just now.

Still, in all the time I'd known Jai, almost nothing had broken his control like this.

The double-speak wall before me shattered into a million shards as a streak of black lightning rushed the room. The table I was bound to crashed into the wall behind it, jarring a groan from between my clenched teeth.

"Goddamn it, vampire. I'm not as indestructible as you," I growled, as the iron-spiked leather was ripped from my wrists and ankles. The pain was intense but short-lived, and I stumbled to my feet, my limbs numb from disuse.

"Spells, mage! They're coming," he roared, darting back out of the room and to the next cell. His eyes were wild and nearly fully black with blood lust, and his fangs were fully distended, their razored edges glinting over his bottom lip.

I scrambled through the debris, feeling the pulse of my magic returning as the effects of the broken, iron-laced restraints and cell walls wore off. Leaving the vampire to tear apart the other cells where our team was hopefully waiting, I focused my attention on sealing the doors leading into our area.

There were so many entrances, though. I wasn't able to get to them all in time, and soon, Council workers were pouring like ants into the room from a corner door.

I barked a laugh as Sol leaped free of his silver cell, shifting in mid-jump and answering the vampire's ungodly roar with his own. Sol landed on a worker's chest and started ripping into him, but the worker managed to toss a potion at the lion before Sol's jaws closed over his throat.

Sol yelped and pawed at his muzzle as a green powder covered his face, burning his fur and skin. Already another worker was running forward with an iron-tipped whip. I lobbed a stunning spell at him to buy the lion some time.

Another of the whips caught my shoulder, and I grimaced, feeling it all the way through my clothing. This fight was going to be ugly.

Still, the Council had underestimated the amount of pain we were willing to endure for our Qilin. I still hadn't seen her, but there was no time to go looking - we were strictly on offense right now.

Jack stumbled into the fray, though he was disoriented and weaker than the rest of us - glancing back at his destroyed cell, I could see he'd been much more heavily bound. Fury washed over me again as I realized how cowardly our Council truly was.

They would pay for every fucking scratch on Carlyle's body, and every minute of worry they'd caused her.

I used my procurement spells to rip the iron weapons from the workers, tossing them through the air to Jack. Soon, he was cracking their own magic back at them. Looking better already, he strode forward, forging a path lined in bodies.

A tidal wave washed into me as Jai splintered Toro's cage, soaking me to the knees. The merman flopped his way into a shift, scrambling for some clothing. I snorted back a laugh - he'd never bothered to master the magic of shifting with clothes intact, preferring to shock people with his naked body.

"Watch your bait and tackle, fish," I called as he struggled into a pair of wet pants. He grinned cheekily and twisted just in time to throw a deadly-looking punch to a Council worker creeping up behind him.

I procured him an iron-tipped spear of some sort, searching the fray for our last member - I had yet to see Killian's bulky form or bright red hair anywhere.

Jai soared over my head with a massive jump, crushing a worker beneath his boots as he landed. The squish of organs and crunch of bone made me wince, but I was glad he had the stomach for it. Sol had rallied from the potion, and Jack was showing off now, cutting workers down nearly as fast as they were coming in.

We were finally making headway, and the rust was

chafing away from our teamwork. The Council's training had never exactly prepared us for this sort of ambush, but each of us had the necessary skills.

When we came together, we fought as a formidable force.

"Killian?" I called, still scanning the chaos. All the cells were busted open, but the fae still hadn't made an appearance. Jai reared back to me and gestured to Carlyle's cell before slamming his fangs into another worker's neck.

I hurried toward the broken box, shoving spells at a few workers who had somehow slipped past the others. Climbing into the remains of her room, I finally found the fae, slumped against the corner of the cell.

Angling myself so I could see if anyone came up behind me, I knelt to check his pulse. I nearly toppled over when my hand went right through his body.

What I'd thought was Killian was nothing more than smoke - an illusion created with his glamor. Since I'd disturbed it, the magic dissipated, and the image of his body faded until there was nothing left.

I shot to my feet and bolted for where Jai had a blood-soaked body clutched in his hands.

"Where are they, vampire?" I cried, needing to know as badly as I needed to breathe. My mate was missing. My brother was missing. My team was struggling.

We had so much potential power between us, but our magic was still being dampened by the amount of iron woven into every surface here. Our strength was waning, as more and more workers found a way in.

Retreating, we began to form a blockade, shoulder-to-shoulder.

"Where's the fae?" Toro called, and Jai looked at me,

his eyes accusing.

"Glamor," I spit at him - I'd done nothing but remove the illusion. "Where's Carlyle?"

"Fucking two-faced, dickless, half-balled, cane-up-his-ass Ringmaster," Jai growled, and I struggled not to smirk. His anger-fueled insults had always amused me, but now was not the goddamn time.

Jack's face had grown dark with rage, and he flicked his two whips in tight circles, keeping a pair of workers back. "I'll kill that mage," he muttered. "He's gone too far, too many times."

"Why did he take Killian?" Sol asked, shifting back and tugging up his shirt to wipe blood from his mouth.

"He didn't," Jai answered, crouching low in preparation for the next wave of workers. "I don't know what happened to the fae."

I started to wonder if Killian had managed some trick, but then the Council workers were on us. I could immediately tell a difference in their training, and I exchanged a glance with Jai.

We were fucked - the first batch had been the grunts, sent in to die.

This group must be the special ops teams, trained to the same level as we were. They also had the distinct advantage of being fresh to the fight and well-stocked with magic.

"We need a way out of this room," I said, glancing at Jack. "It's killing us." His jaw clenched, and he nodded, tossing the whips to Toro. Crouching down behind us and pulling his arms in, he shifted quickly into his dragon form, jumping into the air and spreading his wings wide. There wasn't enough space in the room for him to actually fly, though the ceiling had good height.

Jack flapped until he'd cleared the debris and bodies, then screamed, barreling toward one of the walls.

He knocked a good dent in it, but it was something much sturdier than drywall. Fire engulfed the ceiling as he tried a new tactic, and the air pressed down on us with a fierce heat as we battled our way forward.

Jack slammed his body into the wall again, and I gritted my teeth, knowing he'd be in pain later - he might even have broken bones. Dragons healed fast, but we needed to be ready to move him.

I could siphon one or two of them out of here, but my magic was too drained to move the whole group. All of us were running on empty, our power draining too fast under the Council's magic.

Jack wheeled into the wall another time, finally cracking it down the middle. His wings beat at the flames, coaxing them higher, and pieces of burning building began to tumble onto the floor. I groaned as I realized there were more walls behind this room - of course there were.

It would have been too easy if this room opened to the outside.

"We need a new strategy," I called to Jai, even as he ripped apart another person. Just then, the air popped in my ears, in the distinctive manner of someone siphoning into the room. I swiveled in the direction of the noise, arms raised to cast, and my head nearly exploded.

Grunkeld was striding in from the opposite side of the room - the one I'd closed off - and he was accompanied by a face I'd hoped never to see again.

CHAPTER THIRTEEN

DAIR

"Stop!" Grunkeld bellowed, and several of the Council workers began to fall back, retreating toward the door at the Council leader's orders. Toro and Jack paid no attention, chasing more of them out of the room.

My attention was locked on the woman standing behind Grunkeld - *Regina*.

She met my gaze for only a second, before glancing away with an embarrassed expression. My nerves ratcheted even higher. Why was she here, and what had she fucking done?

"Fucking Gina," Sol growled, sounding so much like Killian that I glanced twice at him before turning back to Regina.

"Cease your battling," Grunkeld called again.

"You've gone too far, Grunkeld," Jai hissed, the sound carrying across the room, half in our heads and half in the growing stillness. Most of the Council workers had fled the room, and Jack had stopped shooting fireballs for the moment. A few chunks of wall fell, still burning, as he thudded to the ground and drew his great wings in.

My team circled up, each of us watching a different angle, as Jai stepped close to the Council's acting leader.

"Where is the Qilin?" Jai asked, his voice promising the calm before the storm.

Grunkeld held up his hands. "I don't know," he admitted. Before he could get out another word, Jai darted forward, moving like a current of dark electricity.

Regina grabbed Grunkeld and siphoned him to the other side of the room, just barely missing Jai's attack.

"Vampire!" she yelled. "Listen first! The Ringmaster took her and Aleron. We've made mistakes, but if you want your Qilin, we need to work together."

"We?" I sneered, unable to help myself. "Since when do you represent the Council?" She'd been pretty high and mighty when working with us - vowing she'd never go back to them after they'd shamed her family name. "What changed, Regina?"

Her face blanched, and Jai stilled. He glanced at me, and I felt a whisper of a voice inside my head. *She was tricked, just as we were.*

I narrowed my eyes, turning back to her and Grunkeld. I didn't exactly doubt the revelation, but I had a hunch that wasn't the full story.

"What have you told them?" I called, and she trembled. Rage stoked in my chest - she'd shared our secrets.

"Please," she whispered, shifting her gaze to Jai. "I had no choice."

"Indeed," Grunkeld affirmed. "There is always a choice, but we felt Jantzen's Life or Liberty methods were especially pertinent here. Regina gave us what information she could, in order to avoid more of Marcel's unsavory methods."

I shuddered. Marcel was a ruthless fae, well-known in the Council circles for his excruciating methods of extracting information. I glanced to Jai, and his expression confirmed that he hadn't been aware of the fae's presence, either.

"Marcel took an especial liking to your pretty Qilin," Grunkeld continued. Jai roared, echoed by Jack and even Sol, and Regina leaped to siphon Grunkeld out of range yet again.

I had a sickening feeling Marcel was the source of the pain I'd felt through my mating bond.

"Where is she?" Jai raged, pacing in front of me.

"Calm yourself, and I'll tell you!" Regina cried, her voice high and desperate as she tried to track the vampire's erratic movements. "Jantzen took her - he's crossed us again, and we need your help to find them."

I couldn't stop the wry laugh bubbling up from my chest, and as soon as Toro caught my eye, he was chuckling, too.

"Goddamn, you people are a mess," he managed, wiping his eyes. "Why'd you trust that fucker in the first place?"

Grunkeld's face had reddened. "We had no better options! Working with Jantzen allows us to work without Turin. Aleron listens to no-one, and neither does your infernal team. I have a roster of dead Qilin, power-hungry monsters at every turn, and a deadline for destruction we're only guessing at."

"Maybe you need a new job, Grunkeld," Jack piped up, snickering. "I have a few connections with Underbelly - they need a new recruiter."

"Let us go, and there will be no more lives lost senselessly," Jai snarled, gesturing at the carnage on the floor. "We'll find the Qilin."

"And bring her back?" Grunkeld prompted, pointing a finger at Jai.

"Doubtful," the vampire sneered, and Grunkeld drew himself up, ready to deliver another ultimatum.

I stepped forward, my hands spread wide to signal peace - sometimes our leader had the democratic skills of a rabid dog. "Look, Grunkeld. Carlyle is my mate. I won't take your doings lightly, but I do know she's willing to forgive a good deal in the name of helping people. She's a true innocent in all this. Let us go, and let us find her. I won't stop her from helping you then, *if* that's what she decides. None of us will," I added, looking around at the team. I wasn't certain they were in agreement, but none of them spoke up to contradict. Not even Jai.

"Just let us find her," Jack said, his voice pleading now. "Underbelly is no place for a Qilin, even without the Enforcer breathing down our necks."

Grunkeld gasped. "Jantzen has called the Enforcer?" He looked accusingly at Regina, but she simply held up her hands helplessly. I knew Jai had frozen a good deal of her mind - she likely hadn't been able to give the Council anything except our location, which was even less than Aleron knew.

"Just let them go," Regina said to him with a sigh that I thought sounded a little too dramatic to be real. "Their mating bonds will fully activate as soon as they're free from your spells here. They have the best chance of finding her before Jantzen can unlock her powers."

Grunkeld's face looked about to explode, and I could hear his teeth grinding. He wanted no part of this plan. "You're finished here," he growled to Regina. She rolled her eyes, having heard that before. I wondered what non-options they'd given her in the first place.

"It's your only real option," I called to Grunkeld when I realized he was still waffling. Finally, he nodded, his glare almost comical in its hatred.

"Go, then. All of you get out of my sight," he barked, turning his back on us and stalking from the room. I glanced to Jai, and for a moment, I thought he was going to pounce on Grunkeld from behind and eliminate any future problems. He restrained himself, though, and turned to us.

"Move," he said, pointing to the door. "Before Turin joins the party. You - with us," he added, beckoning to Regina.

She spluttered a protest, but her face twisted in agony as Jai spiked his ice power at her, eliminating any other sounds from her throat. We all broke into a run for the exit, Regina hurrying to catch up.

CHAPTER FOURTEEN

CARLYLE

I clung to the Ringmaster as we hurtled through the siphon, although the only thing on my mind was tearing him to shreds when we got out the other side.

We popped back into reality inside a trailer - I would always be able to recognize the inside of a trailer, no matter whose it was, where, or how fancy.

And this one was fucking fancy.

Aleron shifted back into his human form, collapsing into a velvet armchair and surveying the room in disgust. He kept quiet, though.

Which was good, because I had a few goddamn things to say. "Where the fuck are we, and what the hell are you doing?"

"Pretty Qilin with such ugly words," Jantzen tutted, holding his hand up to stop my flood of more, even uglier words. "This is my home - it isn't made of gingerbread and candy, but I'll throw you in the oven if you can't accomplish my task. You will open my Portal, pretty Qilin." He turned to Aleron. "You will help her learn to shift, or you will be the hot one on the hot seat. I prefer you in *my* seat, but not until you're a little more broken."

Aleron's cheeks flushed, and I couldn't tell if it was anger or something else.

"This is Underbelly, then?" I asked, edging toward the door. I wondered how far I could get just by bolting.

"The beast, the belly, the Underbelly Circus of nightmares and dreams come true," he sang.

"You were the only one allowed to dream here, Jantzen," Aleron finally said, his voice bitter.

Jantzen turned and stalked toward him, pressing himself over Aleron and murmuring something that made Aleron squirm in his chair. I saw my chance, but as soon as I palmed the door handle, I cried out in shock.

"Solid iron, of course," Jantzen said, not even turning to look at me. He flourished his fingers, and a set of iron shackles slammed onto my wrists from nowhere, locking me to the wall next to the door.

"Hot damn. Who has shackles on the wall in their living room?" I was trying to keep up my bravado and my confidence, but I was starting to realize this wasn't going to be an easy escape. The Council had weakened me enough that the Ringmaster had the true advantage again.

Plus, he could turn Aleron against me at any minute. I grew still, if only to save my skin against the iron.

Fuck, I wished my cipher nature was resistant to that,

too.

The Ringmaster reached over and picked up the receiver of an old-fashioned golden telephone - one with a cord and everything, like in the movies. He murmured something into it, then hung up and turned to survey me with a nasty glint in his eye.

"You think I only play games. You believe I'm a little rotten in the head." He stepped away from Aleron and toward me, needing only a few steps in the narrow space to get right up in my face.

"Pretty much," I agreed, struggling not to cringe away.

"You underestimate me, as did the Council and many others. I don't *play* games - I win them. And I'm not just rotten in the head." He leaned in, close enough to kiss me. Fuck, I hoped he wasn't going to kiss me. "I'm rotten all the way to my core."

His hand skimmed up my body, barely even touching my sweater but still making me tremble in fear. If he tried to make a move on me, I'd tear my wrists to shreds to get away. I braced myself.

But his fingers stopped at my lips, hovering over them as he gazed at me with hard eyes. There was no lust there. I felt the barest shred of relief come over me, but it was short-lived.

His fingers crammed into my mouth, forcing my jaw wide, as his other hand procured one of those vials I was growing all too fucking familiar with.

I mean, seriously, was all the best magic in tiny bottles? I writhed against the chains and his grip, but the potion still made its bitter way into my mouth, spreading its numbing power down my throat.

I choked and gagged as my muscles stopped

responding. In a matter of seconds, the potion had frozen my lungs to the point where all I could think about was air - oxygen. Needed it. *Now.*

My eyesight darkened, and I vaguely felt someone unlatching me from the shackles. Then I was upside down, thrown over a shoulder and bouncing down the stairs into the night air.

Everything went black as the air in my lungs expired.

KILLIAN

Watching that fuck-faced, nutless bag of rotten dicks mess with my Qilin nearly had me blowing my cover.

I gritted my teeth so hard I was surprised they didn't crack in half in my mouth, but I managed to keep my glamor in place and slip out of the trailer behind Jantzen.

He'd fallen for my tricks twice now, but I couldn't get cocky.

My girl needed me - and I was fucking ready to lay claim to that title, too. Dair and Jai and I were too far up our own asses to realize the good thing we had here. Sol had told me as much that first few nights. He'd warned me not to fuck it up, and here I almost had.

But I was here, I had a beat on the bad guys, and a location on the prize.

I was in a better place than any of them, and I had to make my team proud.

My steps were silent in the grass as I followed Jantzen toward a row of cages. My stomach flipped as I realized he planned to lock my Qilin in a mother-fucking cage.

An iron one, too, by the smell of it.

Aleron strode past me, and I had to dodge out of his way when he nearly clipped my shoulder. Sliding on a pair of leather gloves, he reached deep into Jantzen's pocket and withdrew a key, giving him lovey-dovey eyes the whole time. I nearly hurled.

I still didn't buy their thing. Both of them was playing the other, likely.

Aleron unlocked an empty cage and opened the door just enough for Jantzen to roll her inside. Her body landed on the wooden floor with a thud, and I winced. I darted around them and tried to launch myself into the cage, but Aleron slammed the door too fast, and I had to duck and curl in mid-jump to avoid smacking into the bars.

Instead, I rolled under the cage, into the cool, dark grass beneath.

"Wake her," the Ringmaster said, and I saw just Aleron's hooves as he shifted. What the fucking hell was he doing?

Carlyle cried out, then groaned, and I nearly barreled into their legs. My muscles screamed with tension as I forced myself to stay still.

"Hello, Carlyle," Jantzen murmured. "I understand Marcel tried a few experiments with your power."

She mumbled a weak reply, and my heart constricted. When had she been with Marcel? Holy fuck, was Jai ever going to flip his shit.

"Marcel is a respected man in the art of medicine. His research is greatly copied. However, even he is bound by a few ethical standards. Not many, but a few. I, of course, am bound by nothing." Jantzen laughed.

"You finally fucking make sense, and you're talking

about torture," Carlyle said, her voice rough from the potion, but stronger already. I grinned - that was my savage girl.

"Call it what you want, but your choice will come sooner than you think. Life or Liberty, pretty Qilin. Think about it."

"Neither, because I'm gonna break out of this shitty cage and burn your circus to the ground again."

"No, you will choose, or I will choose for you. I prefer to keep my Qilin alive. Both of them. But I can open the Portal with or without you breathing." His voice grew fierce, and Aleron's flanks trembled as the Ringmaster threatened him, too.

So much for lovers. Looked like they were back to quarreling.

"Blah, blah," Carlyle said, sounding bored, and I bit down on my lips to keep from laughing out loud. Fuck, I loved this girl.

The thought knocked me out of my crouching position and straight down onto my fae ass. Had I really just admitted that? Goddamn, I was in deep. I shook my head, wishing these clowns would leave so I could tell my girl and make her mine somehow, cage or not.

The two of us always had been up for a challenge, after all.

I just needed to give it a little time to make certain the Ringmaster was good and truly gone.

CHAPTER FIFTEEN

CARLYLE

The Ringmaster gazed in at me, unfazed by my sarcasm. He smirked like he knew I was covering up my panic, at least partially.

My body was a mess of aches and pains I couldn't remember having injuries for, and it was really wearing on my resolve.

The real issue, though, was that I hated fucking cages, and this one was the worst yet. I'd gone from a large barrier around our safe house, to a smaller cell, to a minuscule iron cage made for goddamn animals.

I was not a happy Qilin.

"Can I at least get some food? Water? Coffee and sugar? Qilin are better sweetened, you know." I looked pointedly at Aleron, and his Qilin whinnied. I wasn't sure if he was agreeing or not, so I just made a kissy face at him.

He pointed his black horn toward my shoulder - the one with the hole he'd put there - so I decided he wasn't agreeing.

"I'll bring you food at sunrise. Until then, stare at the stars like this might be your last night. Life or Liberty, Qilin. Maybe you'll choose better than your dragon did."

Before I could get a word out, he'd siphoned away. Aleron kicked his front legs high in the air and galloped off into the darkened circus grounds.

Well, fuck. I was royally screwed now.

I didn't have much magic, and all of it was weakened by these infernal iron bars. I briefly fantasized about becoming Queen of the Whole World and outlawing iron.

Then my stomach growled, and I flopped onto my back. Everything hurt, and I was exhausted, starving, and starting to feel downright hopeless.

How was I going to do this? I still didn't know how to shift. I didn't have magic or know-how to conjure up another body-walking escapade, even if I had somewhere to go. I could be hundreds of miles from the Council by now.

I wondered what my guys were doing. I couldn't imagine Jai and Killian taking my kidnapping sitting down, but I had no idea what they could really do about it. None of them would know where I was, including the Council. The Ringmaster had played his cards well.

I closed my eyes and tried to imagine my Qilin inside me. Aleron made shifting look so simple, as did Jack, Sol, and even Toro. I'd seen my pretty Qilin once in the mirror, after the epic fuck and suck with Killian and Sol.

Surely, I could coax her out with what I had left from Killian, plus Sol's mating bond magic.

Thanks to Jai's work tearing down my mental barriers, at least it felt like my mind was wide open. I slipped deeper into a state of meditation, sifting through the memories that had been unlocked and unearthed. They seemed like hazy pictures, though. Something filmy covered and dulled what should be bright, shiny memories.

Every time I tried harder to focus and remember my instincts - to find my Qilin - it slipped away. It was like trying to grasp fog in my hands and hold it tight.

It was like glamor.

If I ever figured out who or what had hidden these things from me, inside my very own goddamn mind, we were going to have *words*. If I had my horn by then, there may even be a bit of shanking.

Cursing to myself, I pulled at the dregs of my magic. The magic from my three mates was there, though nowhere near full strength. I found mere wisps of Killian's green and Jai's dark indigo. Tugging at the green strands, I tried to wrap them around a memory, but they were too weak. I'd used too much at the Council, traveling through walls and watching the Ringmaster get sucked off.

I shuddered and opened my eyes. Fuck, if I'd only been able to control that power and save it.

The minutes ticked by, and nobody returned. The night was still and quiet around me, and after a while, I really did start to watch the stars. I found myself wondering where exactly Haret was - if it were something I could see in the sky if my eyesight were good enough, or if it were another dimension.

A tiny part of me still resisted that it even existed, but I couldn't exactly deny the magic I'd learned or the stories my guys had begun to tell me.

Sighing, I sat up and studied the darkness surrounding me. The moon was nearly full and bright, casting a good bit of light on everything. The few nearby trees were hung with ghostly-looking moss, and the scent of damp ground was heavy in the air - swamp, if I guessed right. There were other cages near mine, but none were occupied.

I wondered if anyone would hear me scream, or if they would even care. Probably they would be powerless to help me, anyway.

I'd have to figure this one out on my own. Somehow.

A soft rustling came from the front of the cage, and I leaned forward. Was there an animal there? A ripple in the air caught my attention, and I gasped as the air shimmered, revealing something that made my poor heart nearly give out in relief.

"Killian," I whispered, as my fae appeared out of nowhere. Not nowhere, though. He must have been glamored - invisible. "How?" My mind was spinning with ideas now. Tears pricked in my eyes, and I blinked them back furiously. I could pull his glamor and find my Qilin. I could get out of this cage *before* sunrise and siphon us both the hell out of here.

He grinned, sensing my excitement. "I stole your trick and followed ya into the siphon. Scariest damn thing I've ever done, but it paid off. Been listenin' and bidin' my time ever since. Ready to get the hell out of here?"

"Hell, yes," I answered, keeping my voice low in case the Ringmaster had spies nearby. I couldn't believe he'd risked his life like that. "I have to learn how to shift, Kills, or they're just going to keep coming after me. I need your glamor."

His face darkened. "Learnin' to shift is what he wants. Once you do, he'll have no reason to keep ya. I heard everything."

"Shifting is my best way out," I insisted. "We want to open the Path, don't we? I have to learn my magic."

He huffed out a sigh. "I'll give ya my magic, but I donna understand how it will help." He stepped close to the bars, scanning them for a way in.

"I'll explain it all if it works. Give me your hand."

He reached his hand between two bars, and I grasped it in both of mine. His cedar and whiskey scent wrapped around me, calming me instantly. I closed my eyes and worked to find his bright green magic. Just like I used to reach into humans' minds and tug at their emotions, I tried to pull Killian's power to me.

It wasn't enough, though. Magic was heavier and harder to pull, and I quickly grew frustrated. We needed to be together, away from these infernal iron bars.

CHAPTER SIXTEEN

CARLYLE

"Savage," Killian whispered, his voice barely a note on the wind. I opened my eyes and found his golden eyes locked on me, intense and challenging. His cheeks flushed to a ruddy color in the moonlight, and he swallowed hard. "I donna know what the future is bringin' us, but things have never been good for me until you. Ya need my power, and it's yours. All of it."

My eyes widened. Was he saying what I thought he was saying?

"You want to be my mate?" I whispered, and his long fingers wrapped around my wrist.

"Aye," he said, and my heart soared. "I only wish I had time to give ya somethin' fancier. You deserve so much more."

"We don't need fancy," I said, grinning. "We just need *us*. We don't even need fucking - Jack and I mated without anything but desperation." And I was babbling now.

He chuckled. "Well, we have tha'. Scoot as close as you can, and I'll make sure ya have my magic." His smirk shot through my heart, straight down to my core. I would have torn straight through those bars if I could, but the strength just wasn't there after everything I'd been through.

But I trusted my fierce fae. Even though I had no idea what he had planned, I needed his glamor. He'd risked everything to be here with me, and I couldn't fail him because of a little fear.

Killian reached carefully through the bars and tugged me forward. His hands grasped my leggings and yanked them just down to my knees, along with my panties. Even half-dressed, I felt too exposed and self-conscious at first - anyone could walk by and see us. I hadn't had a bath in days.

Did he really want to do this, or was he feeling pressured into it?

"Shhh," he whispered. "I'm no mind reader, but I can see how hard you're thinkin'." He put his hand under his own shirt and grasped the bar, with the fabric as a barrier, shrugging when it didn't burn his skin. "It's a little hot." He grinned, then reached behind his neck and yanked his t-shirt over his head in one smooth movement.

Ah, shit, he looked gorgeous in the silvery moonlight.

He'd dropped his glamor, showing me his silvery-blue fae skin. The swirling black ink of his tattoos seemed nearly three-dimensional, like shadows wrapping his body.

I reached through the bars and brushed my fingers

across the pointed tips of his ears, and his eyes nearly rolled back in his head before he pushed my hand away. "When we get ya out of here, I want you to suck those points until I can't remember my name. But na' tonight, Savage. Now, on your back."

I obeyed, and he drew me closer, careful to keep his arms clear of the iron. He raised my legs and rested my calves on the bars, making sure my leggings covered my skin. I could feel the heat, and a slight tug at my nearly-depleted magic, but it wasn't painful.

Killian wrapped his shirt around the bars right in front of my bare pussy, threading his hands through the neck hole to reach me. His hands skimmed up my thighs, and I let go of a soft moan as his fingers caressed the soft skin of my inner thigh.

I wanted him more than ever - all of him. I wanted his muscled weight bearing down on me while he fucked me slow and long, staring straight down into my eyes.

"Fuck, Savage," he whispered, and I heard him swallow hard. Guess I'd said that out loud, too. Damn if Jai's mind job hadn't broken down all the filters I'd been working on. "I wan' that, too. Next time. I'll mate ya now for survival, but I'll fuck ya later for love. Lift your head, though."

I raised up on my elbows, enough to see his face. Staring me straight in the eyes like I'd imagined, he plunged two fingers deep inside me, hooking them against my inner walls to find my highest pleasure.

"We donna have time for slow, but I can still make it good," he murmured. Pumping his fingers hard, he never broke his stare - that fucking heady challenge stare. There wasn't much sexier than Killian's golden eyes locked on mine, daring me to claim his power for myself.

There was a wild look in his eyes, and soon I felt him pushing at his magic, urging it into my body with every motion. I grasped at it and pulled, feeling insatiable and greedy for more.

He added a third finger, fucking me as rough and wild as his fae form promised. I moaned and bit at my lips, wishing I could touch him, just a little. Fuck, I wanted to press my whole body against his. Tonight, these bars were even greater torture than they'd ever been designed to be.

"Lay back an' rest your neck," Killian bit out, and I was powerless to disobey. He grasped my hip bone and urged me even closer. Heat radiated off the iron bars, but I was past the point of caring.

I moaned as he ramped me higher and higher, twisting and hooking his fingers inside of me while his thumb pressed hard on my clit.

My breathing had just begun to grow shallow when he slid a slick finger lower, toward my tight asshole and circled, teasing.

"Yes," I breathed, giving him permission. The tip of his finger barely breached my tight opening, and I cried out in anticipation.

Fuck, so good.

"I'll always make it good for ya," he panted. He reached his other hand through the bars again and raked his fingers over my belly, grasping at my hips to press me down harder onto his fingers, still moving relentlessly inside me.

"Fuck, I wan' you. I wan' ta be buried deep in tha' gorgeous pussy," he growled, raking his eyes over my core. I trembled with the same need, cursing the games we had to play to win.

Tucking one hand under me, he penetrated my ass slow and deep with one long finger, stretching my tight hole, while his other hand pumped my pussy and tugged at my clit.

"Fucking yes," I cried out as he added a second finger to my asshole, and an orgasm bore down on me so hard I forgot where I was while I rode the wave of pleasure. Still, he was relentless, finger-fucking my pussy and my ass at the same time until I came again, my whole body shaking against his hands. The hot ridges of the bars pressed into my trembling legs, and I swear the danger of pain made it that much hotter.

"God, Kills," I panted.

"Quiet, Qilin. I'm na' done," he said, withdrawing his fingers. Moving his shirt again, he somehow tilted my hips up just enough to reach my swollen clit with his tongue. He pinched me against the bars, just at the edge of pain and hot iron. Bracing his hands behind my lower back, he lashed out against my pussy, sucking hard at my clit.

I was so tender I had to dig my fingers into the wooden floor of the cage to keep from shoving his head away, but I could feel the glamor magic pouring into me with every swipe of his rough tongue against my pussy.

"Cum for me, Savage," he ordered, then locked his lips around my clit. My voice was rough as I cried out my release a third time, my grip splintering the planks beneath me as my head thudded back against the wooden floor of the cage.

I was both completely spent and pulsing with Killian's gorgeous, bright green magic. I knew enough by now to understand he'd given me every last shred of it - the ultimate trust that made the mating bond real.

Then I'd poured my healing power right back into him, rewarding his gift and filling his stores to the brim. He would be pulsing with energy, just like me. Once I found my shift, we could smash our way straight out of this fucking place.

"Can you feel it? The bond?" I panted. He had impeccable timing, my fae.

"Fuck, yes, I feel it. We're mated, Savage." His face was so proud, and I just stared at him, trying to memorize that look.

I wanted to keep it forever. When I learned Jai's magic, I'd shove this moment at Killian so hard he'd forget every second of self-doubt and unworthiness his fucking family had taught him.

He'd remember me instead - *us* - and how we'd chosen each other, no matter how many people had tried to choose us over the years.

A delirious grin spread over my face. My fae trusted me enough to lower his guard and let me in. My heart was full to bursting. I wouldn't let him down - I wouldn't let any of them down.

As my breathing slowed, I became aware of the crunch of footsteps somewhere nearby. Killian heard it, too, and dread broke through our giddiness.

"Get out of here," I whispered, panic coursing through my body. "They can't catch you!" I tugged up my clothes, and he yanked his shirt from the bars.

"I won't be far," he whispered, stepping back and disappearing into the shadows. My heart squeezed at seeing him go, feeling like a part of me was being ripped away. I hoped he *did* go far, though. Now that we were mated, it would be so much worse if he were caught.

He'd feared Turin using me against him.

Now, I was nearly paralyzed with the same fear about the Ringmaster. Jantzen would stop at nothing to blackmail me, and a brand-new mate right here in the circus camp would be like Christmas morning to him.

I couldn't see or hear Killian anymore, but I felt his presence like an echoed beat in my heart. I prayed to the moons of Haret that he would just keep himself glamored and hidden and not do anything stupid.

For now, though, I couldn't worry about my headstrong fae. I had a fucking job to do. Killian had risked his life to come give me this holy trinity of orgasms, and I needed to put every bit of that mating magic to good use.

Luckily, the footsteps had faded away, headed somewhere else. I was alone again in the night.

I closed my eyes and relaxed my whole body flat on the floor of the cage, releasing tension from one limb at a time. It wasn't hard after Killian had sucked so much pleasure straight from my core. I pushed his magic into every corner of my body, imagining it seeping into each organ and muscle. I let it spread over my skin, coating my pores.

Then I imagined weaving strands of Jack's dragon magic with bits of Sol's lion shifting magic. Wrapping that rope tight around my doubts to keep them at bay, I reached deep to find my Qilin.

She was there - I wasn't alone, after all. I could feel her stomping her hooves and tossing her mane in anticipation of breaking free from my human body.

Carefully, I let go of each fear I had of shifting - fear of pain, fear of being unable to shift back.

I even did my best to let go of my fear of death. If tonight was my last, at least I would have done some good with my days.

I didn't really think tonight was my last, though. I was pretty sure the universe had a few more games it wanted to play with me.

Come out, pretty Qilin, I whispered to the creature in my head, willing her to break free. *Show me your power. Show me your magic.*

She whinnied and stepped a slender leg out of the shadows in my brain. Her form was still hazy, like she was surrounded by smoke. I couldn't tell exactly what she looked like.

Come out, please. I need you, I begged, imagining her like a goddess I was petitioning for help.

It seemed like she ducked her head in agreement. Then there was a flash of horn and a thundering of hooves as she burst forward, leaping from something in my imagination, straight to something in my reality.

My mind exploded in agony as my body tried to figure out what went where.

I screamed out as my bones cracked and healed, only to twist and crack again beneath the tug and pull of muscle and skin. My whole body was a fountain of pain and confusion, and soon I couldn't even scream.

I just let her take over, hoping she knew what the fuck she was doing.

CHAPTER SEVENTEEN

CARLYLE

I was pretty sure I was going to die, just a lump of pulsating pain, right here on the rough floor of this cage.

Delirious and heaving for breath, I wondered if maybe my Qilin had just been waiting for the right time to break free and shed me like a human skin in one of those alien movies.

I mean, fuck.

My body was still changing, and I wasn't sure if it was any kind of good. It was taking for-fucking-ever. It was nothing like Sol's easy shifts in mid-jump or Jack's elegant transformations. I felt like one of those rabid werewolves from the movies, howling and slobbering my way through hell.

At some point, my body seemed to get the right messages going, though, and the pain calmed down to a dull ache. I kind of hoped Killian *hadn't* been near enough to see this - he'd either be disgusted by his new mate or horrified at what he'd helped cause.

My shattered bones finally started to reform and shape themselves longer. Layers of sinewy muscle wrapped each one tightly, like zipping up a tight dress. The peach fuzz hair on my natural skin thickened and swirled into a soft, downy hide that I expected would be soft as satin, if I could touch myself.

My scalp prickled and itched, feeling like my hair was receding all the way backward, and my ears tingled as they stretched. Even my lips felt weird, swelling like I'd been stung by angry bees.

Nothing about my body felt the same, but as I bucked and bristled my way into my new form, I could tell this was my Qilin.

Feeling a little vain, I hoped she was beautiful, at least. They say beauty is pain, so I better be a motherfucking goddess by this point.

My Qilin was definitely powerful. I felt the magic coursing through my body, despite the iron cage. The bars didn't seem to dampen her magic as much as they did mine.

Rearing awkwardly back on two legs, I screamed my way through what should have been a whinny. My muscles flexed, and my hooves crashed through the wooden floor of the cage, down into the iron bars below.

Ah, shit. Too much power. I kicked and thrashed, only making it worse as my new shape got stuck in the mess I'd created.

I'd fallen through the bottom of the cage, but I was still trapped. Broken boards and twisted iron poked into my belly and horsey ass from all sides.

Something moved in the darkness beyond, and I glimpsed Killian crouched in some bushes. I shook my big horsey head at him desperately - he couldn't come help me. I'd been making so much noise, the Ringmaster was bound to be on his way by now.

Killian half-rose, and I whinnied again, hoping my warning went through. I needed to learn how to push my thoughts, the way Aleron did. No, not quite like him. More like Jai. Yeah, I needed my vampire's power.

Killian seemed to get the message, though, because he knelt back down. His form shimmered with magic, and somehow, I knew he was invisible to anyone else. For some reason, I could now easily see both his fae form and his human glamor layered on top, plus a sort of hazy cloaking layer of invisibility.

I wasn't sure if it was the mating bond or my Qilin's power, though. He was watching me with huge eyes, drinking in my new form, and I shuddered as I imagined him running his rough hands over my spine and through my silky mane.

Trying to be calmer about it, I surveyed the broken cage. I could figure this shit out. I could grab my fae, get us straight back to the Council, and rescue the rest of my guys.

Being more careful this time, I kicked my way free of the bars touching my legs - my *four* legs. Holy fucking shit - my brain was still trying to accept the idea that it was inside a unicorn body now.

The bars groaned as I bent them carefully back with a

hoof. One by one, I moved them away from my body. Finally, the sharpest pain from the iron was gone. My hooves pawed impatiently at the grass beneath the cage, but I was still stuck. Splintered wood crushed into my hide, blocking my way up, and I couldn't duck down enough to fit this new, larger body under the cage.

Steeling myself against the scrape of the rough wood, I tried to scramble back up into the cage. My hooves were too slippery, though - useless without fingers to grip.

Goddamn it. I'd really screwed this one up.

Somewhere in corners of my brain, beautiful laughter began to peal, and the word *dumbass* slipped right to the forefront.

Shock coursed through my body - or was it her body? Was my Qilin talking directly to me now?

Use your fucking magic, the voice prodded me.

I grew still, focusing even harder on what this new body actually felt like. True, so many things were different. But I was the same inside. I had my same memories, my same wants and needs. My same hates.

And when I closed my eyes and focused, I could feel the same well of magic I'd collected from my guys.

Of course. *Fucking brilliant*, I thought at my Qilin. My head tossed without me telling it to, as though she were preening.

I clicked my big horsey teeth together a few times, wondering if I could bite through the bars with Sol's strength. Wood would burn with Jack's fire, of course, but I was too close to it all. I didn't want to end up in the middle of a fucking fireball on top of everything else. Spells were kind of useless without hands to do the motions, and I wasn't sure how glamor or air magic might help.

The simplest solution probably would have been to shift back, but I had no idea how to go about pushing her form back inside mine. She was resisting the idea pretty strongly, too. She wasn't ready to hide again, and to be honest, I wasn't ready for that level of pain.

Eying the bars at the far end of the cage, I breathed in deep, imagining stoking a great fire inside me. If I could aim it right, maybe I could melt the bars without setting the wood on fire. Then I'd work on kicking away the wood and making my way back up and through the hole.

It wasn't an awesome plan, but it was all I had right now.

I coughed up a stream of flames, trying to focus it right on a pair of bars. They heated red and started to slump a little, but when I paused to take a breath, the fire went out because there was nothing for it to burn. I realized this was going to take a long-ass time, and something sharp was about to poke straight up my unicorn ass.

I huffed and wiggled away from the intruding board, then started up the fire again. This time the bars sagged a little more, becoming about half as thick as some of the iron melted. Maybe it wouldn't take as long as I thought.

Just as I was about to give it a third blast, I heard footsteps again. More than one pair. The hairs along my new mane started to bristle as my Qilin identified danger, and I was not surprised at all to see the Ringmaster step from the shadows.

Followed by fucking Aleron, whose lavender eyes were wide with wonder as he stared at me.

My head tossed again, and I mentally told my Qilin to fucking stop it. This male was not one to flirt with.

I started to purposefully think of the things Aleron had done to me, and soon I could feel the horn pulsing on my forehead like an iron rod. Yeah, she hated him, too. Good.

A low, warning sort of whinny came from my mouth, and Aleron stepped slightly behind the Ringmaster.

I would have grinned and flipped him the finger if I'd had one. Luckily for him, he must have been able to tell I was so done with this day. I was in a horn-shanking kind of mood, more than ready for any dumbass who tried to come near me.

"I knew you could do it," the Ringmaster said, his voice seething with excitement. "You're even early for the sunrise ceremony." He gestured at the pale crease of color on the horizon, and I groaned in my head.

Fucking Ringmaster. Of course, he'd been waiting and watching for this moment. Probably eating popcorn in his trailer or making Aleron do lewd things to pass the time. My Qilin form was the whole reason I was here - I knew that.

I'd just hoped to have a few more minutes with my new body before someone busted in, trying to use it. Like just enough minutes to break free and go riding into the sunrise with my fae on my back. I snorted, surprised at how much the noise sounded like me.

"Let's get you out of there," the Ringmaster said, pulling out a key and unlocking the door of the cage. Like that would fucking help. But then he started casting spells, peeling the boards away from my flanks one by one.

"Are you sure you want her free?" Aleron asked, and I snapped my teeth at him. Thank fuck he wasn't trying to get in my head, though if he did, maybe I could learn that trick, too.

"How else will she open the Portal, darling?" Jantzen said, sliding Aleron a look of glee. I forced myself to stay still while he continued to extricate me from the messy shards of wood and iron.

I had no plans to open that Portal, but he didn't need to know that yet.

CHAPTER EIGHTEEN

SOL

Dair, Jack, and I were huddled in the floor of the van where Jai had dumped us.

Almost as soon as we'd reached the parking lot, the three of us had been crippled with pain, unable to even stand. I vaguely remembered Jai freezing the locks on a Council van to break in, and everyone piling in around us while he did something to start the engine.

The only explanation for the pain was that something massive had happened to Carlyle, and everyone was scared shitless.

"It has to be her shift," I muttered, as my breathing slowed enough to grit out the words. All that was left now were muscle cramps. I met Jack's eyes, and he nodded, though he looked less certain.

"Then I'm fucking thrilled not to be a shifter," Dair said with a groan as he twisted to pop his back.

I exchanged a glance with Jai in the rearview mirror. He was barely holding himself back from doing ninety, although we still weren't sure where we were going.

We were a team of six again, racing to find our Qilin before it was too late.

Nearly as bad as the pain echoing through our mating bonds was the fact that one of our six was fucking Gina, instead of Killian. None of us had spoken up about our fears for him, decades of training kicking in to make us trust Jai.

I was pretty much betting on the hope that the fae had managed to follow Carlyle though the siphon, because I couldn't face anything else that could have happened.

The only way any of us were handling his absence with an ounce of grace was because we knew Kills would keep Carlyle safe, or die trying. And if he wasn't with her, he'd sure as shit want us going after her instead of him.

"Any ideas?" Jai asked, turning his head to glare at Gina. "We're only a few minutes from a decision."

"One," she admitted, glancing out the window. The Council's property was massive, and we were evidently right on the edge of where its infrastructure joined up with the Texas highways.

"One's all we need, if it's good," Toro said, offering me a hand up into the seat. His glance asked if I'd trust her idea, and I just shrugged. We didn't have much choice.

Gina said, "Underbelly has lots of camps. Texas, California, Florida, Georgia. Probably more than that."

"New Orleans," Jai growled, swerving right at the first

intersection. He'd evidently read her mind, because she huffed and crossed her legs, snapping her lips shut.

"It's the perfect place to hide in plain sight," Dair said, nodding and running his hands through his hair, rearranging the dark curls. "The kids he breaks would just disappear into the crowds. Haretians are drawn there anyway, because they blend right in with the tourists' expectations."

"I don't know exactly where the camp is, but I've heard it's not in the city proper," Gina said. "Likely the swamp, somewhere."

"I want to save our magic. No siphoning in," Jai instructed. "She'll be fine," he added, glancing back at Jack. "Our girl isn't so fragile as she looks, no matter what you three were feeling."

"That much pain should have killed her," Gina snipped, and fuck if she weren't lucky my muscles were too shaky to do anything. God, I wished she weren't with us again, though I totally understood why Jai had forced her along. She knew more than we did, even if that still wasn't saying much.

"We'd know if she were dead. Now, shut it," Dair growled.

Jack nodded, but his face was pale, and the skin around his mouth was tight. I guessed he was probably trying not to relive his years spent as a captive in the Underbelly Circus, and what Carlyle could possibly be going through now.

"Six or eight hours on the road is enough time to hear quite the story from our guest," Toro said, looking pointedly at Gina. Her eyes widened as she scanned all of our faces.

"Yes, please do tell us what you've been up to since we parted ways," Jai sneered, jerking the van a little harder than necessary as he merged into traffic.

"Well," she stuttered, looking like she was about to make some shit up. I settled back in my seat and watched her, shifting just my lion's ears under my long blond hair. Like that, I could hear her breathing catch or her heart rate speed up. If she started lying, I'd know. I also lowered my mental walls, beckoning to Jai to listen in on anything I might hear.

I didn't relish the mission we were on, but it felt damn good to be combining our powers again.

"When I left the beach house, it wasn't long before Aleron tracked me down. He wanted information on all of you - your powers, your mating bonds, whatever. Of course, I couldn't tell him much." She glared at the back of Jai's head, and I smirked, knowing it would have been quite the headache avoiding Aleron's questions.

Literally. I chuckled to myself, wishing Carlyle were here to appreciate a good pun.

"I finally convinced him to quit bothering me for things I couldn't tell him, but he retaliated by tipping off the Council to my position. They, of course, assumed they could break past Jai's barrier."

Ugh. I grimaced. Whatever the Council had tried, it would have been every bit as painful as what Jai had done.

"Let's just say you didn't pay me nearly enough to endure that shit," she added, pursing her lips.

Dair twisted in his seat and studied her, but I didn't see any remorse on his face. "We aren't the good guys here on Earth, Regina. We're not the worst, either, but you knew what you were agreeing to."

She huffed, but she didn't contradict him, either. Frowning, I turned over Dair's words in my mind. I wasn't sure I agreed. We weren't about to play nice when someone tried to cross us, but we didn't go out of our way to hurt people, either. We acted out of defense for our team, not general malice.

"Keep going," Toro prompted, fidgeting. "I want to know more about the Council, not that asshole who can get in my head."

"There isn't much to tell. Once they got wind of my job with your team, it was over for me. I've been under the special care of Grunkeld and Marcel ever since." She winced, and we were all silent. Marcel's tricks were legendary, although none of us had directly experienced them.

"Do you know anything about Turin's role?" Jai asked.

"They'd love to be rid of him, but I get the sense that he knows too much. The Council has been filled with dirty fae for years - Turin is just the scum that's risen to the top."

"Grunkeld mentioned the fae and the mages are clashing even more now, though," Dair pointed out.

"There are three parties battling it out for the Path, now. The fae, the mages, and the Ringmaster. Whoever gets access first can control passage - money, power, prestige."

Dair nodded, glancing at Jai. "Everyone was working together when we first signed up. It seems everyone's growing desperate."

"The Council has mismanaged their resources and squandered every lead they had," Gina said, rolling her eyes.

Jack whirled on her, nearly snapping his seatbelt. "Qilin are not *resources*, you stupid bitch."

I startled, but as I realized he was right about what Gina had just said, anger swelled in me, too. The mood in the van grew hostile, and Gina held up her hands.

"Those aren't even my words, boys. You asked for a recitation, and you're getting one."

My ears perked up, though. She was lying. I hissed the intel to Jai in my mind, and he gave the briefest nod. I scented her sweat in the close air of the van. Gina would cross us if she could - she wasn't about to throw her hand into the pot for saving a Qilin unless it benefited her in some way.

It wasn't exactly new intel, given her history, but it might prove useful anyway.

As the drive wore on, we asked her more questions, but unfortunately, she knew even less than we did about the most important things. Finally, we settled into a tense sort of silence as we watched the miles tick down, bringing us closer and closer to where we hoped the Ringmaster had brought Carlyle.

CHAPTER NINETEEN

CARLYLE

I was almost free of the cage, and every muscle in my Qilin body was tensing to fight my way out of this circus act before the Ringmaster could force me to open the Portal.

I still wanted the Path to Haret to be open, so everyone had the freedom to travel home, but if he were the one controlling passage, we'd all be fucked. I was hoping my guys could help me navigate the Council people until we found a few who weren't so corrupt. Hey, I was a dreamer.

My front and back were thankfully free, but I was still pinned on both sides, keeping me from sprinting away into the nearby fields. My Qilin was stomping and huffing, anxious to explode into a run.

There was enough sunlight now to actually see my surroundings, and the circus was starting to come to life.

Behind me was definitely the beginnings of a swamp - clumpy trees, soggy grass that might not even be solid, and low-hanging moss. I eyed the shadows, wondering how many alligators waited just beyond my hooves. That was about all I needed to top off this piece of shit week.

I could make out rows of cages in the distance ahead, and the colorful pinwheel-shaped tents beyond that. I'd seen more than one small figure scuttle past, keeping to the shadows but still trying to get a peek at what was happening. A few adults had gathered too - big, burly men watching from a good distance and discussing something with big, burly hand gestures.

I guessed even in the Underbelly Circus, a Qilin was a rarity.

If the Ringmaster wasn't so fixated on this Portal thing, I'd probably be learning to prance or jump through flaming hoops, or some shit. Maybe giving little human kids pony rides for fifty bucks. Posing with brides in puffy dresses.

My rambling mind was brought back to my current problems by Aleron climbing up into the cage with me.

What the fuck was he doing?

He knelt by my side, laying a light palm on my neck. "Keep the fuck still, or I'll tell him about the fae you have stashed around here somewhere," he whispered, barely moving his lips.

I startled against his hand, and panic flooded my brain. How did he know about Killian?

"Yes, I can smell him on you," he continued. "I have to say, I'd still take you. If you're not worried about the fae, I could always just shift along with you and give these creeps a real show. My Qilin thinks yours is just *perfect* for mating," he hissed. I snapped my teeth at him, but he leaned away.

Smirking, he tucked his long white hair behind his ears and pulled open the leather satchel he was carrying.

Before I could barely understand what was happening, he'd slipped a fucking harness over my neck and was tugging a goddamn bit into my mouth.

I gagged on the bar and chomped down, only to feel sparks of pain radiating through my teeth and all the way to my brain.

"Iron, genius," Aleron muttered, taking advantage of my shock to tighten the buckles on the harness. Even the leather straps were braided with iron, I realized. The more I yanked against the binding, the tighter it pulled on my skin.

Holy shit, did I ever want to bite a chunk out of him. How could he do this to one of his own?

He backed away and jumped down out of the cage.

My whole body had started trembling, and even if I could have gotten free, at that moment I felt too weak to run. Between the harness and my fear for Killian, I was feeling dull pull toward passivity.

Fighting it, I whinnied and tried to rear up, but too many sharp things bit into me, and the whinny turned into a screech. My muscles were spasming even more now, and it felt like my bones had turned to jelly. I couldn't feel any of my magic now - the leather and iron braids were making me numb to everything. My world shrunk to a pinpoint as my vision blurred and my legs buckled beneath me.

"She's shifting back," Aleron cried suddenly, and the

133

Ringmaster darted forward as if he could stop what was happening to me. Even I had no idea how to stop it, though.

Pain wrenched my muscles away from the bones as they cracked and crumbled, shifting back to my shorter, more delicate human bones. Finally small enough, I fell down onto the grass under the cage. My skin felt loose and saggy, until it began to tighten and shrink around my regular form. Hair fell into my hands in great tangles as my mane shed itself from my scalp, and my teeth felt too big for my stretched lips until they sized down, too.

Within a few agonizing seconds, I was huddled on the cold ground under the remains of the cage, naked and shaking so hard my teeth were rattling together. At least I could spit out the fucking bit now, but the harness was still tangled around my body.

Well, fuck. This was going to complicate things.

"Get her," the Ringmaster barked, and before I could pull myself together, Aleron had crawled under the cage and was dragging me out, wincing as his hands touched the harness again. He hauled me to my feet, and I tried to cover my body, but all I had was my hair and my hands.

"Calm down. I don't want to look at you," Jantzen said, rolling his eyes. "Women's bodies are too soft and round." He made a face that I would have laughed at if the circumstances were different. Instead, I was slumped against Aleron, barely able to stand.

"What happened?" I asked, too disoriented to care which of them I was addressing this question to. As my senses adjusted back to my human body, I started to wriggle my way out of the harness.

"Your shift is unstable," Aleron said, staring hard as I

twisted in his grip. He evidently didn't have a problem with women's bodies, and as soon as the harness dropped to the grass, I yanked away from him. I pulled my hair over my breasts and covered my crotch with my hands, glaring at him.

"No shit, it's unstable. But why?" I darted my gaze around the area. My situation hadn't exactly improved. The iron bars were still at my back, and I was hemmed in by Aleron and Jantzen.

From somewhere behind them, an even worse sound began to reach me - the clanking of chains.

Ah, fuck, no.

Four of those men I'd labeled spectators were now readying long lengths of iron chains, each with an adjustable shackle on the end. They were edging closer, too, and I had nowhere to run. I just hoped Killian didn't try to come to my rescue - this was so not the time for a two-on-six fight.

"Why did I shift back?" I repeated, wondering if I could duck and roll under the cage before they could get around it. There was still the swamp, though. I didn't think I had enough energy to siphon right now. The numbness from the harness was still heavy in my muscles, and my magic was barely a tickle in my chest. Maybe I'd used too much when I shifted?

"I don't know," Aleron admitted, looking back at Jantzen with a shrug. "Shifting is different for everyone. Maybe it's the way you were raised human." He spat the last word like it was a disease.

"Well, you managed it once. Do whatever you did before. Shift again," the Ringmaster demanded.

"Ah," I stammered, pulling my hair farther over my

breasts. There were way too many eyeballs on me right now. I definitely couldn't explain Killian's special sort of encouragement, and I didn't want to give them any ideas, either.

"She smells like sex," Aleron murmured, leaning in for a totally inappropriate sniff. Well, so much for him keeping Killian a secret.

Without even a thought, I backhanded him. He hissed a curse and shoved me backward, pressing my bare back against a few of the iron bars.

I screamed and tried to twist away, but Aleron went flying before I managed. Fresh pain coursed through my body, and as I fell to my hands and knees, I saw Jantzen pointing his cane at Aleron, who was now flat on his back in the grass.

"Not another finger on her, or our deal is off," he said, his voice low and threatening. "I need both of you, and I don't have time to repair a damaged Qilin. You know as well as I do that you two are a precious commodity."

My back was throbbing, but my anger over the injury was nothing compared to the fiery rage I felt at being lumped together with Aleron as a goddamn *resource*.

"Get up," Jantzen snapped at me. He muttered a spell, procuring some sort of robe for me - the satin kind an old man might wear to smoke a cigar in. I tugged it on, wincing as it brushed my back. My body was healing, though, and even faster than normal. My fingers brushed over my shoulder as I eased the robe on, and I startled.

I pulled the fabric aside and stared down at my shoulder.

The hole where Aleron had stabbed me was gone - the skin was fresh and smooth, as if the whole thing had never happened.

"Fascinating," the Ringmaster murmured, noticing what I was looking at. "Your light healed his dark. This... this is unexpected."

I yanked the robe closed and cinched the belt, glaring at him. I really, really wanted to ask him what he meant, but my pride wouldn't hear a word of it.

He just stared back at me silently for a long moment, dark eyes flashing in the early sunlight. Then his eyes narrowed as a cruel smile spread across his lips. He snapped his fingers and pointed over my shoulder.

I looked reflexively, but there wasn't anything there. As soon as two of the men started for the bushes behind me, though, realization crashed through me. *Fuck.* Somehow, Jantzen had found Killian. I had to do something.

I darted to the right, taking advantage of the gap where Aleron had been standing. I was hoping to distract everyone so Killian could run, but the other two men were ready. They each caught me by one arm, and as much as I struggled against their grip, I wasn't stronger.

We were pretty evenly-matched, actually. The only way I was getting free was if I ripped my arms off, and that seemed a bit counter-productive.

Then one of them managed to snap an iron cuff on my ankle, and I yelled out in rage. I yanked out of his grip before he could tighten it too much, though.

If I never saw another goddamn iron chain again, it would be too soon.

My magic immediately dulled even more. The men surrounded me, and I tried to fight back with spells and fists and fire, but everything was a fizzle of nope. A second cuff locked around one of my wrists, and I lost the will to fight back at all.

By this point, I might as well be human.

I'd been at this state more than once. It was time to stop fighting and reassess. It was time to regroup and figure out a new plan.

My head drooped onto my chest as the two men flanked me, hooking the chains together with two more they'd pulled from their asses or wherever. Now I was bound, hand and foot, like a freaking animal. The pose was too awkward to even try sliding my wrists out.

About ten feet away, an unconscious Killian was in the same predicament. The two men handling him rolled him onto his stomach to finish hooking his chains together, and I gasped as I saw the streaks of blood on his back - right where my own skin had been branded by the iron bars a few minutes ago.

I moaned as I realized our mating bond had truly kicked in - in the worst way possible. He'd probably passed out with shock from all the pain I was going through.

"Did you mate with the fae, too?" Aleron growled, instantly guessing the same connection. "Insatiable Qilin," he continued, circling toward me with a predatory glint in his eyes.

"I was gonna take a break from fighting, but if you lay a finger on me, I will kick that dick all the way back to Haret," I spat. I would even head-butt the idiot if I couldn't get my leg up high enough.

"Enough, Aleron," the Ringmaster said, his voice annoyed. I smirked at Jantzen, thinking it was pretty damn funny how Aleron had a hard-on for me and not him. "How nice of you to bring your own collateral, Qilin."

And, I was done feeling cocky.

Damn it, I felt like such a failure. I couldn't control my shift, I was too inexperienced, and with all this iron, I was too weak to do anything. Killian had gone through so much to help me and gotten nothing but captured for his trouble.

I'd been fooling myself into thinking I was powerful enough - that I could handle it all.

"Please just let him go," I said, figuring it was worth a try. "You have me - that's what you want."

"Oh, don't play dumb girl with me," the Ringmaster said with a sneer. "I want so much more than your human body wrapped in chains. Put the fae in one of the empty cages. Iron, of course," he said to the pair of men holding Killian. "As for you, it's on to the Portal."

My beefcake captors nudged me along behind him. I watched helplessly as Killian was hauled away, while I was led deeper into the swampy circus camp.

CHAPTER TWENTY

CARLYLE

To my surprise, we did not end up at a portal, but at the Ringmaster's trailer.

At least, I assumed it was his trailer - it was the same place we'd siphoned into before. Aleron slouched back into that weird velvet armchair, and the two men holding my chains shoved me down at the two-seater table.

"Bring her food - sugary food," the Ringmaster commanded one of them. The other settled across the table from me, one hand still looped through the chain like I could really run away from anything at this point.

"You're going to give her sugar?" Aleron asked, aggravation lining his face.

"She is light," Jantzen answered, as if that explained

everything.

Aleron just glared down at the floor, mumbling something under his breath.

"Care to explain?" I asked, because why not. I wasn't going to turn down food in any form at this point. I'd eaten next to nothing for fuck knows how many days. The idea of sugar had my mouth watering so hard I could almost choke on my own spit.

"Qilin who feast on sugar stay light. Qilin who deprive themselves go dark. I need one of each," the Ringmaster said, surprising the shit out of me with a real answer. I glanced to Aleron, who was still acting like someone had kicked his puppy.

"So, you really *haven't* eaten sugar in a long time?" I asked, remembering the first time I'd met him. He'd mentioned something about missing sweets, and I'd just thought it was weird.

"We do what we do for the reasons we do," he muttered, sounding way too much like his ex.

The trailer door opened, and a plate of random shit was set before me. There were two hard, store-bought cookies, a scoop of butterscotch pudding, and a handful of chocolate candies.

"Seriously?" I said, rolling my eyes. I shoved a cookie in my mouth anyway, following it up with a dozen or so of the candies. Someone handed me a glass of water, and I sighed. "Would it be too much to ask for a cup of coffee?"

"Yes," Jantzen said, smiling.

"Just so you know, this isn't the way to a girl's heart," I said, gesturing to the plate. I didn't even have a spoon, so I used the other cookie to scoop up the pudding. I was not a fan of the stuff, but food was food. Sort of.

It didn't take long to finish the meal, if you could call it that. I did feel better, though. The sugar was waking up my spirits, and I thought if I could find a way out of these chains, I'd probably have my magic back.

"On with the show, then," the Ringmaster said, throwing open the door to the trailer. My handlers edged me back outside into the grass. "Shift," he continued, slamming the door behind him and Aleron.

"I don't know how to just *do* it," I insisted. "My Qilin is shy."

Aleron snorted, glaring at me. "Nothing about you is shy."

"Not me. My Qilin," I snapped back, and his eyes grew wide. He turned to the Ringmaster, and they had some sort of weird eyebrow conversation. "What?" I demanded.

"You and your Qilin are not separate entities," the Ringmaster said, assessing me with new interest. "You need to stop denying your very nature, or you'll end up splitting your consciousness into two minds. That would be interesting, but not entirely useful."

I stared at him - he'd been making way too much sense lately. I should have expected something like this.

"You don't *have* a Qilin. You *are* a Qilin," Aleron said, slowing down the words like I was an idiot.

I shook my head. I'd heard her voice in my head, and I'd felt her emotions. But it wasn't my voice or my emotions. Was it?

I closed my eyes and tried to tune out all the weirdos watching me. I sank into my mind, opening up to meditation, and called to my Qilin.

Where are you? I asked.

There wasn't any answer. Were the iron bands too

strong? Were they blocking her voice?

"I'm just a vessel," I mumbled, opening my eyes. "I take others' power and channel it. I hold the Qilin like I hold the guys' magic." I didn't understand how I could be something my whole life and not know it.

"Then channel her, if that helps," the Ringmaster said, an edge to his voice. "I need that horn!"

"How do I actually do it, though?" I asked again, still frustrated that I had nothing concrete to begin with. "I need these chains off - I can't even feel my magic, much less my Qilin."

Jantzen just shook his head, tapping his cane on the ground impatiently.

"Have you ever pushed your body to its limits? Done a sport or an exercise where you had to force yourself to control every muscle beyond its normal state?" Aleron asked.

"Ah, no. I don't think so," I said. I tended to stay away from extreme exercise, for the most part. Then again, I could think of a few times in bed where my body was pushed to its limit…

I felt my cheeks grow warm, and Aleron smirked. "Get out of my head," I growled at him.

"Not in your head, Qilin. Your dirty mind is written all over your pink cheeks."

I huffed and crossed my arms over my chest. "What's your point?"

"You're in control of your body. As long as you believe your Qilin is separate, you're undermining that control. Take it back, and get your shift under control," he replied.

I grumbled to myself, aggravated that my guys weren't the ones teaching me this. I didn't want to be an apprentice to these two assholes.

The Ringmaster began humming to himself and flourishing his cane, tapping at the ground near my feet now. It started as an annoyance, but as he tapped closer and closer, it felt menacing. When I glanced at his face, I saw evil grinning back at me.

"Shift," he whispered, striking my bare ankle. The pain that shot through me was instant and buckled my knees, bringing me to the ground before him.

Aleron began to back away, as though even he didn't want to watch this show.

"Life or Liberty, Carlyle. Take your pick," the Ringmaster continued, striking the ground again, barely an inch from me, then rapping my other ankle.

"Fuck you," I managed to say around the groan of pain. Fuck, I hated that cane. I just needed more time. More practice.

The Ringmaster whipped his cane in a circle, then drove it straight at my forehead. Agony radiated through my mind, paralyzing me from even moving away. He bent low, staring into my wide, frozen eyes. Taking the cane away, he smiled and whispered again, "Shift."

Gasping for breath, I dropped to all fours in the grass. I closed my eyes, desperate to do anything to avoid that pain again. If I ever got my hands on that fucking cane, I would splinter it right through his heart.

"You aren't the first to say that," Aleron mumbled, and I clamped my hands over my mouth. Goddamn no-filter mouth.

"Shift!" the Ringmaster roared, startling me so badly that I actually fell into the process somehow. My body shook and cracked its way through my second shift ever -

no less painful, but a little faster, maybe.

Trembling, I pushed up on four legs before them. The stupid iron chains were still locked on, too tight and resting just above each hoof now. The iron must not be preventing my shift, then, like it prevented my magic. It reminded me of Killian's description of glamor - how it was part of him and his inner magic.

Was it possible the Ringmaster was telling the truth?

The Qilin voice inside my head was silent. Maybe my Qilin really *was* me. Maybe she was the better version of me. Stronger, mouthier. More fucking magical.

I'd seen plenty of mugs and t-shirts advocating to be yourself, unless you could be a unicorn.

Well, now I could be both.

Making a conscious effort to change my internal monologue, I went through all my Qilin parts, claiming them. Not separate, but part of me. I straightened *my* long neck and tossed *my* head, enjoying the feel of *my* silky mane.

It felt so right, too, that I nearly forgot all about the Ringmaster watching me. I whinnied in excitement as everything seemed to click into place.

If there was a feeling to sum up finding your one true love right inside your own damn heart, I was feeling it. Sure, I wanted my guys - needed them like air.

But I felt whole now. Complete in a way I'd never felt before. I knew that once I'd mastered my Qilin magic, I'd be unstoppable.

Suddenly, it dawned on me that I wasn't experiencing my Qilin for the first time. The body, sure. But she'd been part of me forever, and her presence had been getting closer and closer to the surface ever since I'd met my

Haretian guys.

Every time I mouthed off to one of my guys and demanded they listen to me - that was my Qilin. Every time I fought back against the Council or any of our other enemies - that was my beautiful Qilin helping me take charge.

She was the me that I'd always wanted to be but had held back because of fear.

Carlyle the human girl had been feisty, but Carlyle the Qilin was ferocious.

I'd just leveled the fuck up.

"Good," the Ringmaster murmured. I swung my head around, pointing my shiny, silver-white horn straight at him.

I could kill him right now and end this shit show.

He chuckled, as though he could read my mind. "Patience, Qilin. You have much to learn, yet." He glanced over his shoulder, and I followed the movement.

Behind me, still draped in iron chains, was my beautiful, redheaded fae.

He was awake now, and his skin had a fine sheen of sweat over it. His golden eyes were locked on mine, but he looked so tired.

"Goddamn, Savage. I never knew bein' your mate would hurt so much," he said, his voice barely more than a hoarse whisper. His lips looked dry and cracked when he tried to smile, and my heart beat double-time as I imagined all the pain I'd shared with him. Tears pricked behind my eyes as I realized he wasn't the only one - probably Jack, Sol, and Dair were going through the same thing, with no clue why.

"No," Killian said, with a fierce look. "None o' this is

your fault. We signed up for it."

"He's right, Qilin," the Ringmaster called from behind me. I turned my body, tripping a little over all four of my legs and their matching chains. "Your mates chose their fates. So, let's go now, before it's too late! To the Portal," he announced, twirling his cane as he marched forward like a fucking band director.

Aleron shuffled along behind him, looking uncharacteristically worried, while I was yanked forward by the circus men. Killian and his pair of goons followed behind us, as we wove our sad little parade straight into the swamp.

Fucking hell. This was not looking good.

CHAPTER TWENTY-ONE

CARLYLE

We weren't quite in gator territory when we pushed through a clump of trees and came face-to-face with what had to be the Portal.

It was just like what I'd seen in my odd dream-walking episode, but in person, it looked so much bigger.

The circular frame was thick and dark, and there were hundreds of shards of *kardia* set into it. My stomach turned as I imagined all these lives lost or ruined. This was a beautiful graveyard.

A monument to mass murder that never should have existed.

"Don't look so glum," the Ringmaster said, taking my muzzle in his palm and petting the soft skin there. It should have felt nice, but knowing it was his fingers, all I could do was shudder. Could Qilin vomit? I was about to find out.

"My masterpiece," he said with a sigh. "My life's work - my chef-d'oeuvre."

I huffed. He could call it whatever fancy-ass word he wanted. It was grotesque, and I wanted no part of it.

"Show her," the Ringmaster commanded, pointing his cane at Aleron. For the second time, I saw a good bit of real fear cross the Qilin's face. It was still good to know he was actually capable of it, but it was terrifying that we were about to do the one thing he feared.

That meant I should be working on an exit plan, pronto. I had no idea how Killian and I were going to work with all these chains, though.

Aleron shifted easily, and I couldn't help but wonder if my shift would really become so effortless one day. He hesitated only a moment before stepping forward and touching his horn to the Portal, slipping it into one of the two remaining holes. I watched, breathless.

None of it seemed to actually hurt Aleron, though. Maybe just his pride.

He withdrew his horn, and the space filled in with a smoky darkness. Smoothly, he shifted back to his human body, clothes and all, like Sol and Jack did. Jantzen nodded at him, and Aleron muttered a procurement spell. The velvet armchair from the trailer settled in the grass, and one of the men holding my chains snorted.

"See?" the Ringmaster said to me, trying to sound soothing, but giving Aleron an aggravated look. "He's still magical. That's the beauty of Qilin. They're a vessel, so the Portal doesn't need to take their magic from them."

I widened my big horsey eyes at Aleron. I really needed to talk, but I couldn't exactly shift back. The Ringmaster would probably murder Killian on the spot.

My mind should be wide open, though. If Aleron was wandering mentally, he should be able to step right in. Hating every second of it, I yelled an invitation into the void of my mind, like I had many times with Jai.

Aleron's lavender eyes slid to mine, and excitement zipped through me.

Whose magic does it take? I asked, seeing the blank spot the Ringmaster wasn't mentioning.

Aleron shrugged, plopping into the chair and crossing his legs. He glanced at Jantzen. "She asked about my mates. My mates are fine, or I would have felt their pain," he said, not exactly answering my question.

I want to see them, I insisted, ignoring the fact that he was basically tattling on me.

"Well, they aren't here," he said, shrugging. "Now, hold up your end. It isn't like you have a choice, anyway, so stop acting like you do. It's a pointless waste of time."

I didn't like where this was going. What if the magic was something I couldn't replace, like a mating bond? What if one of my guys was hurt when I did it?

The Ringmaster stepped toward me, and Killian was brought into my line of vision. "I guess I'll have to play with the fae, then."

I shook my head and whinnied, my mane swinging from side to side. *Leave him out of this,* I hissed in my mind, knowing it was just as pointless as everything else. Aleron just sighed, and the Ringmaster didn't even react, if he could hear me at all.

"Open my Portal, dear girl, or this fae is gator food."

His cane hovered over my skin, and I felt the crackle of power and the promise of pain. I flinched away as the cane traveled toward Killian's chest. I didn't see any other choice. I glanced at Killian, and he nodded.

"We'll manage it, Savage," he murmured. "Whatever it is, we'll manage."

My heart soared a little at the words I'd used with Dair not that long ago. He was right. I couldn't prevent every bad thing. I could just do my best and deal with the fallout.

The Ringmaster turned back to me and skimmed his cane across my spine. It felt like tiny needles pricking my skin, drawing my magic closer to the surface. He ducked into my line of vision, his black eyes flashing. "Just to be perfectly clear, I can use this to suck you dry, Qilin. I can take your magic from your body any time I want. I thought you'd choose Life, but I'm open to hearing another word. What will it be?"

I trembled, hating that everything I'd worked so hard for was down to this one sucky moment.

If I picked Liberty and managed to escape, he'd only keep hunting me until he found me again. He'd send the Enforcer after me. His eyes narrowed with the promise that if there was a next time, there would be no choice.

Still, if I picked Life now, I might hurt one of my guys or even my own magic.

The Ringmaster began humming an off-key tune and backed away, pointing his cane at Killian again.

Aleron rose and came to stand next to me, leaning into my ear. "You'd give anything to save them. So save them." He gestured to the Portal. "Open that, and Jantzen has no more need for you, which means he has no more need to hurt that fae."

Still, I hesitated, really not trusting them. Not wanting to take the step that I knew I had to take.

Aleron shook his head and stepped back. "*Try* to be logical," he said with a sigh, as though I were being dense. "When you pour water from a cup into a pitcher, then from the pitcher into another cup, the first cup isn't harmed. You're a vessel. The magic you hold inside you isn't tied to your mates."

I took a deep, shaky breath. It did make sense. Sort of.

Except that nothing about the mating bonds worked the way I'd expected them to. I'd never expected to feel the guys' pain, for example, or to be able to sense when one of them was nearby.

But the longer I debated, the more I started to accept I really didn't have a choice.

My choice had been made for me long before I'd even met my guys. It had been made when the fae and the mages started battling for control of the Path.

It had been made when the Qilin had been hunted nearly to extinction, leaving Aleron and me as the only two left to do the job of thousands. Leaving us as pawns to those with more knowledge and power.

I didn't like it, but I couldn't fight it. Not today. Not like this, with Killian as a pawn.

My head lowered, and my horn pointed like a lance toward the shimmering Portal. Trying to ignore the triumphant grin on the Ringmaster's face, I stepped close enough to rest my horn on the edge of the last empty hole.

Taking a deep breath and praying I could deal with whatever happened next, I slid my horn into place.

It was pretty anticlimactic, really.

I didn't feel much of anything until I tried to take my

horn back out.

That's when the pain started. It was like my first shift all over again, only somehow worse. Killian shouted in pain behind me, and my body contorted its way through shifting back into my human form.

My horn was the last part to go, and I felt a *chink* echo in my head as a shard broke off of its tip, sticking in the Portal.

Fuck - what would that mean?

I tried to reach a shaky hand up to find the tiny piece, but I was blinded by the light that had begun to radiate through the Portal, spewing a rainbow of color onto the ground. A roar vibrated through the trees, like a tornado bearing down on us, though there was no wind.

Heaving, I crawled away from the glowing doorway. One of the circus men thankfully tossed me the robe again, but then he proceeded to grab my tangled, loose chains and drag me farther back. Even the Ringmaster had taken a few steps away from the Portal, but he was grinning like a maniac. He clapped his hands as he watched his creation come to life.

The shards of *kardia* were rattling like glass windowpanes in a hurricane. Even the ground around the Portal was rumbling, and I knew I needed to get the fuck out of here.

Unfortunately, I still had a fae and a few dozen feet of iron chains to worry about.

My captor hadn't seemed to notice how my human wrists and ankles were slender enough to slip through the stretched shackles now, and I was waiting for the right time to use this fantastic development. For now, I kept my arms crossed over my chest so the chains wouldn't fall off.

Aleron sidled up behind me, pressing his mouth to my ear. "Get comfortable, pretty Qilin. You're not going anywhere."

"I did it, though - you don't need my power anymore," I protested, knowing it was a weak excuse. Bad guys didn't just let the good guys walk away. If I wanted out of here, somebody was probably going to die.

I had no goddamn plans for it to be me, either.

Aleron's hand snaked around my waist, and I twisted away from him. He kept a hold on the robe, though, taking advantage of the Ringmaster's distraction to keep whispering in my ear. "See, I've been thinking that over, and I don't think I can let you go. I think you really are the light to my dark - the only way we'll both make it out of this alive is together." His breath made my skin crawl, and I imagined how satisfactory it would be to stab him with my new horn.

My shift was so unstable, though, that I wasn't even sure I could scrape together enough strength to do it again. Besides, I really needed to conserve any magic I had left to get Killian and me out of here.

The Ringmaster began to giggle like a kid and clap his hands, and I snapped my attention back to the Portal. It was so bright now that I could barely look at it, and all the rainbow colors had been washed out by the blinding white.

Except for the very center, where the dark hole Aleron's magic had filled was steadily growing.

"You promised," Aleron shrieked suddenly, releasing me and stumbling backward. "Traitor!"

"Hush," Jantzen cried, pointing at me, but yelling at Aleron. "I'll keep you both from him if you listen! But the irony. I love the irony!"

"What is he talking about?" I yelled, tearing myself away from the circus men, too. One of them actually took off running as Aleron continued to scream curses at the Ringmaster.

I wriggled out of my too-large shackles and shed my wraps of chains. Summoning a bit of Dair's yellow magic, I sent a bolt crackling toward one of my captors, and he ducked. The magic hit another one behind him, though, and the third backed off when he saw his buddy convulse like he'd been hit with a taser.

"It's the Enforcer," Kills called, struggling desperately against his own iron. I stumbled to him, and none of the men stopped me. It seemed the threat of the Enforcer coming after them was more terrifying than whatever the Ringmaster might do.

"He hunts Qilin, and you two just unlocked the door to let him in."

"Fuck," I groaned, tugging at his chains, too, trying in vain to rip them away. Irony wasn't even the half of it. "We have to get out of here." I could see it better, now. The dark shape in the center of the Portal was most fucking definitely the enormous, bull-like Enforcer.

"The beast is hungry," the Ringmaster called over the growing roar from the Portal. "The Enforcer must be fed. If you run, he will chase!"

Aleron started to tremble, his gaze darting wildly between Jantzen and the Portal. I could tell he was thinking of running anyway.

We'd just opened the door and invited the monster in for dinner.

Evidently, one of us could be the main course.

"Get the fuck out o' here, Savage," Killian growled in

my ear. His chains weren't going anywhere.

I clung to his neck, my arms like a vise around him as I kissed the soft skin behind his ear.

"Don't ask me to do that," I begged, even as he started to grasp my waist and push me away.

"I canna handle it if your pain is because of me. Donna do that to *me*," he whispered, his fingers tugging my face up. Staring fiercely down at me, he kissed my mouth rough and fast, pouring his desperation into the kiss. "All my life, I've fucked up everythin'. Let me do this right."

"But it's *not* right," I whimpered, trying to shake my head. We had to make our move now, before the beast broke through.

"It's right for me. Now, donna make this hard, Qilin. *Go*, and let your fae take the fall. I'll survive if I'm still - he prefers the chase. I'll find ya. But if something happens to *you* because of me? I won' survive. Na' me," he said, his sharp edges softening as something I never thought I'd see crept into his eyes.

I brushed my fingertips over his cheekbones, collecting the tear from each eye like it was an elixir of life. The tiny moisture soaked into my skin immediately, and I loosened my grip on his neck. I knew what I had to do, but I fucking hated it.

My heart went numb as he pushed me away, shoving at me hard enough to make me stumble. He never once broke eye contact with me as I backed into the trees, tears streaming down my face now.

"Run, Savage," he whispered. "Run faster than the beast."

CHAPTER TWENTY-TWO

CARLYLE

"Don't run," Aleron bellowed behind me, but I trusted my fae.

I ran like hell because I needed to stay alive.

Behind me, I heard the Ringmaster begin to cackle. I registered the screams of a man and the wet, gnashing sounds of someone dying. I didn't feel pain, though, so it wasn't Killian.

I kept running, ignoring every sharp thing stabbing my bare feet and the stitch in my side. A Qilin form would have been useful now, but I was terrified enough without adding a painful shift. Besides, maybe the Enforcer wouldn't know I was a Qilin if I looked like a girl.

Ah, no.

Crashing sounded behind me, along with a horrifying snort and snuffle noise that could only be the bull beast thundering after me.

"Run, run, as fast as you can, pretty Qilin! The Enforcer is coming for you. He'll grind your bones to make his bread. He'll-"

Thankfully, my breathing soon started to drown out the rest of the nursery rhyme cocktail the Ringmaster was tossing back. I bit down on a scream as a pinecone wedged into my arch, then a branch whacked my ribs, nearly stealing my breath.

I could tell the thing was closing in. I couldn't outrun it - I'd have to use magic.

Now that the iron was far behind me, my body was coursing with magic again.

Gathering my focus as best I could while being in a dead damn sprint, I pictured the beach safe house where we'd been captured from - it wasn't the best, but it was the first place I thought of.

Siphoning had to be precise, and my brain was too scrambled to cobble together another location this fast.

Ducking behind a fat-trunked tree laced with moss, I heaved out the words for the spell and twisted my fingers, just as the wood above my head splintered and shattered. A meaty paw loomed in front of me, and I shrieked just as the siphon sucked me from between the Enforcer's enormous hands.

I fought my way through the dark siphon, operating on pure willpower to force away my panic. I absolutely had to focus on where I was going. Finally, I made it out the other side, sprawling into the hot noon sand at the edge of the beach house - right about where I'd been stabbed by that asshole Qilin.

The magical barrier had crumbled while we'd been gone, and I staggered to my feet, searching the beach for signs of danger.

"Ah, fuck," I whispered, as the air around me crackled and popped with the sound of a siphon. Without even looking back, I broke into a run across the packed wet sand.

It had followed me.

My throat constricted as the snorting of the beast reached my ears. I risked a glance back, just in time to see it throw its massive head back and roar. The Enforcer locked me in his beady black eyes and charged.

I fought back a pointless sob and combed my mind for another place to siphon, even as I pushed my body to its limit. I had to be faster - it had followed me here the same way I'd once followed the Ringmaster.

I imagined my bedroom inside the house and siphoned there a split second before the thing caught up with me. Ducking below the window frame, I heaved and struggled to catch my breath. I'd bought myself a few seconds, but I knew the Enforcer wouldn't be fooled long.

It was twice the size of any of my guys - maybe even three times. I had no idea what magic it had, other than siphoning. Was it a type of mage? A shifter?

Fuck, I had no idea what I was really up against.

My stomach flipped as I realized there was really only one place I could go at this point - back to the motherfucking Council.

My guys would be there, and hopefully the Council could keep this thing from devouring me or whatever the hell it wanted to do. They would at least try to protect me.

I was valuable to them.

I heard doors and walls crashing downstairs, and I knew it was do or die. Screwing my eyes shut, I imagined my cell in the Council. I had no idea where it actually was, but I remembered every fucking inch of that room.

Growling out the spell, I twisted my fingers just in time, siphoning out of the room as the Enforcer was charging and bellowing up the stairs.

The room I landed in was not the room I'd imagined, though.

I stood on shaky legs, catching my breath as I surveyed the chaos of the cell I'd stayed in. Shock coursed through my chest as my eyes darted around. The double-speak wall was shattered. The cells across the hall were demolished. Blood sprayed across the once-pristine silver floors.

There was a fucking burned hole in the wall and ceiling.

"What the hell?" I mumbled, stepping over a pile of rubble. My nerves were a twisted mess - this blood better not be my guys'. But where the hell *was* everyone?

I pulled the stupid satin robe tighter around my body and checked the floor for sharp things as I hurried toward a door at the far end of the room. Surely, there were still people here somewhere.

The first door I opened led to a camera room, and I grimaced as I saw each of the cells on a screen. Yeah, someone had certainly gotten an eyeful of me. A couple of times. The room was empty, though, and I peeked out into a hallway lined with more doors. Shit - I didn't have time for a self-directed tour of the facilities. I needed to find protection before the Enforcer siphoned here, too.

"Hello?" I yelled, jogging down the hall and banging open doors at random.

Finally, a Council worker rounded a corner, doing a double-take when he saw me.

"Don't you fucking dare flash a potion at me," I snapped, holding up both hands. I didn't trust a single person in those white and silver chain-mail things. White knight, my ass. "Is Turin here?" It was time to bargain.

The man stammered something that could have been yes, then darted into a nearby room. I followed him, finding him on some sort of comm system.

"She's back, sir. Yes, sir. Of course, sir." He hung up the receiver and eyed me with obvious worry.

"I'm not here to hurt anyone. Just take me to Turin, leave the sneaky potion shit alone, and we'll all be cool. Okay?"

I was surprised when he actually nodded. It was kind of nice, actually, to be respected for the hell I could raise. I decided I liked this particular minion, for now.

"Turin is in his office. This way," he stammered, pointing down a hall. I nodded and padded after him, feeling slightly more in control of this mess. Maybe I'd get lucky and Turin's office would even have a coffee machine.

Soon, I was being ushered into a plush room with dim lighting.

Turin was standing before a set of floor-length curtains, holding one open a few inches to see outside. Only a strip of sunlight made it into the room. The door closed with a click behind me, and I turned to see the worker still there.

"It seems ya have a story to tell," Turin said, glancing at me over his shoulder. My heart twinged as his faint accent reminded me of Killian.

"Looks like you guys do, too," I shot back. "Where are

my guys?"

"Who else have ya told, besides this worker?" he asked, ignoring my question.

"I've been a little busy not dying, so nobody, including this worker," I shot back. "Where are my guys, Turin?"

"I don't know," he answered, turning fully from the window and walking the straight line of sunshine toward me. "Grunkeld handled that situation."

"Handled? What kind of situation are we talking about?" I stalked forward, meeting him halfway with my hands on my hips. He was tall and well-muscled for an older fae, but after playing hide-and-seek with the Enforcer, I wasn't exactly intimidated.

"Where the fuck are they?" I asked again, pulling together a few crackling strands of yellow magic. I assumed I would have felt pain if Jack, Sol, or Dair were harmed. But not Jai or Toro.

"I do not know," he said, his words slow and icy. He wasn't backing down from my magic, either. "Where is my nephew?"

"I doubt you truly care, but he's chained in iron in a swamp with the Ringmaster and fucking Aleron," I hissed. "I only came back here because I'm being chased by something called the Enforcer, which I was forced into letting free by opening the Portal with my Qilin horn. It followed my siphon twice before I got here, so you might want to check the cameras for a huge, motherfucking bull."

I finally had Turin's full attention. He stared at me, muttering my words back to himself like that might help him understand better.

As soon as he opened his mouth to ask me more

questions, I held up a hand. "Not another word until I get a hot shower, a full meal, a huge mug of coffee, and some clean goddamn clothes."

He glanced to the worker, whose eyes were as round as the coffee mug I'd demanded. "Bring her the things she's asked for. Tell no one wha' has happened, or your life is forfeit." He reached into his suit jacket and pulled out two small vials. "Do your job well, and I'll give ya the gold one. If I find out you've breathed a single word outside this room, it's silver."

"Yes, sir," the worker stammered, backing toward the door. Turin held him in a menacing glare until he'd gone, then locked the door behind him.

"We donna have much time," he said, turning back to me. "This place is filled with cameras. How did you get in, anyway?"

"I siphoned into my lovely old cell, only to find what looks like a war zone."

"Impossible," he scoffed. "How did ya get in?"

I tilted my head at him, noting how his accent thickened when he was ticked off. "I siphoned in," I repeated.

"You canna siphon into the Council. It's blocked from all magical entry."

I snorted a laugh. "Well, then check all those stupid cameras. Unless I'm still strapped on Dr. F's table, and the last couple of days has been one long, fucked-up acid trip, you guys have some security updates to do. Besides, the Ringmaster was siphoning in and out of my cell the whole time I was here."

"It's only blocked for entry, not once you're inside." He began to pace, looking excited. Me, on the other hand?

I was feeling an epic nap coming on. All the adrenaline from the past couple of days was finally filtering out of my poor system, and I yawned so wide my jaw popped.

"What about the Enforcer? If I siphoned in, he could, too."

"Fine. I'll have one of my men monitor the cameras," Turin said, waving a hand as if he was simply humoring me. He still didn't seem to believe anyone could siphon in. "Here," he continued, his voice calmer and a little kinder than I'd heard it before. "I have my private quarters just through this door. Take your shower, and I'll bring in the food and clothing when the worker returns."

"I don't trust you," I murmured around another yawn. Still, it was encouraging that the Enforcer hadn't shown up - it was way past the time it had taken him before.

"Then don't trust me. But think about my motives - I want the Path for myself. Jantzen has the Portal, thanks to you. Grunkeld doesn't know you're here. This is my chance to win you over. Why would I do anything underhanded?"

I considered, trying to find holes in his logic, but in the end, it was pure exhaustion that won me over. I followed him into an equally plush room that had a small sitting area, a bed, and a bathroom.

"I'll put everything here," he said, indicating a small table in front of the overstuffed couch. "You can nap there. I won't bother you for a few hours. I evidently have some research and reconnaissance to do."

"Yeah, you do that." I shut the bathroom door behind me, locking it even though I doubted it would help if anyone really wanted in.

The shower was the single best experience I'd had

lately, aside from Killian's magic fingers, and I was a much, much happier Qilin when I stumbled out of the bathroom, wrapped in fluffy white towels, and saw a tray with a pot of coffee, cute little crustless sandwiches, and a dozen or so bite-size frosted cakes.

"Fuck, yes." I sighed, sinking down into the couch. I even didn't bother with the clothing, chugging a full mug of coffee and swallowing two cakes nearly whole.

The coffee soothed my headache and the sugar spoke to my soul. My eyes were drooping shut in minutes. My body was so happy at finally being pampered that it shut my brain up completely, and I was able to snuggle up and sleep without worrying or even dreaming.

CHAPTER TWENTY-THREE

CARLYLE

The creak of a door opening jolted me from sleep, and I sat up, disoriented and clutching a towel around myself.

As my eyes adjusted, I gradually remembered where I was, why I was naked under this towel, and why Killian's uncle was standing before me with a fresh pot of coffee.

"Bless you, my child," I muttered, reaching for the pot with grabby hands. He raised an eyebrow, but he set the pot down and poured me a mugful.

"You may want to get dressed. We have some work to do," he warned, indicating the clothing still sitting on the table. I held up a finger, pausing to take a gulp of the scalding coffee. It burned all the way down, but it was so worth it.

166

My body was healing at lightning speed, anyway - I could feel it working already.

Scooping up the clothes, I hurried into the bathroom. It was a simple set of exercise clothes, like the army might issue for PT, and I slid into the comfy pants with a sigh. He'd even guessed pretty close on a pair of running shoes. I bounced on my toes as I braided my messy hair, ripping off a strip of the t-shirt to use as a hair tie. I shouldn't have slept on it wet, but I wasn't trying to impress anyone here.

"So what do you have for me?" I asked, returning to the couch and picking up a triangle of cheese sandwich.

"I was in another part of the complex when everything happened, so I've had to make some inquiries beyond what they initially told me. When Jantzen took you, Jai was in the room with you, correct?"

I nodded, already picking up another sandwich.

"Evidently, the vampire went a little berserk. He went beyond any power we had tracked in him before, tearing through the cell itself to find you. When it was apparent you were gone, there was a bit of a scuffle." Turin smiled when I choked on my food.

"Bloodbath," I corrected, remembering all the damage in the room I'd siphoned into.

He shrugged. "The vampire freed the whole team, and they were in the process of fighting their way out when Grunkeld intervened and bargained with them."

"For what?" I asked, wondering what exactly Grunkeld could offer my guys.

"He claims they volunteered to bring you back here to open the Path, but I think tha's unlikely."

I rolled my eyes, nodding. My guys would never want me back here.

"For now, Grunkeld is still unaware of your presence here. If he finds out, he will certainly begin preparations for you to do just that."

I snorted. I had no intention of opening the Path without the support of my guys. "You still haven't answered the question of where they are."

"Unfortunately, I don't know that for certain. Grunkeld is weak - he let them go without a fight. They took a van, an' I would guess Regina is directing them to the New Orleans circus camp you've just escaped, since tha' was one of her only valuable pieces of intel."

I spluttered, spraying sandwich crumbs onto the couch. "Regina? That bitch is back?"

Turin handed me a napkin, looking disgusted, but I didn't have time for his sensitive fae feelings.

"Why was fucking Regina here?" Damn it, I was going to horn-shank that woman one of these days. I could feel it coming on.

"Before we even brought in your team, Aleron tipped us off to her location. We brought her in for questioning."

"With Dr. F? Marcel?" I asked, hopeful that Regina's questioning had been painful. Turin nodded, and I clapped my hands like a kid. Then I started to process the rest of the information he'd just given me, and I groaned. My guys were heading straight into the mess I'd just hauled myself out of.

I was gonna have to go back and get them. I shoved a whole little cake in my mouth to stop the cursing that was bubbling up.

"She has little left to bargain with, even in Haret," Turin said. "I would watch my back around her - a woman who's had a taste of privilege and power, only to lose all of it, is a fierce contender indeed."

"Well, I'll rip her tongue out if she tries to taste anything of mine," I said, the words coming out in a growl. I couldn't believe I had to deal with her *again*.

She had nothing on me in the fierce department.

"Be careful which enemies ya cultivate, Qilin. Regina may be a disgrace to her family name, but in the mage world, her family is na' to be meddled with."

"Like your family?" I asked, raising an eyebrow at him. "Where's your branch on the family tree, anyway? Are you related to Killian's mom or dad?" I didn't know which of his parents was worse, but I had a feeling Killian was going to have a lot to deal with if we ever made it back to them.

Turin scoffed. "I would na' claim his father. His mother is my sister. She is fierce as a fae is made."

"So she's the abuser?" I asked pointedly. "The one who's worked so hard to tell Killian he's worthless?"

"She's a mother of warriors and kings, little Qilin. If she finds one of her brood lacking, she'll try ta kill it ta make it stronger. It's the fae way of things."

"And what if she just kills it?" I demanded, thinking about how I might have to add her to my horn-shanking list.

"Then it was na' strong enough ta worry about." Turin's gaze was steel, and I could tell he believed every damn word he was spouting. There was no arguing with that level of crazy.

"I guess I have one hell of a meet-the-parents coming up, then," I mumbled instead. "What did you find out about the Enforcer?"

"The rumors of it working for and with Jantzen appear to be true. The creature was bred and blessed to be an ultimate weapon, with the height of tracking abilities - it's only a matter of time until it finds you here. It can siphon like a mage, and it controls the fire and earth elements like a fae. It if tastes your blood, it will sense you nearby like a vampire."

"Can it speak? Like, is it more creature?" My guys and Jantzen had been calling the beast a "he." Not that I thought I'd sit around and try to reason my way out of being eaten, but maybe this thing had a soft spot. Maybe it could be bought.

"From what I know, it seldom has an independent thought. It is like the dogs humans use to track criminals - ruthless, intelligent, and single-minded."

"Fuckity-fun, then. Guess I need to armor up."

"You canna fight it, Qilin," Turin said, spilling into derisive laughter. "Qilin always fall before the Enforcer. It has gathered thousands of your kind."

"And done what with them?"

He shrugged. "The rumors say killed, but I donna quite believe that."

"I'll be the first to fight it, then. Like you said - a woman who's had a taste of power is fierce. Well, I'm halfway through tasting the rainbow, fae. I like my odds."

He frowned, and I guessed he had no idea what I was talking about. Probably for the better. "I will help you if you promise to work with me instead of Grunkeld. Jantzen's Portal will be null once the Path is open. Believe me, Qilin. You donna want the mages in charge of the Path. Na if you love your pretty planet."

I eyed him, finishing off the last of the food. I didn't trust him any more than I trusted Grunkeld, but I could use an ally right now. He was surely planning to use me until I wasn't useful anymore.

I had no problem at all doing the same. I stuck my hand out, hoping it wasn't like a mortally binding contract or anything, like in the movies. "Deal."

"Excellent choice, Qilin," he said, though his smile couldn't hide the slight grimace he made when shaking my hand.

CHAPTER TWENTY-FOUR

CARLYLE

"Do you have a plan, then?" Turin asked, trying to be discreet as he wiped his palm on a napkin. Geez, it wasn't like shaking my hand had given him a contagious disease. I rolled my eyes.

"I don't suppose Grunkeld gave Jai a cell phone?"

Turin rolled his eyes back.

"GPS tracking on the van?" I tried.

"Perhaps," he allowed. "I'm certain they'll be at the circus by now, unless they stopped to check other leads."

I considered. If they were at the circus, chances were they'd be in trouble. Of course, the Enforcer may have gone back there, too, which would mean I'd be in trouble. I felt like I also needed to keep my mind open to the fact that Turin might want me back at the circus for some reason, too.

I wouldn't pretend to know everyone's motives. Just because Turin had fought to stay at the Council, didn't mean he'd stay if there was a better option.

I stood, stretching my muscles. I could feel my magic swirling, strong and ready inside me. I was fed, rested, and caffeinated. If there was going to be trouble, this was as ready as I'd be.

"Let's do this," I said, cracking my neck.

Turin raised a brow. "I'm not going with you."

"Ah, come on. It'll be fun," I prodded. I didn't know why I was bothering - I didn't actually want him along. Probably I just like to see how far I could push him. "Do you think the Enforcer will just go back to the circus if he can't find me?" I wasn't sure I wanted to be walking right back into the clutches of something I'd so narrowly avoided.

"I have no idea," Turin drawled, settling back in his chair like he was about to read the Sunday paper. I huffed. He was a terrible partner. "You'll have to siphon back blind and take your chances, I guess. Unless you want to stay here, help me open the Path, and wait for your mates to return in the comforts of my office." He spread his hands wide. "I'll bring you all the coffee and cakes you can eat, little Qilin. Consider it."

I did, for about half a second. Then I screamed, because it felt like someone had stabbed a knife straight in my palm, right at the crease of my thumb. Turin shot to his feet, scanning the room wildly with glamor spells. We were alone, though.

"What the fuck?" I ground out, pressing hard into the

cramp to try and relieve the pressure. There wasn't a mark on me, though, and no blood or external evidence of the pain. "What was in that food you gave me, asshole? What did you do?"

"I did nothin'," Turin insisted, hovering over me with a worried look on his face. "Could it be your mates?"

My jaw dropped - of course he was right. This was the mating bond. Someone was in pain, and I was feeling it. I gritted through another scream as the tendons in my thumb felt like they were being ripped away, and the bone cracked in two. My stomach flipped in nausea at the sensation, and my head spun with confusion at feeling the pain but seeing nothing physical.

I realized it felt like someone was tearing my thumb away from my hand, and that's when I knew.

"Fucking *Ringmaster*," I spat. He had one of my guys - I'd bet a month's supply of sugar on Killian - and he was in revenge mode. Kills had taken his thumb, and Jantzen would be up for a bit of eye-for-an-eye, if I knew him well enough.

"Turin, it's been real. I'm out," I said, giving him a half-ass salute. Before he could scramble close enough to grab my arm, I closed my eyes and threw myself into the siphon. I hoped to hell the Enforcer had grown bored of the beach safe house, because that's exactly where I was headed.

We'd been taken by surprise with no time to pack everything up. With any luck, we still had weapons stashed there. Even if the Council had done a sweep, I was hoping it was unlikely they would bother to haul in all of everyone's random shit.

The house was dark and quiet when I popped into the

kitchen, ducking behind the counter to gather my breath and listen for signs of the Enforcer. The counter was cold and bare, and I felt a pang of loneliness as I remembered Jai making me strawberry shortcake here. My blood heated as I remembered the kiss I'd stolen from him. I'd give about anything to have that night back.

Our frustrations had been so small and simple compared to what we were dealing with now.

Listening carefully, though, I forced myself to move, heading down to the basement training room. Opening the weapons cabinet, I grinned - I'd been right. I stripped off the sweatshirt Turin had given me, leaving just a tank top.

Rummaging in the trunk of gear, I found a knife belt and a few sheaths that I could tighten to my wrists and ankles. I filled each slit with the largest knife I could find.

Magic was good, but sometimes a girl just needed to throw a blade.

Something stirred in my chest, and I felt the stomping of my Qilin. Of course. I didn't need man-made blades. If I could manage my shift, I'd have a permanent blade smack on my forehead.

If I could manage my shift, that was.

I grabbed the sweatshirt and headed back upstairs. Part of me wanted to keep going through the rooms to see what else had been left behind, but I knew it would just be stalling. I had everything I needed right inside of me - my mating bonds, my magic, and my Qilin.

It was time to find my guys.

Closing my eyes, I took care to imagine the swampy area around the cages where I'd been held in the circus. I didn't want to siphon directly back to the Portal, and I sure as hell didn't want to end up in Jantzen's kinky living room. The cage seemed like the least likely place to find trouble.

Pulling myself into the spell, I propelled my consciousness forward.

Halfway through, the pain hit, nearly knocking me sideways into the infinite blackness. I drifted away from my destination like a traveler lost in space. The only thing holding me to reality was a slim line of determination.

Sheer stubbornness pulled me through the siphon, and I bit my lips so hard I drew blood as I tried to avoid screaming. Fuck, these mating bonds were some strong shit. Evidently, this was the balance for the passion we shared.

Finally, I landed in the grass, sprawled underneath the broken cage. It was kind of brilliant, actually, and I spent several minutes just catching my breath. My thumb had calmed down a bit, though it still ached in the oddest way. My skin felt like it was on fire, though, and I was betting on iron fucking chains.

Crawling out from under the cage slowly, I crept toward the bushes Killian had been pulled from. It was hard to believe all that had happened barely twenty-four hours before. It was dusk again, and I sort of wanted to wait until full night. That would make things harder for me, too, though.

I wondered if I could figure out any of Killian's glamor and make myself blend in, or even invisible. I had no clue how it worked, but I figured it was worth a try. I focused on the well of power inside me, isolating the pulse of bright green. I was pleased to see how strong it still was. We'd truly mated.

My fae was really, actually mine.

A twig snapped nearby, reminding me I didn't have the luxury of gloating. I ducked down into the shrubs, imagining the glamor like a cloak around me, making my whole body invisible. I mean, I'd seen the movies. It could work, right?

The problem was, I couldn't tell if it *was* working. I looked the same. Readying a knife and a spell, I made my way as quietly as possible out into the open. A young guy was walking nearby, looking like he'd been patrolling. I realized I could smell him, though, so he must be human and not magical.

I crept behind him, staying to the shadows as much as possible. My foot crunched a dry leaf, and he swiveled, his eyes looking straight at me.

My heart pounded, and my grip on the knife felt slick and sweaty. But he kept looking, his gaze sweeping beyond my body, then back around. I didn't dare move or even breathe until he'd turned and started walking again, even though I was seething with excitement inside.

I'd really done it - I'd created some sort of glamor to make myself invisible!

I followed the guy with more confidence now, still keeping a good distance behind him to account for any noise I might make. He must have reached the end of his patrol, though, because he pivoted and nearly plowed back into me as he started the trek back toward the cages.

I dodged out of the way, ducking behind a trailer. I was in the middle of camp, now, and I was starting to recognize the general area where the Ringmaster's trailer should be. Yep, there it was. The lights were on inside, too.

Still no sign of the Enforcer. It was damn good, but it

was also keeping me nervous. I had no idea when the bull creature might bellow its way back into my life and try to eat me or whatever. Shivering, I pressed myself close to one of the Ringmaster's windows. He'd seemed like the kind of guy who would prefer blackout curtains, but there was a good section of open window.

Peering inside, I glimpsed Aleron, reclining in that stupid velvet armchair.

No Jantzen, as far as I could see.

But there was another person inside. A woman, by the shape of the shadow. A tall, impossibly skinny woman in a dress.

I groaned, biting my lips shut when I realized it had been out loud - fucking Gina was in the Ringmaster's trailer.

Was she being held there? A sliver of doubt crossed my mind. Maybe she'd been captured, just like my guys, and the Ringmaster just hadn't chained her yet. I felt like such a big person, giving her the benefit of the doubt.

Then she crossed in front of the window and leaned low over Aleron, pressing her breasts in his face. I almost vomited up all my lovely coffee and cakes as I saw his hands reach around and grope her ass. She sank into the chair with him, spreading her knees wide across his lap, and her head fell back as his hands drifted beneath her dress.

Yep, I was gonna be sick. I slid down the side of the trailer, crouching in the grass. Goddamn Gina. She'd sold my guys out - I'd bet my horn on it.

I was going to shank her.

But first, I was going to find my guys, so they could watch. Not this - nobody needed to see this. My guys deserved to see a bit of old-fashioned revenge.

CHAPTER TWENTY-FIVE

CARLYLE

I forced myself to gather my senses and focus. If the guys were here, I might be able to feel the pull of our mating bond. I might even be able to reach Jai if I got close enough. I checked my magic. The glamor seemed strong around me, and I wasn't tired or weak.

Steeling myself, I rose and slunk forward, sticking close to the shadows of each trailer. I could do this. I *had* to do this.

There were a lot of people still milling around, but my glamor seemed to be working. A few seemed to sense my presence, but I didn't stay in one place long. Moving as quickly as I could while staying quiet, I made my way toward the swamp where the Portal was. The bonds hooking me to Jack, Sol, Dair, and now Killian were feeling stronger.

Peeking behind a tree, I saw how right my instincts had been. The clearing before the Portal was teeming with activity.

The Portal itself was glowing with energy, and the sight made me a little sick. All that stolen magic. I shook it off and took stock. There were probably a dozen circus workers. I didn't smell anything to do with emotions, either, so they were likely all Haretians with a fucking variety pack of powers.

I took a deep breath. It would be okay - I had my own variety pack. Sure, they were chained to the damn trees, but we could manage it. Okay, maybe a few of them might be drugged and unconscious. Been there before.

Ah, shit. Toro was, as usual, the wild card.

He was somehow half in and half out of the Portal, his torso hanging at an awkward angle. And of course, he was unconscious, which was probably a blessing. I just hoped he was still breathing and in one piece. I didn't *actually* want him sliced like a sushi roll.

The Ringmaster was pacing before the Portal, muttering to himself. Crazy lunatic. The only good thing I could see about the situation was the Enforcer was nowhere to be seen.

"This will never work, Jantzen," a voice called from the opposite side of the clearing. My heart leaped as it recognized Dair's elegant accent. "You may as well let one of us track Carlyle. The Council hasn't been successful with the Path in all these decades - what made you think you could do any better with your homemade Portal?"

The Ringmaster ignored him, pacing faster and making

odd hand gestures like he was writing in the air. He looked like the world's nuttiest professor tripping on acid.

I counted - Dair was awake but thoroughly chained. Jai looked about halfway conscious, his eyes sliding around like he was struggling to focus on anything. Jack and Sol were definitely out - there were several men guarding each of them, and I guessed my shifters were the big physical threat.

Killian was definitely worse for the wear, not counting Toro's situation. His shirt was bloodied, and although I couldn't see his hand from this angle, I was pretty sure it would be down to four digits. His whole face was a swollen mess, which probably explained the migraine I'd been fighting.

Thank fuck the mating bond wasn't exactly literal. I didn't think I could handle all of their pain in full force. Once we got a breather, we'd have to work out some sort of protection from that sort of threat. Our bonds were our most powerful weapon, but they could be deadly if turned against us.

Jai? I called out in my mind, repeating his name as I crept closer. He blinked in confusion, and my anger grew. He must be drugged, in addition to all the chains. I only hoped the Ringmaster was too distracted and none of these workers were vampires or other mind mages.

Boss! I tried, nearly to his tree.

Carlyle? Finally, an answer. My heart pounded in relief.

I'm here in the clearing. What the fuck happened? I asked.

Thank fuck you're safe. You shouldn't be here, but I knew you'd come. Even in my mind, his tone was all alpha and shit. He also didn't bother answering my question, and I rolled my eyes.

Y'all are such damsels. I'm always coming to rescue you, I teased, and I could feel him bristle. *Listen. I don't know what you've seen, but I was forced to open the Portal. The Enforcer is loose, just like Austin said.*

He tried to push Toro through. Got stuck. They need your power with Aleron's to open it again.

I bit down on a sigh, leaning against his tree. Of course, the Ringmaster would be experimenting with my guys. They were expendables for him. I needed to get Toro free, but I also needed a place for us to get to, and a fast way to get there. I glanced over to where Dair was still heckling the Ringmaster.

When we get free, we're going to need a safe place to siphon, and we need it fast. Can you ask Dair about the lodge?

The idea had come to me on the spur of the moment - it was one of the only places I'd been recently that wouldn't have many traces of us. Probably Jantzen didn't know about it, and even if Regina could guess, I thought it was worth the risk. Going back to either safe house would be a bad idea, and I wasn't experienced enough to siphon to a weaker memory.

Besides, I still wanted to try out that ginormous hot tub pool thing.

Dair approves, Jai returned in my mind, and I grinned. It was a plan, then. *He wants you to let him go first, though, to make sure there aren't any hidden problems.* Jai snickered, and I knew the smooth wording had been the mage's, not my rough and wry vampire. Sure, Jai was reserved, but he'd never been proper the way Dair pretended to be.

Tell him to grab whoever he can and get the fuck out of here. I'll follow when I figure out Toro. We need to do this fast, so he can't call for reinforcements or summon that fucking Enforcer. Tell Dair to keep mouthing.

I slid behind Jai's tree, keeping a careful watch on the men surrounding him. I waited until they were distracted with Dair's antics, then I used my knife to cut into the pad of my forefinger. I heard Jai take in a rattled breath as the bright bead of blood appeared, and I smiled to myself. My vampire had no idea what was coming next.

Open wide, boss, I whispered in his mind, just as I reached around the tree and crammed my finger between his lips. He moaned as the blood touched his tongue, and I felt the sharp prick of his fangs descending. My eyes rolled back in my head with pleasure as he sucked the pad of my finger deep into his mouth, his fangs dragging along the skin.

You're a miracle, he whispered in my mind, using his tongue to push my finger free of his mouth. I felt my cheeks flush with the compliment, but I had no time to return it because he threw his head back and roared. The noise shook the whole woods and rattled the magical shards in their frames.

The men assigned to watch Jai turned, and I saw the raw fear on their faces. They knew. I watched as my quiet, reserved vampire distended his jaw to snarl at them. His muscles strained against their chains, pulling the links apart one by one until they fell to the ground with a clang of menace.

I turned away when the screaming began - as grateful as I was to Jai for using his vampire mojo on these men, I didn't really want to see it. I turned my attention to Dair, thrusting my arm behind his back and siphoning him right out from under the chains.

He landed neatly in the grass a few feet from the tree, a

grin on his face. "Clever girl," he said, touching my lower lip with his thumb before pivoting and performing the same trick with Killian. The redheaded fae stumbled into me as soon as he was free, wrapping his arms around me as though he'd been afraid he'd never be able to do it again.

I grimaced when I saw his hand, bloodied and - yep, missing a goddamn thumb.

"He's paying for that," I hissed.

Killian nodded grimly. "With fuckin' interest."

"Get out of here," I hissed to Dair, shoving Killian back at him. He'd already grabbed Sol's limp form, and the three of them siphoned into thin air. Jantzen roared a curse behind me, and I heard the splitting of wood as Jai started to rip Jack free from his chains.

I rushed the Ringmaster, tossing a spell at him before he could tell I was there. He cried out in pain but retaliated faster than I'd expected. A stunning spell hit me square in the chest, and I fell back on my ass, my glamor sliding away.

"Qilin," he sneered. "Come to join the party, then? We have fresh fish and seared dragon meat."

"Yeah, well, I know someone who's getting a piece of mage ass right now, and it isn't yours." I hauled myself back up, palming a couple of knives because the metal made me feel better.

They came in handy, too, as one of the dumbass men ran at me from the side, shifting into some sort of mountain lion. I whipped a knife straight into its chest, following up with the second in its gut, and it screamed, falling to the ground. I swiveled back to the Ringmaster, but he'd taken the opportunity to scramble for the Portal.

A flapping commotion above me had me ducking for cover, and I groaned inwardly as Aleron's Qilin form landed in the clearing with a crash of wings and hooves. I groaned out loud when the last lady I wanted to see slid down from his back, smirking at me like she'd won the damn lottery by betting on this sorry-ass ticket.

CHAPTER TWENTY-SIX

CARLYLE

"Oh, Carlyle," Gina said, smoothing her dress and stepping away from Aleron's Qilin form. "What a waste this all is. Can't we come to an agreement?" She spread her arms around the clearing like she had something to offer. Jai finished off the last of the circus men and started stalking toward me. Out of the corner of my eye, I saw him rip away his shirt and wipe the gore from his face and neck.

I smiled at him once he was clean - shirtless Jai was a definite improvement.

"Well, Jantzen," I called, still looking straight at Gina. "If this is your new negotiator, I have to say you have even worse taste than I thought."

Dair popped in just then, and I noted how calm he looked despite the evidence of a fight on his clothing. Aleron did that sort of horse screaming thing and charged, but Dair was faster. He locked his arm around Jack and siphoned out of the clearing so fast Aleron had to skid on the damp grass to avoid getting his horn jammed in the tree.

I laughed, raising my eyebrows at Gina. "Now, this was hardly a fair fight. Face it, Jantzen. My guys are more powerful than your grunts on a bad day, *and* I'm the better Qilin."

"You barely know how to shift," Gina scoffed. "Yes, Aleron told me. Your power is unstable, at best. You've picked the wrong mates, little Qilin."

"At least I have mates," I said, rolling my eyes at her.

"Oh, couldn't you tell?" She took a step back toward Aleron, and I grimaced. Surely not. "That's right. Jantzen and Aleron have made me the offer of a lifetime."

"Do tell," I managed to say without vomiting.

She ran a hand through Aleron's mane, and his wings trembled. Jantzen looked a bit murderous, but still somehow triumphant. I narrowed my eyes, trying to unpack this oddball development.

"I've agreed to become Aleron's mate and share my power with him. In return, I'll get unlimited travel rights between Earth and Haret, and all the protection the circus has to offer. It's more than my own people ever offered," she said, not hiding the bitterness in her voice.

"Ah, not sure if you've noticed, but those unlimited travel rights might involve a side trip to the morgue," I pointed out. Toro was still dangling from the glass, and I was trying not to think about the idea that maybe he wasn't making it out of this one.

"This Portal has much more promise than any attempt at the Path ever did. Face it, baby Qilin, you're standing on the wrong side. I might be able to convince Aleron to take you, still, though."

"Fuck that. I'm not being sister wives with you." I felt Jai press into my back, his solid, silent body reminding me that he was still here, and still waiting on me to make a move.

Something about that realization made me even bolder - my boss-man vampire was letting me take the lead on this one.

Guess it was time to lead.

I turned to Jantzen. "So, instead of getting your middle school girlfriend to ask me if I like you or not, why don't you tell me how to get Toro out of that thing?"

The Ringmaster stepped forward, brandishing his cane. "Why don't you tell us how you managed to escape my Enforcer?"

I shook my head. "No deal. Where is the bull, anyway?" I glanced at Aleron, and even though his lavender eyes were set in his big horsey head, fear surfaced at the mere mention of the creature.

"He isn't allowed to return without you," the Ringmaster said, smirking at me. "But since you've so conveniently delivered yourself, perhaps I should call him home?"

Aleron huffed, and Jantzen smiled, slow and cruel. Ah, there was still some shit going on there.

"Do what you want," I said with a shrug. "I'll just do the same thing I did before."

"And that was?" Jantzen prompted.

I smiled, all nice and sweet and shit. In my head, I admitted to Jai all I'd done was run like hell. He kept a straight face, though. His hand snaked around my waist, and if it hadn't been for Toro, I'd have siphoned the hell out of there and ended our problems.

As it was, I sort of hoped Dair would stay away. I didn't need any more distraction. One wrong move here, and one of us would be toast.

I already ordered him not to return, Jai said in my mind. *I'd be here alone if I could.*

I tensed, mentally warning him not to make any plans for that.

"Well, since we seem to be at a standoff, how about I gloat a little?" Regina said. I raised an eyebrow at her. Surely, she wasn't going to do the classic bad guy thing, where they brag about all their accomplishments? "It doesn't matter where you siphon your ragtag harem to, little Qilin. The Enforcer will always find you. The Council will be hunting you, too. You're a dead girl walking, and you're even less intelligent than I guessed if you can't see which side is going to win this war."

And, there she went. I sighed. "I'm about to be the crankiest fucking unicorn you've ever met if you don't shut the hell up."

"Not likely," she said, slinking toward me. "I've already made deals with people you don't even know yet. Wherever you try to hide, someone will find you. Every time you take a mate, I'll put out a hit on him. The only one I'll keep? Alisdair. Aleron knows how to force the mating bond, and I'll be using it to gather the most powerful families in Haret to our cause. He'll make such a handsome trophy husband on my arm. Just try and stop me, little Qilin, and you'll see how the big girls fight."

Jai stepped back, which meant he'd read my fucking mind before I'd lost it.

I shifted in less than a second, screaming through the pain like it was the knife edge of an orgasm. Anything my body felt was worth what I was about to do. Not only did I hate this chick with an unladylike passion, she'd just threatened every one of my mates.

She'd threatened the future of the people I'd been working to protect - those of Haret and Earth.

And, she was really fucking annoying. I was done making excuses for either of us.

My hooves felt light as air and solid as stone as I charged her, ducking my head. My ears barely registered her scream as the wind tore through the silky hair of my mane.

My horn slid so easily into her skin, slipping straight between her ribs like a blade through hot butter.

Something registered in the deepest part of me that I was taking a life, but it was overruled by the strands of fury squeezing my soul. This woman wasn't worth a single second more of my life, and she sure as fuck wasn't going stay loose in the world as a threat to those I loved.

I only stopped charging when I rammed straight into the Portal behind her. My horn screeched like nails on a chalkboard as it tore into the magic shards. It was nothing like before, when I'd just filled a blank spot.

This was a rending, and I felt it in every cell of my body. Toro's body tumbled to the ground, and I was barely cognizant of a flash of movement as Jai snatched him away.

I tossed my head, and Gina's body went flying. Her

heart slid off my horn and landed on the ground with a wet plop.

That sound - the squish of flesh and blood where it shouldn't be - was what yanked me back to the horrible thing I'd done. Except I didn't feel horrible. Hollow, maybe. I certainly didn't feel triumphant. But a pulse of rage in my horn told me I'd do it again if needed.

My Qilin form faltered and flickered like an image pixelating before it disappeared altogether, and I stumbled down onto the grass, naked and shaking.

I rolled to my stomach and dry-heaved into the swampy grass.

As if on cue, Dair siphoned in. He took in the bloody scene and panic shot across his face, but I heard Jai yell something at him. Dair grabbed Toro, the two of them disappearing again into a siphon.

It was just me and the vampire. He knelt and pulled me to him, his hands sliding up my bare skin. I slumped against him, barely able to stand. How the hell was I going to find the strength to siphon?

"Take your time," he whispered, steadying me. "Aleron and Jantzen are gone."

I lifted my head and blinked around the clearing. Damn. It really *was* just me and the vampire. I glimpsed Gina's body, crumpled against a nearby tree. A huge, bloody hole gaped in her chest where I'd stabbed her.

"Well, that makes two," I blurted, trying not to think too hard about the fact that I had just stabbed someone to death, the way Aleron had. *No.* Not the way he had - there was a huge damn difference between Austin and goddamn Gina.

"Two what?" Jai asked, combing my hair back from my

face.

"Two dead girls who tried to get my guys." The joke fell a little flat, but at least it allowed me to begin separating out my guilt at Gina's death from my satisfaction that maybe she'd gotten exactly what she deserved. I'd killed that harpy girl in straight self-defense. I'd shanked Gina to protect my mates, who were worth a million traitors like her.

"You're a Queen, Carlyle. That means you'll have to make difficult decisions sometimes. Do things you wish didn't have to be done."

My stomach lurched again, but my heart hardened like my horn had. I'd never set out to be a killer, but this was war, and she'd been an enemy, straight and simple.

"Should we destroy the Portal?" I asked, looking over at the frame instead. I'd made a pretty good dent in the magical pieces.

Jai shook his head. "He'll only build another. Let's go. I don't want to be here if they return, or if the Enforcer is on his way."

I shuddered. I didn't have the strength for that kind of fight right now.

I sighed, burying my face in his neck. I gathered the strength he was offering and tugged us carefully into the siphon. "As long as I get the spoils of war," I whispered, but the words were lost in the darkness of the siphon.

We landed in a delicious tangle in the living room of the lodge, and although I could hear the voices of the rest of the team nearby, I needed a few more moments with my vampire boss.

I kissed the hollow at the base of his throat, letting my tongue drag up the column of his neck as he leaned his head back. His long hair was out of its usual tight bundle, and the silky strands tickled my forearms. My hands slid down his bare skin, skimming along the sinewy muscles of his back, then up his chest.

I stroked along his snake tattoo, and his breathing grew ragged. I held back, anticipating the moment when he would inevitably run.

But he didn't. His hands wrenched my naked hips flush against his, and I felt his length, hard against my soft.

"Carlyle," he rasped, just as his mouth fastened on mine. He managed to keep his fangs tucked away, but I didn't need them. I wasn't backed against a wall this time or caught between a fae and a vampire.

I was locked between his chest and his arms, and a sweeter cage had never been made. I moaned into his mouth as he ran his tongue along mine, sucking gently before turning fierce. The kiss seemed to go on forever, until I thought I'd forgotten how to breathe.

Releasing me slowly, he tasted my air a second longer, then stepped away reluctantly.

It was only then that I realized just how much of an audience we had. Only Toro and Jack were missing, and I could glimpse them through the open door leading to the small pool. Reclining in the water, Toro was looking better already, and Jack had his eyes closed, but a soft smile on his lips.

"Your Queen," Jai murmured, stepping back even more, his black eyes locked on mine.

For a panicked second, I thought he was going to kneel before me, but then he smirked.

"Time for me to clean up and rest. We'll take a day here, then reassess," he said, his voice back to the firm alpha boss. The others nodded, and he headed for the bathroom. I felt all the adrenaline from the last several days begin to drain away from my body. I stepped back just enough to fall onto the couch behind me, and Killian laughed.

"Someone take care of my new mate while Dair takes me to the tailor to get a thumb sewn on."

I shot up to join them, but Sol caught me around the waist. "Let someone else do it, shortcake. You've done enough. Why don't we join the others in the pool?"

Dair smiled. "Agreed. We all need to replenish our stores. I'll order food and take care of this ugly mess." He gestured to Killian, who glared, but it was half-hearted.

Grinning, I allowed Sol to tug me into the room with the pool.

CHAPTER TWENTY-SEVEN

CARLYLE

The tiled room actually had a small rinse shower in the corner, which was where Sol led me first. I flushed as I became more aware of how I naked I still was, how exceptionally dirty, and how my audience now consisted of Jack and Toro as well.

"Let me wash you?" Sol asked, turning on the nozzle and testing the temperature. I nodded and leaned against the tile wall, resisting the urge to cover myself. Hell, so many people had seen me naked lately, it shouldn't matter.

But I wasn't exactly sure how Toro fit in yet, and part of me was just nervous to hear their reactions to all that had happened.

Gina was nobody's favorite, but would any of them see

me differently now?

Sol coaxed me away from the wall, wetting down my hair with the warm stream. His strong fingers massaged sweet-smelling shampoo into my hair, working a moan from my mouth as he scrubbed away all the dirt and grime of the Council, the Circus, and the fight at the Portal.

He added conditioner, letting it soak as he soaped my body. He worked to massage away some of the soreness in my muscles, and I leaned my forehead against the cool tile in relief.

"Shifting fucking hurts," I mumbled, and chuckles from three men reached me. I glanced around at my shifters, finding them all nodding.

"Only at first, though," Jack said. "Your body learns."

"I wish you could've been the ones to teach me," I added, staring down at the bubbles swirling into the drain in the floor.

"Shortcake," Sol whispered, pulling me close. He was still in his clothes, and my hug soaked him, but I suddenly felt like I never wanted to let go.

"I killed Gina," I whispered, my chest shuddering as a sob threatened my composure. "I pierced her straight through the heart, Sol."

He hugged me even tighter, murmuring something I couldn't understand as I shook in his arms. I wanted to be strong, but I never wanted to be a killer.

"We've all killed, shortcake," Sol said, his voice loud enough to reach the others. "We've all felt what you're feeling, too."

"It's as bad as shifting at first," Toro admitted.

I looked up to meet his eyes, fear rising in my chest at his comparison. "I don't want it to get easier, though."

"No, honey," Jack said, hauling himself out of the pool to take me out of Sol's arms. His wet boxers were plastered to his thighs, but the rest of his body was naked. I noticed his wounds and burns from the chains had mostly healed already. Were we all healing faster?

His hands slid down my sides as Sol rinsed the conditioner from my hair and washed away the final bubbles.

"Come soak with us," Jack said, his voice husky with desire.

"This lodge room was a fantastic idea, shortcake," Sol said, and I heard his wet clothes slap the tile floor as he stripped. I turned to smile at him, finding he hadn't bothered with boxers. My smile fell into a snicker as he shrugged.

I let them help me down into the pool and onto the low bench that lined each edge of the pool. I stretched my legs and pressed my feet against one of the jets, groaning as the water massaged my aching soles. They had adjusted the water temperature to pleasantly warm, and as I settled against Sol's muscled arm, I started to feel more like myself.

"Yeah, this room is heaven. I think I'm in love with you," Toro said, groaning as he sank deeper into the tub. I couldn't quite see his body under the swirling water, but if I had to guess, I'd say he was naked, too.

"Get in line, fish," Jack drawled, slinging an arm around my waist beneath the water and leaning in close for a quick kiss. "You have the best fucking ideas, baby." His lips tugged at mine and made the kiss something worthy of talking about, his tongue tracing across my bottom lip before plunging deep into my mouth and tangling with my tongue.

The water lapped at my breasts as Sol adjusted his position behind me, and I caught his smooth, summery scent just before he pressed my knees apart and knelt between my thighs on the bottom of the shallow pool. He was tall enough that we were eye-to-eye when I slitted mine open around Jack's kiss.

"Keep going," Sol whispered, sliding a firm hand up my thigh. His fingers caressed my folds, circling my clit gently, and I moaned into Jack's mouth.

Toro cursed softly from the other side of the pool, but he didn't come closer. I cut my gaze to him. Maybe he liked to watch, too?

Sol's fingers pushed inside me, twisting and pumping, and Toro's eyes widened as I held his gaze. Jack's lips slid along my jaw and down my neck, and Sol leaned in for his turn with my mouth while Jack lifted one of my breasts above the water's surface, sucking my nipple into his mouth.

I was so hungry for my men that I would take them in any combination - we'd earned this fucking interlude, no matter how brief it might be.

I could see just the shadow of Toro's body beneath the water, but his arm muscles bunched and rippled. He was pumping his own cock, watching us, and my core thrilled at the attention I was getting, both to my skin and my ego.

It was such an aphrodisiac knowing I could cause this kind of need in each of my guys.

I reached beneath the water and pulled Jack's cock free from his boxers, stroking its smooth length slowly while I stretched and wrapped my legs around Sol's torso. I drew him in, then widened my legs and reached for his cock, too. Guiding him to my aching pussy, I turned my face back to Jack and used my tongue to beg him for more kisses.

Sol got the idea and scooted me to the edge of the bench before plunging deep inside me. I cried out as the water splashed up around us, but Jack fastened his lips on mine, tongue-fucking my mouth, He knelt up to give me a better grip on his cock, and he took the opportunity to grab both my breasts in his hands. His thumbs rolled and tweaked my nipples as Sol thrust slow and deep inside me.

I lost myself to the sensation of being filled and fucked, caressed and cherished.

I fell so hard into the zone of pleasure with my mates' touch that Sol's growling release came without much warning. He nuzzled past Jack and claimed my mouth as he thrust several more times, each more tender than the last as he milked his release. He was telling me without words how worried he'd been, and how much he'd missed me.

"I'd stay here forever, but I don't want to be greedy," he whispered. Then he interlocked our fingers and moved aside, nodding to Jack. My dragon surged in, cupping my face with both hands.

"Fuck, honey, I need you. I was so afraid," he whispered, his eyes a little wild. I pulled him in close with one hand, urging his cock to my core. I wasn't nearly finished yet. I turned my mouth to Sol and gave him a passionate kiss, then I arched an eyebrow at Jack.

"Bring it home, dragon," I teased. He didn't waste any time, sliding one hand under my back and lifting my hips. He slid his body beneath mine, seating me in his lap.

I caught Toro's heavy-lidded stare as Jack lined his

cock up and began thrusting inside me from beneath. His tongue darted out to lick his lips as he watched the water lap at my breasts. I watched him watching, and the sensation was so much more erotic than I'd thought it would be.

Sol moved around to my front then, and I locked my arms around his neck to get the resistance I needed to really ride Jack. Sol lowered his mouth to my breasts, sucking and biting at my nipples as Jack's hands locked on my hips. I leaned forward and bounced and rolled on his cock, chasing my orgasm as I kept my eyes on Toro.

Soon, though, Jack's cock found my favorite spot inside, his fingers found my clit, and I lost my ability to concentrate on anything more than pleasure.

Riding Jack so fast the water splashed up around me, I cried out as my orgasm rolled through my body. Sweet bliss spread through my muscles as I felt Jack pulse inside me, and my head fell forward onto Sol's shoulder as he supported me, kissing the side of my neck. Jack's hands smoothed down the length of my thighs, loving my body, and I felt my heart calm and swell.

These were my men, and they weren't judging me for what I'd done. They'd been afraid, and now they needed me. They'd helped me come back to myself, using the cover of the water to wash away the shame I'd been feeling.

"Well, well, no time wasted here," Dair said as he entered the room, his velvety voice like another balm to my ears. Fuck, I'd missed them all so much.

"I told you I wanted to come back here and try the pool," I answered, pulling away from Sol and smiling up my mage. Maybe we'd been in the pool longer than I'd thought, because he'd found the time to shower, too. He looked fresh and yummy enough to eat, in a relaxed pair of linen pants and a navy polo that showed the depth of his eyes.

"Killian's fine," he answered before I could ask. "Fucking fae somehow managed to keep his thumb in his back pocket the whole time, and they attached it back like new. He's sleeping off the pain-blocking potion now."

"I always knew that fae had his thumb up his ass," Toro joked, and I snickered. I rubbed absently at the spot on my own hand. I hadn't felt anything there while they'd been gone, so it must have been a good potion for once.

"I also brought clothes and the food should be here any moment," Dair added.

"Fuck, I think I love you, too, mage," Toro said, hauling himself out of the water. He was definitely naked, and by the look of his cock, he'd gotten a good bit of satisfaction from our time in the pool, too. He caught my gaze and winked, and I decided I was okay with what had just happened.

Maybe next time I'd give the fish a better role than spectator.

Dair raised an eyebrow and stepped away to avoid being splashed as the rest of us got out of the pool. Sol handed me a fluffy towel, and I started wringing out my hair.

"How about this, Cariño?" Dair murmured, handing me one of the thick white robes I'd worn on our last visit. I sighed and smiled as he wrapped me in it, pulling me close.

"I don't know how we did it all, but we did, and I'm so fucking glad to have you all back," I said, hugging him tightly.

"*You* did it - you have some stories to tell, little Qilin." For some reason, the diminutive didn't bother me at all from Dair. Thinking of telling him about Gina made me nervous all over again, though. Would he think I'd gone too far?

"Later," I said, pulling away. I just didn't want to talk about it all right now. He caught my hand and led me into the living room, where everyone had gathered. Beautiful men were sprawled all over the rustic furniture, and I took a few seconds to take it all in.

Sol was in sweatpants only and taking up half the leather couch, long legs spread in front of him and arms behind his head as he laughed at something Jack was describing. Jack had pulled on a t-shirt and jeans. He sat in a wide armchair, one ankle propped on his knee and looking as relaxed as I'd ever seen him.

Toro had ignored the clothes altogether and just knotted a towel around his waist. He was checking under all the lids on the cart of food Dair had ordered, sampling a little of everything with delicious little groans.

Killian was the only one not clean yet. He was stretched sideways across another armchair, his muscled forearm covering his eyes from the light. His chest rose and fell peacefully, as he somehow slept through everything.

Dair's hand rubbed at my neck, urging me forward, and just as I entered the room, so did Jai, from the opposite side.

He was freshly shaved and still shirtless. His dark jeans rode low on his narrow hips as his arms reached back to bundle his damp hair. The sight took my breath away, and his gaze flicked up to meet mine as he must have caught the tail end of my thought.

His dusky skin flushed a tiny bit, and my heart leaped.

Instead of throwing myself at him again, though, I stepped away from Dair and toward the food. My stomach rumbled, and Toro turned to grin at me. He handed me a plate, and I filled it quickly with all sorts of cheese, crackers, fruit, and sweets, of course.

The guys began to crowd around, and they quickly found a piping pan of lasagna, several juicy steaks, and a plate of spicy-smelling wings, as well.

"I ordered pretty much everything they make," Dair admitted as we all sat again to dig in. Even Killian woke enough to eat, though he was still bleary-eyed and clumsy with his plate.

"So, as much as I'd love to stay here forever, what's next?" I asked, dropping my plate on the coffee table and sitting cross-legged before it.

"We need a new safe house," Sol said around a mouthful, resting his head against the couch. He looked exhausted - all my guys did, despite the showers and clean clothes.

I sighed. It would be nearly impossible to get another house set up without our funding from the Council. It was pretty damn hard to steal a house.

"Not a house. We need a safe *boat*," Jai corrected with a smile.

"What?" I asked, as pretty much everyone turned to our leader.

"Fucking genius," Jack said, shoving a bite of rare steak in his mouth. The others nodded, and the excitement in the room grew.

"We know the Enforcer is an excellent tracker, but he should still be limited by his senses. It's nearly impossible to track scents over water," Sol explained to me, his summer-sky eyes sparkling.

"I've never been on a boat," I confessed as Dair settled himself next to me on the floor.

"A yacht," Toro piped up, grinning as he went for seconds. "We need to steal us a fucking yacht!"

"Cariño doesn't approve of stealing," Dair teased me, his warm palm sliding up my leg under my robe. My stomach lurched as I remembered what a hard time I'd once given him about stealing. Now, I was a murderer. Talk about hypocritical.

"Ah, well," I stammered, distracted by where his fingers were headed. "I could probably make an exception, as long as it doesn't hurt anyone."

His fingers reached the top of my thigh, and I wanted to feel everything he might offer. I needed more pleasure in my body to drive out the pain in my heart.

"No more pain, unless you ask for it," Dair whispered, leaning close and nipping at my neck. His fingers cupped my pussy, but no more. My cheeks heated with anticipation. Instantly, six sets of eyes were locked on me. "Fuck," I breathed.

My group of shifters and a vampire would be well in-tune with the increase in my heart rate and pulse.

"Now, that's a fantastic idea," Dair said, his voice barely more than a growl. "Though I'm not as keen on an audience as you seem to be, Cariño."

205

CHAPTER TWENTY-EIGHT

DAIR

I'd been playing nice all evening, watching my Qilin have her fill of the others, but it was my fucking turn. I needed to make sure she really was okay - something in her mannerisms were still off. She was pushing reality away instead of dealing with it, and we didn't have time for the shit to hit the fan if she denied herself now.

Jai caught my eye from across the room and sent me a warning to keep it quick. I pushed down on the flare of anger. The fact that he wasn't rushing me out the door to steal a boat meant that he sensed it as well.

Our Qilin was struggling to keep her happy face on.

"Team, we get eight hours here. Not a minute more, and it's already been two. Gather your strength, because we break at four," Jai barked, eliciting groans from the men.

I leaned in to whisper again in Carlyle's ear, pinching the delicate skin at the top of her thigh. "That's hardly enough time for me to tell you how displeased I really am. You put yourself in so much fucking danger, Cariño."

She shuddered against me, and I felt the heat of her pussy flare against my fingers under her robe. Her anger was flaring, too. Good. I wanted it to surface. My Qilin couldn't be a Queen until her anger reflected outward instead of eating her alive from the inside.

I needed to wrench it out of her, forge it into something pure, and shove it straight back in her hand as a weapon of righteous fury against Jantzen, Aleron, and the Council.

"Come," I bit out, standing and holding my hand out to her. Her lips parted at the simple word, and my lips twisted. I had a plan. It would work, too, as long as I was brave enough to carry it out.

Carlyle stood, glancing around the room as if asking permission from the others. I bit down on a hiss - my Queen didn't need their permission. I yanked her into my side and pulled her into a siphon before she could realize what was happening. When we slid out the other side, she swallowed a tiny scream.

We were on a flat, cold ledge of stone near the top of one of the mountains surrounding the lodge. The night sky above us was filled with pinprick stars, and the dark valley below was dizzyingly far away.

"What the fuck?" she mumbled. "I thought we were going to the bedroom."

"Tell me what happened," I demanded. Jai had caught

glimpses of it when we'd been at the Council, and he'd given me a few of the images. The gaps were what I was worried about.

"When?" she asked, avoiding the question. I grasped the back of her head and twisted her face to mine, taking her mouth in a quick, harsh kiss.

"Don't play stupid with me, Cariño. We don't have much time."

"Fuck off, Dair. It's been a long-ass week, so I'm sorry if I need a little goddamn clarification."

I slid my hands down her neck and across her shoulders, pushing away the robe. Her pure, bare skin glowed like the moon above us, and I ached to leave my marks on her.

"What happened? Every time I wasn't there to see it - what the fuck happened?" I said, keeping my words tight and controlled. She glared.

"Well, first there was the fae doctor who glamored Aleron to look like Killian and kiss me. Then the tests. The crazy fucking Ringmaster telling me I could have one of you, then failing to deliver. Then bringing me Killian, only to make sure every creep in the building had camera access to us fucking for power exchange. Ah, there was Turin, who is double-crossing everyone he knows, including us. Jai and Killian fucked me at the same time, even though Jai will still barely kiss me. I did some sort of weird-ass astral projection thing where I wasn't even in my body. Dr. F still saw me, though, and I got the great fun of watching Aleron suck off the Ringmaster. Is that enough fucking information, or should I start on day two?"

Her voice had been rising with every word until she was practically screaming into the night.

"It's never enough," I whispered, procuring the robe straight off her body.

She stood before me, naked, seething, and practically spitting. "Of course, it's not enough. Why would it ever be enough? I'm just one goddamn person, Dair."

"You're not a person," I reminded her, struggling to keep my tone even after all she'd just told me. "You're a Queen."

She whirled, turning her back to me and staring out into the night. After a few moments of silence, her shoulders slumped as the guilt and self-flagellation began. I knew the process well - I'd seen it a thousand times in Killian, and more than I cared to admit in myself.

"I'm not, though," she whispered. "I'm just a carnie kid, struggling to keep my head above water in a world I know nothing about. I just want to forget it all happened."

"Is that what you did in the pool with Sol and Jack? Forget?" I prompted. She was smarter than this. Her guilt was repressing her instincts in the same way her human upbringing had held back her Qilin shift.

"Yes," she mumbled, glancing over her shoulder at me.

"It doesn't work for long, though, does it? Is that what you're hoping for with me, then? To make you forget?" I asked, propping my hands on my hips and glaring down at her.

Her eyes shone with unshed tears, and I almost lost my nerve. This had to be done, though. Jai couldn't trust himself to do it yet, and none of the others had the slightest idea what she really needed now. Their touches were centered on what *they* needed - each of them desperate to reassure themselves she was here, and whole.

"Do you?" I asked again, my voice hardening.

Finally, she nodded, turning fully back to me. Her body trembled like a leaf.

"Well, sorry to disappoint, but I won't do that."

Her eyes widened in shock, but before she could bite out a sarcastic answer, I snatched her to me, taking her lips in a consuming kiss. Her body grew compliant in my arms, and as much as I relished her softness, I knew she needed to learn to be hard as well.

"On your knees," I whispered, stepping back from her. "And I'll give you what you *need*."

She obediently dropped to her knees on the stone, and I twirled my fingers for her to turn. She did, facing out into the shadowed valley. I bent and pressed against her shoulder blades until she was on hands and knees, only inches from the edge of the cliff.

Her ass was in the air, displaying her beautiful body to me, with all its dark places open to the moonlight above. I ached with hunger for her, but I knew we had to get through this first.

She needed so many kinds of strength, and my magic had nothing to do with what I could teach her.

I stripped off my own clothing, feeling primal and powerful in the night. This was my mate, and it was my duty to protect her, even when she was her own worst enemy. Kneeling behind her, I bent and pressed my face to her pussy from behind.

Her scent was intoxicating, not to mention the sweet juices that coated her already. I licked through her soft folds, my cock jumping at her moan.

I sat back on my heels for balance, grasping her hips and holding her in place while I lashed her slit with my tongue, scraping my teeth over her sensitive clit.

"Dair," she moaned, pressing her body back into my face. Fuck, I wanted to be inside of her.

But this was a game, and she'd just broken a rule.

I lifted a hand from her hip and brought the flat of my palm swiftly against her ass. The smack was cold and sharp, echoing beautifully in the night. I followed it up with another in the same spot, because she didn't expect it. Her cry was so sweet I almost did it again.

"Do you feel weak or powerful?" I asked, and she twisted her face to look back at me.

"What?" she asked. I repeated my question, though I knew she'd heard me.

"I don't know," she answered, and I sighed. It was progress, though not much. At least she wasn't lying.

"When you decide to be powerful, you get to cum," I said. "You're a Queen, Carlyle."

"So everyone keeps saying," she muttered, hanging her head.

I bit my tongue against giving her any other clues. Instead, I pushed a finger into her pussy, coating it in her wetness. I pumped her a few times, but I knew one finger would never be enough. I pulled it out and circled her tight asshole. She moaned as I pushed just the tip of my finger in.

I knew what she'd done with Jai, and I was fucking jealous.

It made me a little rougher, but she didn't seem to mind.

I wet a second finger in her pussy, then went for her ass again.

"Yes, Dair," she moaned, pressing back into my hand. My cock was stiff and heavy, aching to be inside of her, but she wasn't ready - not in either of the ways I needed.

I cracked my palm across her ass again, just as I spread my two fingers wider in her tight hole, stretching her.

"Fuck," she panted, and I admired the print of my hand across her creamy skin.

"Are you feeling weak or powerful?" I asked, hoping.

"What the fuck does that even mean?" she snapped, and I sighed. The cool night air was working against me, as was Jai's impatient nature to be on the road early. I closed my eyes and focused on a bottle of oil I knew was at the lodge. I whispered the spell, and it dropped into my hand. I spread a bit of the oil on my fingers, then pumped them in her ass, faster now.

Lining my cock up with her pussy, I gripped her hips again and thrust inside both her holes at once. God, she felt like the heaven I didn't deserve.

As soon as she made a noise, I let go of her hips and spanked her ass again, thrusting hard. Her palms slipped on the ledge, and she scooted an inch closer to the edge.

"Dair," she gasped, and I heard the clattering of pebbles falling down the mountainside. "We need to scoot back."

"No, you need to own your power," I snapped, picking up my speed. Fuck, she felt so good. My cock glided in and out of her pussy almost too easily, and the oil made her asshole so tempting.

"What the hell power do you want from me?" she said, bracing her hands more securely on the rock. I knew her palms would be sweaty soon, and she wouldn't be able to grip the edge forever. She needed that fear to find her courage. She needed to find the edge so she could leap over it.

"All of your power," I ground out, pulling my fingers and cock out. I lined my tip up with her asshole and pressed against it. "Weak or powerful?"

"Which answer gets you to fuck me proper?" she growled. She kept still this time, though, instead of pressing herself onto me. "Good girl," I murmured.

I grinned and smacked her ass even harder this time. She jumped, and I gave a smooth push into her ass, pausing about halfway to let her settle before fully seating myself.

"You think you're weak," I said, beginning to move inside her. "You think you've been *lucky* to get out of the traps laid for you. You think all of us are more powerful and more magical than you - that you're just a vessel for our power. You're fucking wrong!" I gave a violent thrust, and her hands slipped forward even more.

She gasped as her head hung over the edge of the cliff, but still, I didn't stop.

"You think you've done horrible things, and that guilt is corroding your power. You failed your shift," I accused, smacking her ass hard. As she cried out, I continued, "You opened the Portal even though you knew you shouldn't." I spanked her again, just as hard. Her cry was rougher now, needier, and my cock twitched inside of her. "You might have saved a few of your mates, but you killed a woman and let the Ringmaster and Aleron escape!"

I smacked her ass three times, with quick, flat-handed movements, and she shuddered beneath me.

"You're not a good girl, and you don't deserve to cum," I whispered fiercely, leaning over her back.

She hung her head, her body slowing. I gritted my teeth. This was what she needed. I knew it, but I hated breaking her like this.

"You're weak," I said, drawing my cock out of her and sitting back on my heels. She crumpled into herself, and it about broke my fucking heart.

The night was silent around us, and I allowed it to settle. She needed the silence to face her thoughts.

"I did the best I could," she murmured, finally. Her words were muffled against the rock, but I still heard them.

"Your best wasn't good enough. Wasn't powerful enough."

"Fuck you," she said, but it was still too weak.

"I like my women powerful. It's no fun to play with a weak woman," I said, meaning every word of it. As my words hung in the air, I felt the shift in her mood, like lightning crackling across the sky.

"You like me, though." She pushed up and turned to look at me. Her face was cold and calculating. So fucking clever and beautiful, that I nearly lost the game right then.

I kept quiet, though.

"You like me, and my body." She inched forward, her knees farther apart as she approached me. She looked down pointedly at my cock, twitching for more of her body. "You like my mind. You think I'm clever," she said, nearly startling a gasp from me. Had she just pulled a thought from my mind?

Still, I kept silent and motionless.

"You don't think I'm weak." She was barely an inch from me now, as she slid into my lap like a viper. "You think I'm the very essence of power, all bottled up for no good reason."

"You've never been more right," I whispered, my heart

soaring at her words. She'd figured it out, and so much faster than I'd ever hoped. "You've never been just a vessel, Qilin. Stop keeping your power stoppered."

She pressed herself to me and yanked my hair, opening my mouth to hers. Her lips teased across mine, and her tongue flicked over my skin, never quite giving me what I craved. Touché.

"I guess if I'm all-powerful now, I don't have to be good," she whispered, standing and turning her body. Lowering herself into my lap again, she leaned forward just a bit. "I want your cock in my ass and your fingers in my pussy. And I want it good and *powerful*," she ordered, smirking back at me.

I groaned as I hurried to comply. "Next time, the game is different," I whispered as my cock sank deep into her ass.

"Less talking, more fucking," she said, beginning to move against me. I snickered, pressing my fingers into her pussy while thumbing her clit. I pushed her back on all fours for the best leverage and sped up.

Just as she started to pant her release, I bent low over her back. "Next time, the power to cum won't be so easy to command. Queens have to keep leveling up," I reminded her, thrusting and pumping as hard as I could. I felt my cock swell inside her, burning for release.

Just as the orgasm exploded from me, I pushed off on the balls of my feet and shoved us forward over the edge of the cliff. We sailed together into the empty air beyond.

Her cries of pleasure shrilled into a scream, but even as we plummeted through the air, I felt her instinctual power crackle around us.

She swirled the air around us to slow our motion,

calling on Killian's magic. She pulled us into a siphon just a few feet above the treetops.

I fell out of the siphon in an ungraceful heap, straight onto the cold stone of the same ledge where we'd started. Carlyle landed like a perfect fucking superhero, her long, white-blond hair rippling in the breeze she'd created. Her lavender eyes flashed in the moonlight, and she glared at me so fiercely that if I'd been a lesser man, my dick would have shriveled up and fallen off.

"I know what you did," she said, her words flying at me like knives. "And you're goddamn lucky to be alive."

"I don't believe in luck," I said. "I believe in power and practice."

She watched me a few seconds longer, her expression unreadable. "Since you're all about leveling up, I expect next time to be even better."

"Don't worry, Cariño. I'll always have new games ready for a good girl." I smirked at her in the cocky way I knew she liked, and her eyes narrowed.

"Promises, promises," she whispered. She bent and grabbed her robe, then pressed her fingers together and siphoned away before I could step forward and join her.

I chuckled to myself as I pulled my clothes back on. I wondered if she would have still left me here if I couldn't siphon.

My game had been a dirty trick, for sure, but something had clicked into place for her tonight. I'd felt it in her movements when we fucked, and I'd seen it in her eyes when she landed.

She was shedding her human nature and becoming more fully Qilin.

As a shifter, she needed to come to terms with her

other side, and Qilin weren't all sweetness and light like the unicorns humans had imagined. The team and I would be there to make sure she didn't go dark like Aleron, but if she didn't find her full inner power, none of us would survive what was coming.

CHAPTER TWENTY-NINE

CARLYLE

I siphoned back into the living room and snatched up the bundle of clothes meant for me, not bothering to connect with any of their stares.

My insides were a mess of knots, and I wanted to be alone for a few goddamn minutes to sort it all out.

I locked myself in the bathroom and took a quick shower, washing away the grime from the rock ledge and the cum leaking from my body. Fucking mage.

Sure, that had been an epic orgasm. Evidently, Dair's edge of pain was even better with a side of crazy thrills.

But were Dair's tests any better than Dr. F's, when it came down to it?

I knew he'd been trying to get me past my guilt of

doing so many things wrong. As I let the scalding water beat down on my skin, I tried to assess if it had worked. I *did* feel more powerful now - like I could handle more of what was coming our way without breaking down.

Did I also feel emptier, though?

The only other Qilin I knew was powerful but empty of emotion. The two often went together. I'd seen it in history class, and recently, up close and personal. I didn't want that. Too much emotion was bad, but so was too little.

It wasn't me, and I didn't think a good Queen should be devoid of emotion, either. Could I be powerful without giving up my emotion?

All my life as a human had been spent rebounding from others' emotions, then learning to protect myself from being overpowered by them. I'd drawn emotion from LuAnn's clients like I drew power from my men. Well, not quite the same way, but still.

My eyes flew open as I realized I'd been cordoning off my guys' power the same way I used to with clients' emotions.

I'd been imagining a vessel inside me, where the magic stayed. I thought of it as Dair's spells, Killian's air, and Jack's fire. Never mine.

I'd also been keeping my Qilin separate.

With a flood of understanding, I thought I knew why my shift was unstable.

"Jai," I yelled, projecting his name inside my mind, too. He couldn't be far. Within minutes, I heard the doorknob rattle. Shit, I'd locked it. I started to step out of the shower, but before I could get there, a spark jumped through the metal. The door swung open, and Jai stalked in, closing the door behind him.

He surveyed my bare, wet skin with interest, but he didn't approach. I turned off the water and reached for a towel.

"How much time is left?" I asked, drying myself.

"Two hours."

"Could you pull me into someone else's mind?" I asked, and his eyes widened. "With their permission, of course."

"I've never tried. It might work, though. What do you need?" he answered. I pulled on my clothes.

"You, Jack, and somewhere big enough to hide a dragon."

He eyed me, but I didn't offer any other details. He could have scraped them from my mind, I was sure. He stayed out, though, only nodding and slipping out of the room.

A few minutes later, I was dressed and ready to go. I was still worn the crap out, but I figured I could sleep when we got wherever we were going next.

Sol, Killian, and Toro weren't as patient, though, and when I walked into the living room, I found each of them dozing. Dair was poring over a laptop with Jai, and Jack wandered in just as I was about to ask about him.

"Can I borrow your dragon?" I asked, sliding my arms around his waist in a hug.

"Of course, honey. Where do you want to go?" He glanced to Jai for permission.

"I'm coming, too. Qilin's choice," Jai replied, a tiny smile edging onto his lips.

"Dair will know where we are," I said, giving him the side-eye - I figured the ledge we'd just been on was high enough to be out of sight. I stepped forward and grabbed Jai's arm, keeping my other one locked on Jack. I siphoned the three of us out of the room instantly, landing where Dair and I had just been.

I guess the mental images from our game were still pretty fresh because Jai looked at me and smirked.

"Ah, so, when I shifted, I didn't have wings," I started, ignoring the flush in my cheeks as Jai's lips twisted even more. Yep, he'd definitely gotten a few vibes from what I'd just done on this ledge.

"Qilin don't *all* have wings," Jai said.

I shrugged. "But I want them. You guys told me my form would come from my mates, and Jack has wings."

"I'm not sure that's how it works," Jack said uncertainly. "I mean, you already found your form. How could you change it?"

"If I get another mate, wouldn't it change then?" I asked. They both considered. "Besides, if the shift is really part of me, and I can play mix-master, I should be able to play with my form a little. I just don't know how."

"That could be true," Jack admitted, glancing at Jai. "Like how shifters can learn to keep their clothes or not."

I snorted. It figured that Toro would have skipped shifter class that day. "Anyway, I want you to go through your shift as slowly as possible, so I can learn how it happens. I don't have years to perfect this. I'll be lucky to get a week's peace to practice."

Jack nodded. "Stand back, then." He gestured toward the rock wall behind us, while he stepped closer to the ledge. Before I could explain what I wanted Jai to do, Jack had shifted. It was a little slower than normal, but not much.

I frowned, admiring the heaving ruby-colored creature before me as he spread his leathery wings wide. I hadn't felt any pain at all through the mating bond. "Why is my shift so damn painful?" I asked, not really expecting an answer.

"Back, dragon," Jai called up to Jack's enormous head, bobbing above us. Jack drew in his wings and tucked his head, shrinking and folding in on himself until he stood before us as a man again. "Let me into your mind," Jai said. "I'm going to try and pull her in, too, so she can feel the shift as it happens."

Jack looked doubtful, but he nodded. Jai settled down on the ledge, pulling me into his lap. He tugged my shirt up so my bare back was pressing directly to his skin, and his hands wrapped around my middle.

"I think taking you with me will be easier if we're already physically joined like this," he whispered.

"Not complaining," I murmured, sinking into his body. Jack looked mildly annoyed, but I smiled at him. "Show me your shift, dragon."

"Slower this time," Jai warned.

I closed my eyes, feeling Jai circle my mind like he was circling my body. It began to feel a little like my dream-walking or out-of-body experiences, as I started to see things through Jack's eyes. I could see myself and Jai, sitting against the side of the cliff. Looking down, I could see Jack's body as if it were my own.

My limbs began to ache as he started to shift. It wasn't exactly painful, but as his skin parted down his spine, I grimaced at the sensation. It was like peeling off a layer of dead skin after a sunburn. The bones and muscles were the same. I felt the ache and pull of strain. So shifting did hurt

Jack a little - just not as much as it hurt me.

Somehow, that made me feel better, like I wasn't so abnormal.

When the wings started to form, I tried to track the process, but my mind just couldn't keep up. My eyes opened, and I saw Jack before me in full dragon form again. I sighed and leaned my head back on Jai's shoulder.

"This isn't really giving me what I wanted. It's too fast still, and I don't want to waste all his energy in case we need it."

Jai rested his cheek on my forehead, his fingers absently stroking up and down my sides. I shivered a little at the slight tickle, and Jack huffed. A flare of jealousy echoed in the corner of my mind, where I was still listening in on his thoughts.

Before I could react, Jack whipped back out of the shift and settled on the rock before me. "I don't think I can go any slower than that. Maybe once you get your shift down, we can worry about the wings."

"She may need physical contact," Jai said, pressing my hips harder into his. He sent Jack the barest hazy glimpse of what I'd done with the vampire and the fae in the Council. My core flared with desire just remembering it.

"Are you fucking kidding me? You guys were doing that while I was chained to a table?" Jack grumbled.

"I'll make it up to you," I promised. "Please, can we just try?"

"I'm not complaining about physical contact," he said, shaking his head. "But can't exactly shift while I'm fucking you. I'd tear you apart."

"Try just the tongue, then," Jai offered, like we were discussing where to move the furniture. "I can move fast enough if you lose control. I'll just throw us off the cliff. Carlyle can handle what comes next."

I bit down on a groan. So he really had seen my memories of what had happened with Dair. *Fucking nosy vampire*, I thought at him, and he snickered. He tugged my shirt up even more, exposing my breasts to the cool, early morning air. The sun was just barely starting to rise, and I knew we'd be out of time soon.

"Fine. Do it," I said to Jack. I mean, really. Why would I turn down a bit of tongue action from my dragon?

Jai reclined a bit more against the rock, and Jack reached to slide my pants down. He settled himself on his belly between my legs. Jai hooked his knees under mine and widened his legs, pulling mine with them. I was completely open to Jack, and he growled in appreciation. As Jack's tongue slid through my folds, Jai's hands moved up to cup my breasts, his thumbs rubbing lightly over my nipples.

I fell into the sensations, letting my mind float on pleasure. I could still feel Jai in my head, and Jack's mind was nearby and open, like the valley below us.

"You taste so good," Jack murmured, then swirled his tongue around my clit, keeping the pressure teasing and light. Jai's hand kneaded my breasts, and his lips dragged along my collarbone. I could feel his cock growing hard behind me, and I nearly wished for those silver-walled cells, just so he'd feel confident enough to fuck me again.

"One day," he whispered in my ear. "You're getting stronger, as am I. When you control your magic, and I control my bloodlust, then I will ask you to be my *aima*, if you still want me."

"I will," I replied, the word ending on a gasp as Jack

fastened his lips around my clit and began to suck. He pushed two fingers deep inside me, and I felt my thighs begin to tremble. Jai pressed them wider, pinning me open for Jack, and his fingers grew rougher on my nipples.

"Start the shift," Jai commanded.

I squirmed as the sensation of skin separating down my spine joined the bliss of Jack's tongue. My mind struggled to make sense of the contrast.

Jack's wings came first this time, their weight pressing his body flat against the rock, and mashing his face against my pussy. He sped up, eager to finish his job before the shift was complete. I felt the odd push of gravity on my back, as though the weight of wings was pressing me down, too.

The spiral of orgasm began, and Jack pulled away, roaring as the last bit of his shift took his mouth from my body. The snap of wings and a gust of air pressed me back into Jai, whose fingers had replaced Jack's tongue.

Still holding me wide, he pinched one nipple hard and pumped his fingers inside me, scraping along my sensitive inner walls to push me over the cliff of a second orgasm. I cried out and shuddered in his arms, cumming hard around his fingers.

My mind dipped and swooped as though it had fallen off the cliff and joined Jack flying through the valley below. I felt the wind along my body as though I were the dragon - the currents stuttering over my scales and all the nerves along the fine edges of my leathery wings.

Thanks to Jai's connection, I didn't feel like I was watching Jack. I felt like I *was* Jack. I saw the beautiful garnet magic swirling inside him, shifting with his intentions to make either form and whatever motion he required.

"Oh," I murmured, suddenly understanding I'd been looking for a physical, whole Qilin inside of me to change into, not for the violet-hued magic I knew was also there.

Opening my eyes, I sank back into myself and my physical reality of being held tightly in Jai's grasp, naked on a cliff while I watched my dragon mate soar toward the sunrise.

Twisting my face up to meet Jai's dark eyes, I smiled. "I think I know what to do now."

"Good," he said, his hands stroking up my body. "Do it, then, Qilin."

I sat up and reached deep inside to find my own magic. I visualized myself pulling and shaping the violet strands like clay to form a Qilin with wide dragon wings. This time, instead of looking for a creature inside of me, I asked the magic to make me into the creature.

And for a shuddering split second, it did.

The pain was still there but lessened. For the barest moment, I raised myself on four legs instead of two, and I felt the phantom weight of muscles and bones bearing down on my back, struggling to spread into wings.

Then my strength spluttered, and I collapsed back into my human form, panting.

Jai smiled at me, handing me my clothing. "Progress," he said gently. I nodded, trying not to feel disappointed. I really wanted to figure this out.

Just as I finished dressing, Jack swooped back in. Shifting in the air, he landed in a sexy crouch, rising to grin at me.

"I saw it," he said, hugging me tightly. "You did great."

I grumbled to myself, but they both just laughed.

"This takes time, honey. Shifters learn to shift like they learn to walk - gradually and with lots of tumbles," Jack reminded me.

"I know," I sighed. We just didn't have months to sit around waiting for me to figure it out.

"Siphon us back," Jai said, confirming what I'd just been thinking. "It's time to find a boat."

CHAPTER THIRTY

DAIR

While Jai, Jack, and Carlyle had been gone, and the others slept, I'd stayed busy finding a boat.

I'd been to a handful of cities along the southern Atlantic coast, and I could picture a good marina or two. We'd have to choose carefully and make use of Killian's glamor, but I was certain we could siphon in, find a mid-size yacht that wasn't in use, and make our way into the middle of the ocean for a while.

The pop of Carlyle bringing them back echoed in the room, and the sleepers began to stir.

"Show me," Jai said, coming around to check the computer screen. He nodded when he saw the map.

"I was thinking I can siphon Carlyle there to get a

visual, then the two of us can work to bring everyone in. There are shops nearby for food and a bit of clothing. The marina is here, and there should be several choices based on this satellite image." The image was a few days old, but there were always larger boats coming and going in these ritzy areas.

Jai nodded, scanning the screen. "Good. I'll come with you on the first siphon if you can manage two."

"Of course." I could probably get everyone there myself, but it would deplete me enough that procurement would be difficult. Besides, Carlyle needed the practice.

Jai clapped his hands. "Everyone up. We're going."

They were all up in moments, and only Killian still looked half-asleep as I gathered Jai and Carlyle to me, pulling us into the siphon. I landed us under the cover of an alley between two restaurants.

"The marina is that way." I pointed, and Jai nodded, buttoning up his shirt before striding out of the alley. He was a little exotic to fit in among the locals, but he also had a dangerous air that would make him unapproachable. Hopefully, nobody would bother him while he was scoping the boats. There was a low Haretian population in this area, as far as I knew. What we were doing had its risks, but we'd managed before.

"Take a good look around," I warned Carlyle. "Be certain you can bring someone back here."

"I'll be fine," she said, her voice too light to fool me. I didn't press it, though. There was a time for that, and this wasn't it. She explored the small alley for a few more minutes, then nodded. "Back to the lodge," she said, siphoning away before I could grab her. Stubborn Qilin. I was smiling, though, as I pulled myself through the same

229

spell.

I grabbed Jack, and she took Killian, then I doubled back for Toro while she transported Sol. Soon enough, we were all safely in the alley.

"You guys know the drill," I said, looking around at the team. They all nodded - our usual MO was to have Sol, Jack, and Toro gathering food, clothing, and a few weapons. Killian and I helped by either glamoring the items or procuring them straight out of the store. Jai always went off on his own to secure the house.

"What about me?" Carlyle asked as the guys began to scatter.

"Come to the grocery with us," Sol suggested. "You can pick out your favorites and help us glamor the cart right out of the store."

She rolled her eyes, but I noticed she didn't say another word about her moral high ground. It wasn't that any of us wanted to steal - we just didn't have a lot of options.

"I guess these people have enough," she grumbled, gesturing around at the fancy boutiques and gourmet groceries before following Sol down the street.

I stopped Killian before he could follow. "You won't find anywhere to buy a knife around here. I'd suggest going invisible and wandering onto some of the yachts, then meet them to grab the food."

"Can do," he said with a grin, his broad form flickering out before my eyes.

I ducked into a nearby shop, making detailed mental notes of where certain clothing items were laid out in the store, including sizes and fabrics. At least I was dressed similarly to the wealthy humans in the stores. I knew I'd have to work quickly and only take a few pieces from each store, though, since they were tiny shops.

It was a study in sleight of hand, really. Not too different from the card tricks human magicians performed.

After studying a large leather satchel in the window of one store, I stepped outside and between two cars. After tossing a distraction spell - which was really just a bit of noise and a flash of light people always turned to look at - I immediately procured the bag right onto my shoulder and crossed the street, blending into the other shoppers.

Nobody noticed a thing.

I repeated the pattern again and again as I made my way down the street toward the marina. The bag was heavy on my shoulder when I spotted Jai, speaking to a young kid who was probably a dock worker.

He saw me and beckoned.

"Here's my Captain now," Jai said, creating an accent that made it sound like he was still learning English.

"Sorry, sir," the boy said to me. "I just usually know all the boats here, and I hadn't seen the one your employee was describing." The kid was giving me too keen an eye for my liking.

"Thank you for working to keep the marina safe," I said, taking Jai by the elbow. "I'll be sure to mention your service to your manager. We can handle things from here, however."

The boy nodded and moved away, but I caught him glancing over his shoulder more than once as he made his rounds.

"Nosy kid," Jai growled.

"You should have just waited for Killian or Carlyle to glamor us," I said, grinning. "Places like this always stereotype, and between your skin color and clothing choice, you don't stand a chance of boarding one of these things unnoticed."

Jai flashed a tiny hint of fang at me, but I knew it wasn't a threat. He just hated being forced to steal as much as Carlyle.

"There are several unoccupied," he said, keeping his voice low. "I think that one at the end is a good size, and I just saw the owners leave. Just filled the tank, too."

I eyed the boat and glanced over my shoulder. The kid wasn't around anymore, but I tugged Jai back into the shadows before siphoning us right onto the main deck of the yacht. It was a mid-size, probably sixty feet. Jai used his magic to gain quick entry, and we explored the stateroom and two smaller cabins.

"It will be tight," I admitted. There was plenty of room up on top, though.

"I don't want anything so large it's suspicious when we have to make port. Toro can spend time in the water," Jai reminded me. ·

I shrugged. It was gorgeous, of course. There was a very nice deck for sunbathing and an ample, slatted-floor area with cushioned seating and good shade. The kitchen even had a full-size refrigerator and nice appliances.

"You stay here, then. I'll collect the others," I offered. He nodded, and I dropped the bag of clothing onto the main bed, which might hold three of us if we didn't move much.

I siphoned back to the alley, pleased to find everyone waiting. Killian was standing in front of what looked to be an empty shopping cart. I could see the hint of glamor shimmering over it, though, so I guessed it was probably filled to the brim.

"Jai's holding the boat. I'll siphon back there with this cart, then come back for you," I said.

"Why don't we just start walking that direction?" Carlyle asked. "It seems like an awful lot of magic to waste."

"There's a nosy worker down there. He's already suspicious of Jai," I answered.

She smirked. "Human?"

I nodded.

"Let me handle this one, boys," she said, already striding off toward the marina. Killian snickered, muttering something about how the kid was a goner.

"Well, are you going to follow her or not?" I asked, trying to hide my annoyance. She was perfectly capable, of course. I just didn't like the idea of her on her own.

"C'mere an' I'll give everyone some glamor," Killian said. "Na quite invisible, but at least the right clothes for this snotty place, an' faces nobody will remember." He dropped the magic from the cart and started to apply it to Jack, Sol, and Toro. Soon I was staring at a group of all-American blond frat brothers, looking like they were off to party on their father's boat.

I couldn't help but snicker at the makeovers, especially Toro's. He just flipped me the finger as they all sauntered away. I had to admit, they fit in perfectly. I grasped the cart's handle and focused hard - it would be easy to scatter all these loose items in the siphon. Imagining the shaded area on the boat and hoping Jai had managed to keep the owners away, I popped out of the alley and right back onto the boat.

"Damn," Jai said, as soon as I landed. "They went all out."

From the shelter of the pilot house, I scanned the docks. Our frat boys were making their way toward us at a good pace, but I didn't have eyes on Carlyle.

"Shit," Jai muttered, peering at the street leading to the docks. "The owners."

I cursed and siphoned straight down to the dock, hoping nobody would see. I forced a grin and waved at the group of four I knew were my team, leading them to the boat quickly.

"Where's Carlyle?" I hissed. Panic and confusion crossed their faces. "Kills, with me. The rest of you, on board now. The owners are coming."

I heard the engine fire up behind me even as I spoke. Sol and Jack darted on board, while Toro knelt to begin the unmooring process. I felt Killian's glamor settle over us as we strode the length of the dock, looking for our Qilin.

I heard her giggle before I saw her, and as soon as I saw her, I wanted to commit murder.

The kid from the docks was leaning way too fucking close, grinning and chatting her up like a little prick.

"Easy," Killian whispered.

"Head back to the boat," I growled. "I'm on it."

"Carlyle," I barked, breaking into their conversation.

She gasped, her eyes wide enough to let me know she was acting.

"Daddy!" she cried, and my blood heated. I'd never much liked that sort of whiny play, but if she wanted to submit to me, I'd certainly take it.

"You've been quite bad today," I ground out. "Quit running away, or I'll have to punish you."

Her cheeks flushed pink, and I smirked. That part

wasn't acting. I reached forward and yanked her to me, much too close on my cock for the boy to interpret us as father and daughter.

"Uh, excuse me," he stammered, backing away.

Just before he was out of sight, I cracked my palm across Carlyle's ass, and she let out something between a gasp and a moan.

"Promises, promises," she whispered, reminding me of our time on the ledge the day before.

"Promises I intend to keep," I said, slanting my lips over hers and taking her mouth fiercely. I pulled us into a siphon, reaching toward the boat that Jai was already guiding out of its place. I stumbled as we landed on the deck, and Carlyle pressed up against me even more.

"I was just distracting the poor kid," she said with a grin, her hand pressed against my waist for balance. "You didn't need to give him a heart attack."

"Nonsense," I returned. "I just gave him the best image he could want when he's in bed by himself tonight."

"Ew," she laughed, peeling herself away from me long enough to look around. Jai was maneuvering us closer to open water, and I could just barely see the owners running down the length of the dock, shouting in vain to stop us.

The others were gathered at the rail, and Sol laughed as he tossed the empty shopping cart overboard.

"Welcome home, Cariño," I said, spreading my arms wide to indicate the sea beyond.

"I could get used to this," she said, stepping forward and beginning to explore.

CHAPTER THIRTY-ONE

CARLYLE

We'd been at sea all afternoon, and I could no longer see land anywhere. It was both frightening and exhilarating.

My guys had pulled through again with this amazing idea - I was confident that the Enforcer couldn't possibly track us way out here.

The only dark spot in the whole thing was that evidently, Sol was not well-suited to the water. Killian had been poking fun at him all day, teasing about the kitten who hated water, but I'd seen Sol hang his head over the rail more than once. He'd finally retreated to one of the bunks below, waving everyone away.

I only hoped he'd get used to it.

So far, the others had been relaxing. As for me, though,

I was determined to continue to work on my shift. I didn't want to be the weak link that broke us. I'd worked enough with Jack for now, and Sol was out of the question. I still had one shifter left, though.

Toro had jumped overboard more than an hour ago, and as I watched him play in the water and dive for shells, I decided it was time I included him in the magical mix.

Maybe getting a bit of his bright blue magic was the missing piece of my Qilin puzzle. It couldn't hurt to try - I had a pretty good idea it would be fun as hell, actually.

I leaned over the railing of the yacht, waiting until I saw the merman's dark skin flash through the turquoise water.

"Toro," I called. His head bobbed to the surface, and he grinned. Shaking the water droplets from his face, he flipped his tail hard beneath the water. The momentum forced him up and out of the ocean in a graceful flip, and he somersaulted in mid-air and landed with a smack on the deck next to me.

"Damn, fish out of water," I cried, laughing as he flopped around dramatically, pretending to be suffocating. "Didn't that hurt?"

"A little," he admitted, rolling to a sitting position and shifting back to his human form. I tossed him a pair of shorts from a nearby chair. He snorted. "Are you afraid of a little raw fish?" he asked, gesturing toward his sleek, muscled torso.

"Nah, but it makes the dragon blush." I pointed to the sky, where Jack was circling, keeping watch on us from above. Teammates or not, his eyesight was way too good for Toro to be walking around naked.

"I'll save it for later, then," Toro said, waggling his eyebrows at me.

"Later might be sooner than you think," I said, taking a deep breath to calm my nerves. It was obvious Toro was attracted to me, and I'd admitted my own desire a long time ago. We'd just been pulled in so many directions since meeting - not to mention the small issue of him trying to drown me while he was possessed by an insane Qilin - that we just hadn't been in the right mood at the right time.

"What's the story, then?" he asked, snapping the waistband in place.

"It's not a fish story," I teased, feeling my cheeks flush. Damn, this was hard. I wanted to let us happen naturally, but I just didn't have time.

Not with the Council and Turin searching for us and the Ringmaster and Aleron maybe joining forces again.

"I had an idea about why my Qilin form is unstable - because I haven't, ah, sampled all the flavors of shifter yet," I rushed out.

Toro leaned his head back in a raucous laugh, and I couldn't help but grin. He never did anything half-assed, whether it was as simple as enjoying a belly laugh, or as complex as helping the team finishing a mission.

"Goddamn, Qilin. You're cute, but you need some new lines," he finally said, wiping a tear from his eye.

"Ah, fuck off. It's not like I'm in the practice of picking up random men."

"Random? No. But damn, girl. When you sample, you fucking sample. All the flavors of the rainbow for our sugar-girl." He grinned to show me his teasing was good-natured, and I realized I was feeling a little more at ease already. Once we'd moved on from how Aleron had used us both to nearly drown me at the old safe house, laughter had been our thing.

He was still smiling as he stalked toward me, his light blue eyes twinkling. "So, your place or mine?"

"Surprise me?" The words came out in a bit of a squeak as he crowded me against the deck railing.

"Plan on it," he murmured, his fingers sliding up my arms. His touch was deceptively light for such a big guy, and as he stroked my skin and stared down into my eyes, I started to both relax and heat up. I raised my arms and locked my hands around his neck, pulling his face closer to mine.

He pressed his lips to my mouth, humming as his tongue scraped along my bottom lip. "Sweet," he whispered, just before dipping his tongue into my mouth. His kiss was unhurried and teasing, as his lips nibbled their way around mine, and he tasted my mouth in slow sweeps.

Suddenly, he swiveled me to face the ocean, sweeping my hair to one side and tangling his fingers deep in my curls. He massaged my scalp and tugged my hair while kissing and sucking and nipping along my neck, then my jaw.

His other hand slipped under my chin and turned my face to the side so he could claim my lips again, but he broke away before he'd barely started, returning to my neck and traveling across my shoulder and lower to the tops of my breasts. Pulling lightly on my hair, he opened my neck again and kissed the hollow at the base of my throat before delving deep into my mouth again.

I had no idea which direction he was going next, and his rhythm and intensity varied as much as the ocean waves pummeling a beach. One was light and tickling, and the next nearly buckled my knees.

It didn't take me long to decide that Toro was the best

kisser of the group.

Keeping one hand tangled in my curls, he let the other one begin to travel my curves. His touch was so light it was maddening - as teasing as his jokes and leaving me just as breathless.

Gradually, I became aware of his siren song lilting softly inside my ear, spreading and unfurling inside my chest.

"Don't be nervous," he whispered, just as my nerves started to tremble. Toro was so in tune with me, it was as if he knew what I was going to feel almost before I felt it.

"You're so good," I murmured, feeling my cheeks flush as I realized that really didn't make sense.

"I can feel every bit of water in your body," he confessed, licking up the shell of my ear before dropping his mouth between my breasts, then back against my lips in a matter of seconds. "I can feel it heat or cool. I can feel it tremble with fear or pleasure."

"Damn," I managed, my knees going weak again. His arm circled my waist and supported me.

"I don't want to frighten you. No more siren right now - we'll save my sinker magic for another time. I'd love to get you in the water, though," he confessed.

"Life jacket?" I asked with a hard swallow as his palm slid lower, brushing just an inch above where I wanted him.

He chuckled, and I felt his chest rumble against my back. "Anything for my sugar-girl." He left me for just a few seconds while he rummaged in one of the cabinets on deck. "Here you go," he said, buckling the foam vest snugly around my chest. "I'm gonna have to find something else to lick, though," he warned.

"Surprise me," I said, my voice a little stronger now. I started to turn toward him, but before I could catch his eyes, he bent and scooped me up under the knees. He pushed off the deck in a powerful jump, and I shrieked as we tumbled into the water below.

It was warm and clear, but still a shock to my unsuspecting system. I bobbed to the surface without effort, thanks to my jacket. Toro appeared just inches away, and I looked down as the soft brush of fins found my bare legs.

He'd shifted as soon as he hit the water, and I marveled at how easy it was for my guys.

"Will my shift ever be that easy?" I wondered, half to myself.

"It will, and it won't always hurt. You need practice, like kids need to learn to walk. But you think you need my magic, too, right?"

I nodded, biting at my lip and pushing some of my wet hair away from my face.

"Then lean that pretty head back and watch the sun while I rock your world with my pretty head."

He disappeared beneath the water before I could respond, and I could feel his hands and tongue making their way down my body, stripping off my shorts and panties.

I could sort of see him since the water was so crystal-blue clear, but the ripples around me marred the view a bit. Giving in to his instructions, I rested my head back on the life jacket's pillow and let my body float, weightless and pliant in his hands.

As he began to knead his fingers up my inner thighs, I wondered what it would be like to have underwater sex, without needing to come up for air. Feeling so weightless had to be a thrill, not to mention the nonexistent friction and the crazy poses we could try. My imagination ran rampant until Toro pushed my thighs wide beneath the water and began to stroke the folds of my pussy.

His hands alternated rough and gentle, just like his kisses, and I twisted in his grip. I grinned to myself. Fucking tease.

I felt him rest my legs on his shoulders though, and his arms locked around my thighs, holding me right where he wanted me. His tongue began to flick my clit, just far enough away that I wanted to scream and mash his face to my core.

Then I felt his tail. It curled up behind me, long and surprisingly muscular as it slid down my spine and pressed against my ass, scooting me closer to his mouth. I moaned as his tongue finally pressed hard and flat against my clit, sucking and licking while his tail pulsed behind me, creating a rocking rhythm between us.

Even the surface of the water was sensual as it lapped at my skin. My arms floated limply on the top of the water, and as the sun dried each droplet, rivulets of salty-cool water ran to replace them.

Toro removed one of his hands from my hips, and his fingers found my entrance, pushing inside me and twisting in a slower rhythm than his tail. I felt my thighs begin to tremble as I got closer to orgasm, and I closed my eyes to revel in the sensation as he began to speed his fingers and tongue.

With my eyes closed, I could begin to glimpse the liquid swirls of his bright blue magic, and I opened myself to it, sucking down his shifter power.

My skin tightened and tingled, reminding me of the first few times I'd seen my dragon scales.

My eyes flew open, and I checked my arms. Nope. Still skin.

Would I get mermaid scales, though? Fuck, I hoped so. My Qilin would be so gorgeous with some of Toro's green and blue shades mixed in with Jack's fiery orange and red.

Toro must have sensed my distraction because he totally upped his game with a third thick finger in my pussy. I cried out, and far above me, my dragon answered with a roar of appreciation.

Pleasure rolled through my body like a tsunami, and I was really fucking grateful for the life jacket because I probably would be drowned by now. Every nerve in my body had gone from alert to overload as Toro worked his magic.

Finally, he dropped from beneath my legs, leaving me hanging limp in the water with a silly grin on my face.

Yeah, the fish could stay.

I felt a million tiny bubbles tickle my skin as he suddenly swam furious circles around me before popping up inches from my face.

He planted a sloppy, salty kiss on my lips and laughed at my lazy smile.

"I think you're a keeper," I joked.

"You're fucking right I'm a keeper. I'm your best shot at ever being a mermaid. No girl's turning that down."

I splashed half-heartedly at him, but he just dodged out of the way. "You're not wrong," I murmured.

He played in the water for a few minutes, leaping in shallow arcs that splashed my cheeks with droplets. Each time, I admired the flash of shiny green and blue scales.

"I hope I get some of those pretty scales," I said, as he drew near.

"Me too. I want to make my mark on the Qilin, too." He grinned. I cocked an eyebrow at him.

"*The* Qilin?" I prompted. I wanted to hear it from him. Was he thinking of walking the same path as the rest of the guys?

His eyes widened as he saw how serious I was. "My Qilin," he corrected, his voice rough.

"Damn straight, fish," I whispered, thrilling with the idea that I really might have all of them one day. It would take time - especially if I wanted to avoid Aleron's methods.

My mates would all be here for the right reasons. Not because they were pressured into it, or because I felt like I needed their power.

Because they wanted me for the long haul.

"Haul me in, keeper," I said, smiling. "I want to try my shift again."

CHAPTER THIRTY-TWO

CARLYLE

Of course, the shift still wasn't happening. I was pacing the deck now, trying not to get aggravated as my guys piled on the pressure with their ideas.

"Try it without clothes," Killian suggested.

"You want everything without clothes," I griped, and he snickered.

"Fuck yeah," he said.

"That's how the lions learn," Sol said, and I glared at him for agreeing with the fae. He still looked pretty pale, but at least he'd decided to come up for some fresh air.

"Fine." I yanked my shirt over my head and shimmied out of my shorts and panties. Hands on my hips, I stared them all down. "Now, what?"

I'd been trying to coax my Qilin out again for nearly an hour, and all the guys had offered suggestions, even the ones who weren't shifters.

Needless to say, I was pretty fucking testy.

"Maybe you need some sugar," Dair suggested, procuring a container of my favorite chocolate gelato before he'd even finished his sentence. I was tempted, but honestly, I'd eaten my fill not long ago.

I shook my head and pivoted on my heel, pacing the deck.

I felt like I was on display - like I was the main exhibit of a freak show. They were just trying to help, but I really wanted them to all just go away and let me figure it out.

There just wasn't much private space when seven people were living on a boat, even when it was as luxurious as this one.

Closing my eyes and leaning against the rail, I let myself sink deep into my mind, working to find the meditative state I'd relied on for protection for the last several years, before meeting my guys.

If my Qilin had always been with me, chances were she was hanging out in that safe space.

The deck was silent behind me, and as the minutes passed, I forgot all about the possibility of being watched. The breeze ruffled my hair and cooled the sun's warm rays on my skin. The wooden deck was smooth beneath my feet, and the railing was polished slick under my grip. I let my conscious go deeper, imagining it as deep as the ocean.

I sank all the way into the blackness at the bottom, where all the light was so concentrated it had turned to darkness.

This was where I belonged, really.

Despite my love of sugar and the power I felt when I was seething with colorful magic, I wasn't all rainbows and glitter.

I wasn't a unicorn.

I was a Qilin, and there was a difference.

Something stirred and woke in my chest like feathers ruffling and branches cracking under soft-stepping hooves.

One by one, I sifted through the human ideas I'd held about unicorns, and I rejected each one. Humans could keep their unicorns. I was Haretian, and I was a Qilin. I didn't need tricks - I just needed me.

The more I repeated it in my head, the more solid the idea became. I started to think of my Qilin as me - not as a separate animal I needed to call forward. She wasn't a witch's familiar or a spirit animal.

She was me, and she was made of power. I was her, and I was made of determination.

With my guys, I was made of magic. I was a vessel that could channel magic, and I was determined to channel her form.

My mind turned the puzzle over and over, twisting it like a knotted rope until I could find the end and unravel it bit by bit. The world fell away. I felt like with each mental knot I unwound, I stepped closer to the inner sanctum where my Qilin form had been tucked away most of my life.

Sure, I'd broken her out a few times.

But I needed to coax her close enough to the surface of my brain that I could call on her magic as easily as I called on any of the guys' powers. She was mine - my magic. I'd spent my whole life ignorant of her existence, and my whole time with the guys relying on them to pull me through.

Now it was my turn.

The violet magic in me began to churn, and I felt the last knot unravel. It was like a net holding me down fell away. My body uncurled and expanded, stretching and moving and growing.

I shucked off the expectations of pain, and I ignored the hazy image I had in my head of what my Qilin was supposed to look like.

I shifted, and as the form burst through, I heard my guys again.

Turning toward them, I stretched my neck and preened. I stepped forward on graceful hooves, their hard, gold surface clicking on the deck with the same noise high heels made. My body swayed as I got used to having a horizontal spine instead of a vertical one. I tossed my head, and a flowing lion's mane flashed before my eyes, golden and brushed with soft rainbow highlights.

Wriggling my muscles from top to bottom, I twisted my neck around to look at my back.

There, like the answer to a thousand prayers, were the most fantastically-badass wings a girl could hope for.

It took me a second to pinpoint the muscles that would spread them, but they snapped wide in an instant once I did. Gasps and cheers came from my audience of mates and males, and I would have grinned and laughed if I'd had lips and vocal cords.

Instead, a high-pitched whinny escaped my mouth, and their eyes grew wide.

"Fuckin' siren song," Killian blurted, staring at Toro.

My heart sped up at the idea. I twisted around, peering closer at my body. My hide was white, and it did fucking sparkle. But patches of scales - red, gold, turquoise, and silver - covered all my tenderest parts like armor.

My chest swelled with pride.

I'd tasted all six of my guys. Mated or not, the seven of us made a rainbow with the colors of our magic.

I looked at each of them in turn, nodding my head in a bow of thanks - I could feel Jack's fiery red dragon magic, Sol's orange lion strength, Dair's brilliant yellow spellcasting, Killian's green glamor and air currents, Toro's bright blue water magic and scales, and even a bit of Jai's indigo ice and bloodlust.

All I'd needed to complete the rainbow was my own violet Qilin magic.

Suddenly, my wings itched to be used, and I whinnied to my guys. Running was awkward on the short deck with two extra legs, but I charged the opposite side without a thought of stopping.

Flapping my wings hard, I lifted into the air just in time, my back hooves barely clearing the rail.

It was fucking hard work, I realized, but soon I was climbing in altitude.

A shadow passed above me, and I looked up to see Jack had shifted and joined me. He spiraled down and under me, shooting across the sky and returning with all the glee of a puppy.

As I looked down, I finally caught a glimpse of my reflection in the water below.

My horn wasn't black, like Aleron's, but it was as long as a sword and flashing with menace. Here in the air, in my final Qilin form, I felt like I might actually be powerful enough to beat our enemies.

For the first time, opening the Path seemed like a true

possibility.

Beating the Enforcer seemed plausible.

Raising an army against whatever darkness waited for us in Haret seemed less daunting.

I circled around and flew back toward the yacht, Jack following. Stumbling into a rough landing, I worked to pull my Qilin body back inside. My human skin felt full to bursting at first, but it soon adjusted like it had been before.

Looking up from my hands and knees, panting, I grinned at the collection of men before me.

"I'm a fucking Qilin," I said. I got to my knees shakily and surveyed their faces. "I'm a fucking Queen."

"You're *my* fucking Queen," Jack said, stepping around me and lowering himself to one knee like the knights in the movies.

I laughed, but then Sol did it, too.

Toro joined him, then Dair.

Jai nudged Killian's shoulder, and the two of them dropped together, both looking like they simultaneously hated and loved the gesture.

"Seriously?" I said, feeling nervous. I mean, here I was, naked in the middle of the ocean, with six men kneeling before me.

What kind of drugs did you have to take to end up here?

"Cariño, it's what we've been searching for all these years," Dair said, his soft voice catching my attention.

"I know it seems like a lot, shortcake," Sol added. "But you were born for this."

His words actually pushed me deeper into fear, and I felt my body begin to tremble. Looking down at my slim human limbs and soft human skin, how could I possibly think of battles and wars?

Jai was up on his feet in a flash, his arms grasping mine as he shook me hard.

"No," he ordered. "Never doubt your power. Never doubt yourself or your Qilin."

I tried to nod, but my mind was frozen on the idea of being born for this. "I'm no chosen one. I'm no hero - no martyr," I babbled, thinking of all the things I didn't want to be. "Aleron's the Eagle. Why hasn't he opened the Path? What if I can't, either?"

"Aleron is na' the chosen one - he's the one who fuckin' chose," Killian growled. "He failed because he was cocky."

"And because he's filled with darkness," Jai whispered. I lifted my eyes to his, and for the first time, I understood his fears for us.

"You're not filled with that kind of darkness," I told him, begging him in my mind to believe it.

If I'm not filled with darkness, then why aren't I part of your Qilin form? He asked in my mind. *None of your power reflects mine.*

I frowned. He couldn't be right, but I didn't know how to answer his question. "Maybe I just have your magic, like Dair and Killian. Or maybe I don't have enough of your power yet," I said, but the words felt false in my mouth. He'd given me plenty of power when he and Killian had double-teamed me at the Council.

"My physical form changes, though. I'm not a shifter, but you should have something of mine," he insisted. I thought of his lightning speed and strength - I hadn't felt that, either, though it would have been damn useful.

"Maybe I have fangs," I offered, but he shook his head.

"When you whinnied, I looked. I would have seen them."

"Maybe it's my horn, then," I said, suddenly realizing what my horn had looked like. Not a sword, really. White, gently curved, and glistening - as sharp as Jai's fangs.

His brow wrinkled as he worked through the idea. I stepped back from all of them and closed my eyes, reaching deep inside for those violet strands. Pulling them tight, I called my shift to the surface again and felt my body transform.

There was still an odd discomfort, but the pain was nearly gone already.

Jai gazed at my horn, reaching his hand out to slide his palm down its length. I was surprised to feel every inch of movement, and even more shocked to realize how good it felt.

I'd obviously never had a cock, but I couldn't help but wonder if this was what my guys felt like when I stroked their length.

Jai's eyes were darkening with lust, and before I understood what was happening, he'd pressed his palm down on the tip of my horn, impaling it deep in his flesh.

His blood hit my system like the crest of an orgasm, and my Qilin body shuddered in pleasure.

The shock hit me so hard I pulled my shift in fast, stumbling to my knees before my vampire. He stood above me like a dark god, his eyes solid black and his palm bright with blood.

Moving like liquid sin, he stepped toward me and lowered his body flush with mine. He pressed his palm to my lips, smearing the blood across my gaping mouth.

My tongue darted out to taste it, even as I was horrified at the idea.

The *taste*, though.

Ah, fuck. The taste of him on my lips.

I was lost.

I sank into him, my lips closing over the wound in a fierce suck. He shuddered against me, and his mind flashed open like ice crystals in the sun.

"Fuck," someone said, breaking the spell he had woven around us with his blood magic.

I scooted back, my eyes bugging out of my head. I wiped my mouth with the back of my hand, spreading his blood even more. My pussy clenched at the smell and the taste, and I moaned as I tried to deny myself what I knew I wanted.

What I'd always wanted, deep down.

What he wanted, if his desperate look was any indication.

Jai bolted to his feet and disappeared below deck, and I groaned. My running vampire. I needed to go after him, but his mind was closed to me.

His fear was going to be the ruin of us both.

I was afraid, sure. But it was because it was all so new to me. None of what we'd just done had hurt me. I screamed that thought at him in my mind, but it just bounced off the solid walls of his mental barriers.

"Goddamn coward leader," I grumbled, staggering to my feet. I looked to Dair, still feeling a little dizzy with pleasure. "Wanna procure me a towel and some clean clothes?"

He smirked. "Towel? Of course."

"And clothes," I prompted as the towel appeared in his

hand.

"I rather like you like this, Cariño," he murmured, stepping toward me and offering the towel.

CHAPTER THIRTY-THREE

CARLYLE

The afternoon spread into evening, and then morning again. I filled my time with men and magic, and before I knew it, several days had passed.

The best days of my fucking life.

"I wish we could stay out here forever," I murmured to Sol as he stirred beside me. It was early morning, and the sun was still deciding whether it was ready to pierce the sky above. After a few days of mostly avoiding me because he was embarrassed, we'd discovered that Sol's sickness was actually more bearable when he was near me, so we'd taken to sleeping together under the stars each night so he could get some rest, at least. We'd even brought one of the small mattresses up and made a bed right on the deck.

He pulled my body into his, pressing a soft kiss to my lips.

"Once we figure out the Path, we'll have a lifetime to do things like this," he promised, pulling me onto his chest.

The light blanket fell from my shoulders as I moved on top of him, deepening the kiss. His hands slid up my sides, greedy on my skin. I'd pretty much taken to nakedness lately, and nobody was really complaining. I slid my knee over his chest, straddling him and rubbing myself over his smooth, golden skin.

"My lion," I murmured, feeling his cock harden beneath me.

"My Qilin," he answered, his thumbs brushing over my nipples. I raised up just enough to guide his tip inside me, and I began to ride him. My hips circled slowly as I watched the horizon, feeling wanton and lazy.

Quiet footsteps drew my attention back to the deck, and I saw Toro at the railing. He met my eyes, and a flash of hunger zipped through me. I'd been claiming orgasms from my mates all week, but Toro and Jai had kept scarce. Jai wasn't surprising, but I was beginning to wonder why the fish was holding back.

Even now, when I could see his massive cock standing at attention in the growing light, he didn't move to join us.

"He wants an invitation," Sol whispered, brushing his finger over my clit to draw my attention back to him. "He acts rough, but he has manners."

I grinned. I could do that. Sliding my eyes back to Toro, I lifted my chin in a silent beckoning. He blinked and looked over his shoulder as if to make sure there wasn't someone else there.

"Yeah, you," I said, patting the seat next to the thin mattress where Sol and I were still lazily fucking. Toro made his way over and seated himself on the edge of the seat, still hesitant. I reached for him, sliding my hand around his neck and pulling him down for a kiss.

"Can I surprise you this time?" I whispered against his full lips. I felt them twist into a grin, and he nipped at my bottom lip in answer. With Toro on the seat and Sol and me on the deck, he was at the perfect height for me to get a mouthful of his cock. I pushed him back a little, running my hand down his smooth, dark skin. Muscle after muscle rippled beneath my fingers, and I gasped as Sol began to thrust harder into me.

My need grew, and I fisted Toro's cock, rubbing up and down as Sol worked my body. Toro groaned a curse, and his head fell back against the railing. I wasn't content with just a hand, though. Twisting my body far enough, I licked a solid line from the base of his cock to the tip.

"Fuck, girl," he breathed. "Are you sure?"

I didn't answer with words, letting my mouth do the talking as I plunged my lips down his shaft, sending his cock deep in my throat.

Sol cursed beneath me, and I grinned internally. I didn't know if he'd ever been with Toro, but he certainly appreciated watching. I poured my attention into sucking Toro while Sol kept a steady rhythm beneath me. His hands drifted back to my nipples, rolling and pinching.

I felt Toro swell in my mouth, to the point where I nearly choked on his width.

"Carlyle, I-" he gasped, trying to pull away. I dug my fingernails into his thighs, though, locking him in place. He shouted his release a few seconds later, and I swallowed down every bit of his cum. His legs grew limp under my hands as he struggled to catch his breath, and I swirled my tongue around his tip before pulling away.

"Breakfast of champions," I said, laughing, and he smirked, stretching back against the cushion in a satisfied pose.

Sol took the opportunity to up his game then, gripping my hips and thrusting into me at a punishing speed. My eyes slid closed, putting my focus on the rotation of my hips as I bounced, chasing my own release now. A hot mouth found my breasts, and I clutched at Toro's shoulders as he nipped and sucked my nipples.

Sol pressed a finger to my clit, rubbing furious circles to push me over the edge. Moaning his name, I reveled in the sensation as he continued to fuck me hard, drawing out my release as he found his.

I collapsed against Toro, and he gathered me close. I pulled him down onto the mattress as I slipped off of Sol with a groan. They snuggled in next to me, and I cupped both of their faces in my hands.

"Perfection," I sighed, turning my eyes to the brilliant colors of the sunrise beyond. For once, Toro didn't have anything smart-ass to say, and they both murmured their agreement as their eyes started to slide closed again. They wanted to sleep, but I was energized.

I wondered if there would be any side-trips today. At first, Jai had decided Dair should pop up into various locations around the country, with one of us in tow each time, to throw off any suspicions over what we'd done. The trips carried some risk, of course, but they also gave us the opportunity to stock up on fresh food and listen for any rumors of our long list of enemies.

He'd actually let me go on one trip with Killian, and I was anxiously awaiting another. Jai was calling them bucket list trips, and I had so many places I wanted to see. Sure, I was also anxious to see Haret, but I didn't really know much about it. I'd started brainstorming bucket list trips to take each of my guys on, even though I knew it was unlikely we'd get that much time.

After hearing about all the trouble Killian and I had gotten up to, though, Jack had started calling them sexcapades, and he was eager for his own. Grinning to myself, I admitted Jack's term was probably more appropriate.

Sliding out from between Sol and Toro, I padded to the shaded seating area. Jai was up, of course, already setting out fresh pancakes and a bowl of fruit for everyone when they woke.

Jai was the only one I still felt a little awkward being naked around, and it was more because of his reaction than my discomfort. As I'd expected, he handed me a silk dressing robe Dair had picked out for me, in soft yellow. It had kimono-style sleeves, though, and it always got in my way. I slid it on and pressed a kiss to his cheek before he could angle away.

Leaving the robe untied, I kneeled on the cushioned bench, staring down at the water. It was already warm, and the sun was barely up.

"It's supposed to be almost winter," I noted.

"This is winter, this far south," Jai pointed out, settling next to me. I resisted leaning into him. I knew he'd come to me when he was ready. I was trying to be patient. Just then, the wind picked up and blew away one of the cloth napkins Jai had set out. I reached to catch it, but it fluttered beyond my grasp.

I lost my balance, tumbling into Jai's lap just as my robe flew up, too. I tried not to smirk as my naked ass landed right in his lap. I couldn't have planned it better myself. His hands gripped me tightly to keep me from falling off the bench, and his breath hissed in as his fingers brushed along my new tattoo.

"I still can't believe Killian allowed this," Jai growled.

"Killian is not my boss. I wanted it."

"*I'm* your boss," he continued, his voice rough. I noticed he hadn't pushed me away yet. "I should never have let him take you off the boat."

"Does this mean I don't get any more bucket list trips?" I teased. Jai had told me from the first night I'd met him that I wasn't a prisoner. Now, he couldn't really stop me from siphoning away if I wanted to. I stayed because I respected him.

"It means the next one is mine," he said, his palm smoothing up the tiny stars and moon I'd had inked along my spine. I shuddered as the magical ink flared to life. It changed color like a mood ring, glowing when I was turned on - I was sure it was like a lighthouse beacon about now.

"The next trip?" I whispered, afraid to move in case he stopped touching me.

"The next *tattoo*," Jai said, leaning to kiss along my spine, his tongue tracing each of the tiny symbols. A low moan escaped my lips, and his fingers crept all the way up to the base of my neck. He squeezed, drawing me up straight.

Jai slid the yellow robe off my shoulders completely, and my bare skin connected with his soft, warm t-shirt, then his hard muscles as he drew me against his chest. "I don't want anyone outside our team to touch you," he growled in my ear. "Not even a tattoo artist."

My breath stuttered as his jealousy washed over me, the wave of emotion numbing my neck. His other hand gripped my hip, his long fingers stretching down and down, so close to where my body really wanted them.

"Sorry, boss," I whispered, and his hands wrenched me even closer, the lower one clamping over my lower belly and the other caressing the hollow at the base of my throat.

"You will be," he hissed, though my addled brain heard it as more of a purr. "If it ever happens again."

"This isn't a deterrent," I said, my voice rough with my sudden need for him. When was he going to really let me in?

"What is it, then?" he said, his lips brushing my ear.

"A promise," I answered, going even more boneless against him until he was supporting most of my weight with his hand at my throat. I swallowed, relishing the pinch of his fingers against my skin, and his breath stuttered.

An inch at a time, he drew his hand back from my neck, his fingers gliding across my collarbone until they trailed down my spine again.

"When the sun gets too hot for you later, come find me," he murmured in my ear, and I felt the icy spike of his power against my skin. Holy fuck, it felt good. My skin pebbled with the chill, while the rest of me revved like a furnace.

Risking it, I twisted in his grip, coming face to face with my vampire.

"Fuck, Jai. When will you let this happen?" I pleaded,

my mouth nuzzling his.

He pulled back and stared down into my eyes, silent and unyielding. Eventually, quiet shuffling behind me brought me back to the reality of a crowded boat and the realization that we had an audience.

Sighing, I looked over my shoulder to see Killian and Sol exchanging charged glances. Jai drew the robe over me again and slid out from under me, disappearing into the kitchen.

"He's maddening," I said, staring out over the water. Sol chuckled, coming to sit next to me and filling his plate.

"He's Jai," he said, shrugging.

"He wants Dair and me to go in early today," Killian said, grabbing a plate, too. "We're supposed to scout for some intel on the Council and their progress with the Path."

Dair strode in at that moment, looking fresh enough to have stepped away from a photo shoot. I smiled as I watched him pour a glass of juice.

"Do you want anything while we're out?" Dair asked me, dropping a kiss on top of my head.

"Everything I want is on this boat," I said, trying not to pout that I wasn't invited again.

Jack wheeled in the air above us then, dropping lower and shifting to land on the deck. His hair was as wind-blown as if he'd been flying in his human form.

"Have you been out all night, dragon?" Dair asked.

Jack's excited grin pulled our attention, though. "I found an island. It looks abandoned, but there are some old buildings on it. It's not far - that way." He pointed in the direction of the rising sun.

"We'll check it out, then," Jai said, returning with more

pancakes. "If it's truly abandoned, it might serve as a better shelter for Kana's kids."

I bounced in my seat. "I want to see her!" Jai grinned at that, nodding.

"As do I. It's still too dangerous, though," he warned. I deflated, although I knew he was right. Every one of our former contacts and safe houses were a risk now. We'd been keeping tabs on Kana, and we knew she was safe. I still missed her like crazy, though.

"Ready, fae?" Dair asked, and Killian nodded. They were gone before I could get around the table to kiss them goodbye, and now I was pouting even more.

"It's okay, shortcake," Sol whispered in my ear. "The sooner they leave, the sooner they get back. Besides, I'm pretty interested in solid land - let's check out this island."

CHAPTER THIRTY-FOUR

CARLYLE

It took a little planning, but soon enough Jack and I were flying toward the mystery island, with Toro swimming along below us.

Once I saw the island, I could siphon Sol and Jai there, but someone also had to stay with the yacht to make sure it didn't move. Dair could miss the siphon and end up in the middle of the water. Entertaining, maybe. But dangerous.

I swooped below Jack, playing in the air. Damn, I loved flying, almost more than sugar.

It was tough, though. My muscles weren't nearly as strong as they needed to be, and I was exhausted when I finally saw the island ahead. Jack descended and landed on a strip of white-sand beach, and I tumbled into a shift after him. I'd gotten pretty good at shifting on call, but I was nowhere near graceful.

I also hadn't mastered the clothing thing, so I was naked again. He'd better be right about the deserted island part.

"There's some kind of estate in that direction," Jack said, as Toro shifted and climbed out of the water. "I flew all over, though, and I didn't see any people."

"Maybe it's just a seasonal house," I suggested.

He shrugged. "It's possible, but the grounds were pretty overgrown. Here, climb on my back," he offered to us. "No funny stuff," he warned before shifting.

Toro snickered and pinched my ass. "Nothing funny about this body."

"Shut up, or he'll drop us in the ocean."

"Still don't see the problem," he said with a grin as we both climbed onto Jack's back. He rose gently into the air, flying low over the island. I saw what he meant. It looked like nobody had been here in years. The house was enormous, though. More than enough room for the kids we'd rescued from Underbelly.

"We could even bring more kids here," I said to Toro, growing excited. "We could make this into a little safe haven until we figure out the Path." I didn't think they'd all want to go to Haret, either, although I hadn't told the guys that. Most of the kids were young enough that they would have never been to Haret. If I hadn't met my guys, I wouldn't want to leave Earth at all.

Toro nodded absently, something in his eyes I didn't quite recognize. He hadn't been with us when we'd rescued the kids, but he'd been in captivity before. I reached over and squeezed his hand.

Jack landed in the weedy driveway before the house, and we slid off his back. He shifted back and crept to a window, peering in. "This place is definitely abandoned."

"Let me siphon back and get Jai, then," I said. "You two stay out of trouble."

They barely acknowledged me leaving, already caught up in exploring. I snickered, really hoping they were right. If someone was inside, a naked man looking in their window was going to be an issue. They both had animal instincts, though - they would hear or smell someone coming.

I popped back onto the yacht without any trouble and described the whole thing to Jai and Sol.

"Shit, I wish I could go, but you need to check it out, boss. I'll stay with the boat," Sol offered.

Jai looked regretful, but he still nodded. He handed me my robe again, and I rolled my eyes. I put it on, though.

"We won't be long," I promised, bending down to give Sol a quick kiss. I was kissing one of my men goodbye today, damn it.

Jai tucked his fingers in mine, and I pulled him into the siphon. Fuck, I loved magic. We landed back in front of the house, and Jai tugged me along. I could sense his excitement, which meant he'd been worried, too.

"This is good, isn't it?" I asked as we entered the house, following the voices to Jack and Toro.

"It's very good," Jai said, pausing to turn and cup my face. He leaned in and graced me with an easy kiss, heating me straight through.

Throughout the morning, I was flying high emotionally as we explored. Jack returned to the boat for a while to let

Sol see the island, and we were all excited when Jai's internet research revealed the owner of the island had gone bankrupt several years before. The island itself seemed all but forgotten in a sea of lawsuits and bank paperwork. If we ever got out from the searching eyes of the Council, Jai claimed he could fix it all so the place was forgotten completely.

"The guy's last name was Mulligan?" I asked, reading over Jai's shoulder, once the five of us were all back on the boat. He nodded, tapping away. "That's so perfect."

"Why?" Jack asked.

"Haven't you heard of taking a Mulligan?" I looked around at them, getting only blank stares. "It's a saying. It means a do-over, like when you had bad luck and want to try again."

"Hell yes, that's perfect," Jack crowed, giving me a high five.

A popping noise sounded on the deck as Dair and Killian returned, and I jumped up to tell them the good news. The words died on my lips, though, as I saw their faces.

"What?" Jai snapped.

"The Enforcer," Killian said. "It's loose and on the rampage - there are dozens of bodies piling up."

I gasped, my knees going weak. This was my fault. All those deaths.

"They're nearly all Haretians. Circus people," Dair added. His words did nothing for my stomach, though. These were the people I'd just been so excited about helping, for fuck's sake.

"We have to do something," I whispered, sagging into the nearest person. Jack held me tightly against his chest.

"We will," he assured me.

"And stop thinking this is on you," Jai bit out, whirling on me. "This is the Ringmaster's work, pure and simple. He forced you to open the Portal. He set the beast free. He is the one responsible - *not* you!"

His icy power spiked toward me, and I nodded, trembling.

"I still need to fix this," I said, hating the obvious fear in my voice.

"We will, honey," Jack murmured in my ear. "But we need a plan first."

"It's not hard," I snapped, as fear and shame started to give way to rage. "Dair and I siphon everyone in, we kick ass, then rescue all the circus people who want out!"

Jai immediately started listing problems, complications, and caveats, but I tuned him out. Instead, I twisted in Jack's arms and stared up at him.

"How many people would be loyal to him?" I asked.

He glared. "Very few, and most of those out of fear."

"And what type of magic are we talking about?"

"The Ringmaster kept mostly shifters and mages for his shows. A few fae, but they're harder to tame. Security was usually humans with guns and a handful of vampires or larger shifters."

I huffed. "So, anything goes. We need to find a few mages who can siphon, first," I said, ignoring Jai's continued discussion behind my back. "That way, we can start getting people out of there and to the island."

"Honey, that island isn't exactly habitable," Jack reminded me.

"They've been living in fucking *cages*," I cried, banging my fists on the table. The others stopped talking and looked at me.

"Carlyle, I know. We're making a plan now," Jai said, his voice softer. "Toro, find me a place on that island to anchor the boat. Jack, go do the medieval dragon thing and steal some livestock. Then, we'll start working on how to get people out."

"How are the humans explaining the Enforcer?" Sol asked, as Jack took to the sky and Toro splashed into the water. Jai headed in to start the engine, and I saw Sol go a little green as the yacht began to turn in the direction of the island. He hurried away, clutching his stomach.

Killian shook his head, answering the question for the rest of us. "As far as I could tell from the news reports, someone is glamoring the beast. They've blamed some of the attacks on wild animals. I think the rest is being covered up by the circus."

"Any signs of Jantzen or Aleron? Or the Council?" I asked, and Dair sighed.

"Nothing outright. I expect the Council is doing what we are - waiting to see if the other will show up."

I took a steadying breath and followed the others down into the cabins, where we spent the ride getting dressed and portioning out the few weapons Killian had gotten from the marina. When we reached the island, Toro directed Jai to a secluded cove, away from sight and weather. Once on land, Sol recovered quickly, and he helped fell a few trees for a makeshift animal pen. Jack swooped down, a cow in either claw, dropped them, and made another round.

None of it was perfect, but at least we had a place for any refugees we might pick up.

Now, it was time to fight.

In my heart, I still believed this was my fault. I didn't care what the others thought. This was my mess to clean up, and I'd do whatever it took.

Taking turns, Dair and I siphoned everyone back to the mainland, just at the swampy edge of the circus grounds. I fought to keep my nerves down - the last time I'd been here, I'd been so weak. I'd been unable to maintain my shift, drained by iron, and emotionally unstable enough to kill a woman. Even if she probably deserved it.

"You're stronger than ever now," Jai whispered in my ear as we made our way silently to the clearing.

I nodded, believing him. I had good control over my shift now. I was so stocked with magic that I probably couldn't hold any more. And I'd decided having emotions was a strength, not a weakness.

We'd just have to see if all that was enough.

Jai held up a fisted hand, and everyone stopped short. We ducked behind trees, stretching our senses into the clearing. I began to make out the moans and muffled crying of individuals, plus the snorting and heavy footsteps of the Enforcer. My body recoiled, remembering his noises much too clearly.

There was an odd crackle of fire, too, and as soon as I dared lean around a tree enough to see, I wished I hadn't.

A bonfire had been built in the center of the clearing, with a sort of chandelier strung above it. Ropes draped down from the chandelier, ending at the waists of a dozen or so circus people. The flames stretched upward, licking at the ropes. The ropes were different lengths - some taut and high, but others looping down, too close to the fire.

One caught fire as I watched, and the young man attached to it began to pace. He glanced over his shoulder at the Enforcer, who had circled around to the opposite side of the fire. As soon as the rope burned through, the man bolted.

My heart dropped as he sprinted from the clearing. I clapped a hand over my mouth to avoid calling out as the Enforcer charged after him. He was caught within seconds, and I doubled over, smashing my palms against my ears to drown out the screams and gnashing of teeth in flesh.

I regretted every shred of a second when I'd respected the Ringmaster's intelligence.

This was unbearable.

This had to be stopped.

I didn't even realize I'd stepped away from my tree until a rough hand yanked me backward, and an unfamiliar palm flattened over my mouth.

"Stupid girl," a voice hissed, as I struggled against my captor. "He'll sleep a few hours now unless you interrupt his feedin'." The accent caught my attention. Turin.

I was dragged back into the darkness of the swamp, and I yelled out to Jai in my mind. He gathered the team, and they slunk after me, abandoning the macabre scene in the clearing.

Turin led us deep into the swamp, soaking our legs up to the knees as we walked. I didn't know why we were trusting him, but Jai's look told me to keep quiet. The fae must have given him some kind of intel. Finally, I caught the shimmer of glamor, and Turin guided us into a hidden, one-room cabin.

Once everyone had crowded in and shut the door, Killian turned on his uncle.

"There better be a good fuckin' reason for this," he

snarled.

"Your Qilin mate made me a deal," Turin said with a grim smile. My heart dropped. I'd forgotten all about his deal in the excitement of rescuing my guys and then the bliss of the yacht. "She's no good ta me dead."

"Carlyle," Killian said, his voice so calm it scared the shit out of me. "Wha' did you do?"

"Ah," I stammered. Behind me, Jai cursed, and I guessed he'd already skimmed the info from my mind.

"Goddamn it," Killian cried, banging his fist against the wall. The cabin shook.

"Now, look here, Turin. I need to rescue those people," I began. "None of this is their fault."

"This is war, Qilin. There are casualties. I don't like innocents being slaughtered, either, I assure you. However, if you are eaten by that beast, none of us will survive. Or haven't your men told ya?"

"I know Haret is dying," I said, looking at the floor. "I know the Path has to be opened - not just the Portal. But I won't back down. Those people don't deserve to die."

"They'll die if the Path is na' opened," Turin cried, losing patience. I folded my arms over my chest. This was not a negotiation, no matter what the rules of fae deals said.

I noticed Killian had grown quiet in the corner. As I glanced at him, though, I heard Jai in my mind.

Kills says the deal must be kept. Turin's magic will force you back to the Council, but not us.

I resisted shaking my head - I couldn't afford to tip off the fae. But that wasn't going to work, and I told Jai as much. I wasn't leaving them here to deal with the monster bull.

There is one other way, Jai continued, and I could tell he didn't want to tell me. The fact that he carried on and told me showed just how much he'd come to care for me and respect my abilities - my role not just to fight back, but to decide for myself. To rule.

The bargain does not transfer between worlds, he said, gazing into my eyes. My heart stuttered, and I knew this was the plan. This would work.

We'd try to kill the Enforcer first, of course. But if it didn't happen, I'd draw the beast straight back to Haret.

The circus would be safe, and my bargain would be broken. I'd just have to deal with the fallout there.

CHAPTER THIRTY-FIVE

CARLYLE

Without waiting to see what else Turin had to say, or any sort of warning to my guys, I threw myself into a siphon.

Hopefully, Jai would make them understand.

I landed back behind the same tree. As Turin had predicted, the great red-skinned bull had slumped against a wide tree and appeared to be sleeping off his meal.

The Haretians still tied to their ropes were a mess, though. Some were actively trying to get their ropes close enough to burn through, while others were stretching them to the limit, keeping the line as high as possible. A few had simply collapsed into hopelessness.

One of the girls who was working on getting her rope to burn was facing in my direction. I decided she might be a good first bet. I stepped just past the edge of my tree and waited for her to notice me, then I placed a finger over my lips to indicate silence. She nodded.

I crept toward her, keeping a keen eye on the sleeping monster.

"Don't run," I whispered as soon as I was close enough. "That's what sets him off, and he's faster than any of us."

She narrowed her eyes. "Not if I can get out of these fucking ropes, he's not. Cheetah shifter."

I smiled - I'd picked a good one. I examined the ropes. Of course, they were fucking iron-laced. "Can you help me get some of them out? Or are you gonna go all every-man-for-himself?" I asked her.

"I can't carry anyone. I'm too small for that. But I can make it back to camp and find help."

I considered. That would have to do. "Can you bring me a mage who can siphon? We have a safe place ready. No more circus."

She blinked at me like this was more than she could believe. "Who are you?" she asked, suspicion edging into her voice.

"Look, I don't expect you to trust me, because the Ringmaster probably beats that out of everyone. It's your call if you come back. But I've rescued people from this place before, and from other camps. I'm going to have to face that thing eventually, and I'd rather have as many innocents out of the way as possible."

Her eyes widened then. "You're the Qilin - the light one."

I nodded, grinning. "And I'll help as much as I can. But you can't do anything stupid." I was pleased that she'd actually heard of me - that meant word was getting out that there was hope.

People fought harder when they had hope, and this was going to be fucking hard.

I called a tiny amount of Jack's fire magic to my palm and burned through her rope. She shrugged off the remaining pieces and shook out her muscles. I watched, holding my breath, as she shifted into a small, sinewy cheetah. Slinking toward the tree line, she swung her head around to nod at me, just before she slipped into the shadows and vanished. The Enforcer was still sleeping, and I breathed a sigh of relief.

I prayed she'd come through, but at least I knew the plan was working. Now, I just had to do the same with the others, and fast. The person next to cheetah girl had been watching us, although he was too far to hear our conversation. He made me nervous, though. He looked like a runner.

I was in the middle of giving him the same spiel when I heard the pop of a mage siphoning in. My heart both leaped and fell when I saw it was Dair. Of course, I hadn't expected my guys to stay away for long, but I hated having any of them near this kind of danger.

"I'll get the smallest ones out," he whispered, creeping toward me. He indicated one of the crying ones on the ground nearby.

"Thank you," I said, feeling tears prick behind my eyes. This was so not the time, but damn it, I loved this man.

He used a spell I didn't know to unravel the rope, then siphoned away with the young girl in his arms.

"Are you gonna run or can you trust me?" I asked, turning back to the guy before me.

"I don't trust anyone but me," he growled. I sighed - I'd been on that train before, too.

"Just don't wake the thing up," I said. "Make it past the clearing before you run."

I burned his ropes before he could respond, ducking away to the next person before I could see what his chances were. My heart was pounding anyway - I didn't need to see if this dude got eaten. Dair returned and stole another one, and for a few minutes, it looked like we might pull this off.

We were only halfway around the circle when the beast began stirring. Warning the next couple of people not to run, I rushed through getting their ropes off. Of course, one of the girls didn't listen, and I gritted through the screams when the Enforcer caught her. The only positive was that her stupidity got everyone else to keep the fuck still.

Dair popped in right next to me, and I snatched him close, my arms wrapping around his chest as I planted my feet. He didn't move a muscle, though.

"Maybe it will sleep again," I whispered, my face buried in his black button-up.

"Sorry, Cariño. He didn't even eat that one," Dair said, his voice barely a breath. "Do *not* sacrifice yourself," he added, fiercer than I'd ever seen him. I tilted my head back slowly, finding his navy eyes pleading and panicked.

"I have no plans to die tonight, mage. Did Jai tell you the backup plan?" I asked hurriedly. I could hear the monster snuffling around on the other side of the fire. No doubt it could smell me, which was gross.

He nodded briefly, not looking pleased. "We have no clue where that Portal might open. You could be jumping into anything, Cariño."

"What choice do I have?" I snapped. He didn't get a chance to answer, though, because a roar sounded just behind us. Forcing my muscles to be as slow as possible, I turned and leaned my head back, back, back, until I was staring straight up at the tower of beast. It huffed out a rancid breath, and I forced down a gag. I might never eat meat again.

Behind the Enforcer, I could see people beginning to creep away, getting the hell out of the clearing. I glimpsed my guys, too. All of them had fucking returned, hiding in the trees for the right moment. Goddamn it, I hoped none of them would play hero, either. I shot a mental warning to Jai, asking him to spread it around.

None of us were dying tonight.

The Enforcer pawed at the ground, creating a rippling sort of earthquake. I stumbled, knocking back into Dair. Shit - I'd forgotten about his earth and fire magic. He raised his pronged spear in a huge fist and bellowed at me. Despite the extremely bull-like look he had going down below, there was an oddly human shape to his torso.

"Dair, get the fuck out of here," I said between gritted teeth. I lowered my head and called forth my shift. There hadn't been any fooling the monster with my girl-body last time - might as well use my Qilin strength.

I snapped open my dragon wings, and a few gasps came from the remaining captives. The Enforcer swung his ugly head around, and I whinnied to get his attention back. I beat my wings a few times, fanning the smoke from the fire toward him. He snarled and stepped forward.

I backed up a step, getting pissed when my horsey ass bumped into my dumbass mage.

Jai, I yelled in my mind. *Order them all out of here!*

Through the billowing smoke, I saw my guys finally leading the rest of the captives into the trees. I even glimpsed cheetah girl with a tall, slim boy in tow - hopefully the mage I'd requested. At least that part of the plan was working.

Just then, Dair decided to become my least favorite person. He siphoned straight between me and the fire-skinned minotaur, brandishing his magic like a golden force field. The Enforcer roared, and my heart nearly stopped as he reared back and rammed his spear straight at Dair.

I leaped in and kicked the weapon out of the way, but Dair was already right back in the fight. He was throwing spells faster than I could count them, but nothing seemed to be working. The yellow magic bounced off his cracked, leathery hide like he was impervious.

Jumping into the air, I flew at his neck, intent on introducing my horn to his pulsing jugular. He swerved and ducked, though, his giant arm smacking into Dair as he went. My mage went flying, crashing into a nearby tree and slumping to the ground. *No* - I screamed out a whinny and dodged to go after him, but the Enforcer blocked me, wrenching at one of my wings.

I tumbled out of flight and hit the ground so hard I couldn't breathe. I scrabbled to stand, wincing as my wing failed to straighten properly. A flash of darkness caught my eye, though, as Jai collected Dair's unmoving form. I horn-swiped at the Enforcer again to make sure he didn't turn and see Jai.

Breathing, my vampire yelled before disappearing again.

Thank fuck. The tension around my lungs loosened

just a bit. I decided it was about backup plan time - this thing was too strong for us. It must have a weakness, but fuck if I could figure it out. I needed to end this shit before one of my other guys got brave.

The Enforcer advanced a few more steps, and I backed up on instinct. Then I did it again because at least this way I was putting more distance between the fight and my guys, as long as they stayed put.

I charged toward him once more, lowering my horn like a battering ram. He roared and met me halfway, lunging into the blow and striking my side at the last second. I felt his leathery skin slide against my horn, but it didn't catch. Then I was tumbling, sprawling onto my back in a way a horse definitely should not move.

My spine felt like it was broken, but I forced myself up, corralling the pain the way I used to cordon off emotions. I would heal - I just needed time. I was pretty sure he wasn't supposed to kill me on purpose, anyway. I just needed to get through the fight, take him out if I could.

Force him back to Haret if I couldn't.

Come at me, bitch, I projected, wondering if I could get in his mind. There was no answer, though.

The Enforcer picked his spear up and stepped forward again, crowding me. With a start, I realized I was being herded toward the Portal. That was supposed to be *my* plan. Why did he want me there? Suspicion flooded my mind, but I still didn't have a better idea. Buying time, I sidestepped and pranced closer to the fire. I could handle the heat, right?

The Enforcer followed me, prodding my hide with his spear. Its tip thudded against my dragon and mer scales, and I grinned internally. My special sexy armor might not survive a direct hit, but it was tough. I lowered my horn again, striking at the spear like it was a sword fight. The clang vibrated my head, and a wave of dizziness threatened to suck me under. I'd taken a chunk out of the metal, though.

Stumbling back again, I shook my head to clear the fuzz.

The Enforcer matched my steps, driving me even closer to the Portal. Was it time? I was still afraid, but I realized most of that fear was centered on not knowing what was happening beyond the clearing. I didn't know if the circus people were safe. I hoped my men were. I had no idea if Turin was going to show up and intervene. It was also weird how the-

"That's it, girl!" a familiar fucking voice rang out, like I'd just summoned the devil himself. The Ringmaster strolled into the clearing, doing a fancy dance with his cane and top hat. "Brilliant bloody show!"

I longed to shout something filthy at him, but I couldn't risk shifting back. And there was no fucking way I was opening my mind enough to send him a message. Instead, I ducked my head and charged again at the bull.

This time, I struck a bit of hide, my horn tasting the monster's blood for the first time. It sang through my system like electricity - it was nothing like Jai's. The beast roared, swiping out at me. He clipped my hide right back, and I felt a bit of wetness slide down my flank.

"Yes, yes! Taste the blood! Grind the bones and make the bread!" Jantzen was half-screaming and half-singing at this point.

Fuck, he was a nutcase. I was suddenly pulsing with a blind hatred I was pretty sure wasn't mine - it scorched straight down my horn and seared my insides like fire, threatening to burn away everything good inside me. I tottered back, and my horn dipped into the fire. I screamed as the heat made everything worse, but as soon as the pain came, it left, taking the rage with me.

Cleansing fire?

Holy hell, I could barely keep up with everything that was happening.

Jantzen waltzed by - literally - and cackled as the Enforcer pressed me even closer to the Portal. I could feel my tail brushing against its iron frame. The shards of *kardia* beat like a thousand heartbeats behind me, their magic calling to mine.

Carlyle, now! Through the Portal!

I couldn't see my vampire, but I knew his voice. My heart stuttered as I obeyed without question. My back hoof pressed against the Portal, popping through like it was piercing skin. The sensation crawled all over my body, but I kept going. My other hoof went through, landing on solid ground. At least I wasn't falling into nothingness.

Now I was just half a horse's ass, I thought, nearly delirious in my desperation for this to work.

The Enforcer roared, and I swore the trees shook. The barest shimmer of glamor caught my eye, and although I couldn't be certain, I suspected six men were waiting nearby to follow me down the rabbit hole.

I couldn't decide if this moment was a victory or an epic defeat.

But I took another step, then another, backing slowly into the Portal.

My ass was cold, like winter was creeping up behind me. My front hooves followed until all that was left was my neck. I had to be sure the Enforcer was following me, though. What if it just meant to force me into Haret while it stayed here? Nope, that wasn't happening.

I called my fear to Jai, wherever he was, and suddenly, the Enforcer bucked and screamed. Whirling around, he began clawing at the air. I saw a gaping wound on his back, running with thick, blackish blood. I seized the moment and scrambled out of the Portal, ramming my horn deep into the wound.

The rage was like a blindfold this time, shutting out everything else until all I knew was an insane desire to kill.

The Enforcer stumbled forward and pulled himself free from my horn, wailing and staggering back. Toward the Portal.

Fucking yes!

I sprang forward, aiming my horn for his belly. He curled into himself, stepping back until he was in the place I'd just been - halfway through the Portal. Someone was screaming nonsense behind me, and I hoped it was Jantzen, but I didn't have time to check.

Gathering my strength, I shoved harder at the monster, shanking him again and again.

He was almost through when he lunged forward and locked his paws around my neck. My horn shoved into his stomach to the hilt, pinning me against his heaving body, and we tumbled backward, straight through the Portal.

CHAPTER THIRTY-SIX

JAI

Watching Carlyle tumble through the Portal with the Enforcer nearly ended my immortal fucking life.

My ears were filled with the ferocious roars of five other men experiencing the same, but my mind was as silent as the lakes I'd grown up around. Still, black water at midnight, not even a ripple to disturb the perfect round reflection of Haret's moons.

My body catapulted through the Portal with the others, but my world moved in slow motion.

My *aima* was in trouble, and I wasn't there.

KILLIAN

I was the last one through the Portal, but only because I stopped to blow my cover. I collected every last shred of my power and called every wind in the forest to hurl that motherfucking Ringmaster straight into the heart of his bonfire.

His screams were the lullaby that was going to put me to sleep every night for the rest of my goddamn life.

JACK

The second my body felt the cold night air of Haret, I shifted. My dragon wings strained toward the heartbeat of magic that wove through everything in my home, and I listened with the most ancient part of my soul. *Home, home*, my heart answered. I swiveled in mid-air and darted back to the glowing Portal, screaming down on it with my claws spread wide.

It shattered into a thousand pieces beneath my weight, locking the two worlds apart again.

The multi-colored shards of *kardia* clinked to the ground like hail on a window, each one losing its color as it hit.

The ground below the ruined Portal seethed with a rainbow of colors as the dirt sucked the magic down.

Home, my soul sang.

CARLYLE

Everything fucking hurt.

CHAPTER THIRTY-SEVEN

CARLYLE

"Well, I see you've undone all the goddamn work I did to keep you safe."

I struggled to open my eyes, but it was too dark to see anything anyways. I didn't recognize the voice, either. My muscles were sore, but I remembered them hurting a hell of a lot more before I'd-

Wait. What *had* I done?

"Drink this," the voice commanded, and something warm dribbled into my mouth. I balked at the metallic, salty taste. "Relax, Qilin. It's not mine."

"Your what?" I croaked, noticing my throat hurt most of all.

"It's my blood, not hers."

My heart surged as I recognized Jai's smooth voice. He was agitated. *What is it?* I asked him.

A cackle sounded, and I noticed it seemed to echo like we were inside a small room. My eyes finally slitted open a tiny amount. Jai's face was blurry above me, along with that of a sharp-boned, ancient-looking woman.

"Drink," she repeated, pressing the rim of a cup to my lips again. I grimaced, not liking how the blood coated my lips, sticky and too cold. She tipped the cup, though, and more of the liquid slid down my throat. It seemed to coat and heal as it went, and as strength drizzled back into my limbs, I struggled to sit and figure out my surroundings.

I was naked on a slab table in the center of a narrow stone room. Candles of all sizes flickered around me on the walls. I glimpsed other people gathered in the shadows. *My* people - I did a quick head count and found all six of my guys there. My body rose before it was ready, and the woman shoved me back down with considerable strength. My stomach rolled with nausea.

"Your mates are safe. The minotaur is locked away. My quiet evening at home is ruined."

Jai mumbled something to her, and she chuckled.

"What did you mean, I undid the work you did?" I asked, finally focusing on what she'd said a few minutes ago. The others gathered in close. I sank into their gorgeous warmth as their eager hands each reached for me, pressing into my bare skin.

The old woman surveyed us with a wry look, pursing her lips when Jai added his hand to my thigh. I folded my arms over my chest, feeling awkward in my nakedness. The last thing I remembered was fighting the Enforcer in my Qilin form, though, so it made sense.

"Your mother brought you to me when you were born. She begged me to bind your memory and your Qilin form."

I frowned. Yet another reason to dislike the nameless, faceless woman I'd never know. She'd made everything so much harder than it had to be, but why?

Before I could ask, the old woman turned and glared at Jai with suspicion. "I'm not sure how you broke through that wall, but here we are."

"Yes, Grand-mère. I broke it," he murmured, sounding a little embarrassed.

I would have fallen off the table if I hadn't been in the grips of six strong men. "Grand-mère?" I repeated, just now noting her long, straight hair and dark eyes. Ah, yeah. She looked like a much older version of Kana. Briefly, I wondered if the old woman knew what he'd done to break my mental barrier - fuck, I hoped she couldn't see all *that* in his memories.

Jai tossed me a guilty look that didn't make me feel any better. "Carlyle, meet my grandmother. Former Queen of Seori Sang."

"Former?" I said, feeling stupid because apparently all I could do now was parrot.

"There are troubles everywhere in Haret," she said with a grunt. "I do not relish the work to come."

"Why did her mother want her magic bound?" Killian asked, earning a glare from Jai's grandmother.

"To hide her. To keep her from becoming Queen."

"But why didn't my mother want me to be Queen?" I asked. Was my mother really one of the bad ones, then? It wouldn't be a stretch of my imagination - I'd spent most of my childhood hating parents who had given up a child to foster care, regardless of the reason.

"She should probably explain that herself. Unfortunately, she isn't able to do that." Jai's grandmother sighed, and I knew I'd have to drag the information from her. Some people were just like that - you had to ask for every fucking scrap.

"Where is she?" I asked when I couldn't stand the silence any longer. I tried to keep my voice from shaking, but it was no use. I'd gotten over wanting a mother a long, long time ago.

But I still wanted to *see* her - to ask her some questions. To know what I'd meant to her, if anything at all.

I didn't want her to be dead, right after I'd started thinking she might be alive.

"She's with all the other Qilin, girl. The ones the Enforcer caught."

"Caught?" I gritted my teeth. My first real meet-the-family moment - well, besides Turin - and I sounded like an idiot.

She nodded. "The Enforcer doesn't kill Qilin, though some say it's worse than death, what he does. The Qilin are in stasis, unable to move, use magic, feel. They can think, though. They can regret. They can go mad."

Her last words shot through me like an arrow.

Qilin feared loss of freedom more than death.

"How many?" I asked, my voice tiny in the dark stone room.

"Nobody knows," she said, her voice the gentlest it had been yet. Several beats of silence filled the candlelit room as the reality of the problem sunk in. I'd started my time with these guys thinking I was their only shot at opening the Path - that I was the last Qilin. The end of a hunted race.

Somehow, I'd never felt alone, even as I learned there was literally nobody else like me.

Then, I'd met Austin. Then Aleron. Now, I was learning I had a mother and there were countless other Qilin trapped and waiting somewhere, slowly going mad in their captivity.

"And all for what?" I whispered, my spirits drooping as I felt suffocated by the immensity of greed that had created this mess. Immediately, I was crushed into a fierce hug that smelled of sweet grass and sunshine.

"For everything, shortcake," Sol murmured in my ear, nuzzling against my neck. "We're doing this for everyone who can't."

I smiled into his tangle of blond waves. He'd misunderstood, but he'd refocused me. I didn't need to dwell on the evil that had caused this. I needed to home in on the good which was going to solve it. I lifted my face just enough to press a kiss to his lips. He wasted no time answering it, showering me in kisses that proved his worry.

Jai's grandmother cleared her throat delicately. "Well, I'm sorry I can't offer you more choices than this cold-ass stone table or the ground outside, but I can at least give you some privacy."

"Privacy?" I echoed, biting down on my lip. What was my actual problem?

She snickered. "I don't plan on watching, girl. But the mating magic must be sealed in Haret before we tackle anything else." She paused when I just blinked at her. Was she telling me we weren't mated here? She sighed. "Didn't these men tell you anything?"

"Ah, it's been a damn struggle," I answered, shooting

Jai a look. He smirked, but before he could use his old line about needing to learn at my own pace, his grandmother shooed him out of the room.

She beckoned to Toro, and he groaned. I wasn't sure how she knew which ones I hadn't mated with, either.

"Can we at least get some food?" Toro complained, following like a sad puppy.

"Of course. Who do you think taught that fool grandson of mine to cook?" She cackled again, and Toro perked up. He cast one final longing look at us, then slammed the door shut.

Leaving me naked and alone in a candlelit stone room with my four gorgeous mates.

Honestly, it could have been worse.

CHAPTER THIRTY-EIGHT

CARLYLE

I was spared any awkwardness by Jack - the dragon practically shoved Sol out of the way as he folded me into his arms, lifting me straight off the table and squeezing so tightly I wondered how I was still breathing. Covering my lips with his, he kissed me just as frantically. Sol pressed behind me and began stroking my spine, and I realized my guys were desperate for this act of claiming.

Just like when I'd been kidnapped, they needed to feel my touch to reassure themselves I was here - that I was still theirs.

Sol's arms slid down my thighs, lifting me until my legs were wrapped around Jack's waist, and I was pressed between them. Jack's kisses slowed to a more purposeful rhythm, and I moaned as I felt Sol's warm hands spreading me wider. A finger slid around my thigh and dipped inside my wetness, just as Jack lowered his mouth to my breast.

Killian appeared at my other side, leaning in to kiss me. He suddenly broke away and pressed his face into my neck, his cheek against Sol's shoulder. His hand slid down to my waist, holding me close.

"I can't believe we made it this far," he whispered. "I'll be claimin' you every night of my life, Savage, if ya let me."

My head fell back at his words, and my chest rattled with something that threatened to turn into a sob. I'd been putting on a brave face for so long. I just wanted tonight to be about love, not war.

The room was silent, and then the click-thud of Dair's boots sounded as he joined the group, hemming me in on my other side.

"Cariño," he murmured, dropping a kiss on my shoulder. "Tell us what you want."

I struggled to control my breathing - I didn't want to cry now. Not when I was pressed between four of the most perfect men I could have imagined.

Jack seemed to sense the moment getting too heavy, and he nipped at my breast, then dropped to his knees before me. Sol adjusted quickly to bear my weight, and suddenly, I was spread wide before Jack's devilish mouth. His tongue licked a thick line between my folds, and I forgot all about crying.

"I want it all," I said, the words coming out like a growl. "My rainbow of magic."

I moaned again as Jack tasted my pussy, switching from gentle licks and nibbles to a devouring assault and back again. I felt Sol's hands massaging my thighs where they held me, and my eyes rolled closed as a mouth descended on each of my breasts. Killian was rough and all teeth, while Dair was the fucking tease I expected.

With all of their hands and mouths on me, I came way too fast, but all it did was stoke the fire and get me ready for more.

I homed in on Jack - he needed to be first. My Qilin instincts were kicking in. I was going to mate with all of them, but my gut told me I needed to do it in the same order I'd done it before. I was making a fucking rainbow, after all.

I reached down and tugged at Jack's hair, pulling him up from between my legs. I planted a sloppy kiss on his mouth, loving that he was covered in my scent.

"On the table, dragon," I said, staring into his sky-blue eyes. He gave me a saucy grin and stripped off his clothes, shimmying up onto the table. Sol lifted me up, and I straddled Jack's thighs. My hand went straight for his cock, sliding up and down to make sure it was hard and ready for me.

"Take my magic - claim me before all Haret," Jack said, his eyes fierce. "Dragon and Qilin together again. The dawn of a new era."

My heart surged at his words, and all the candle flames in the room rose like a symphony of light. There was something more than I'd expected at work here - something truly magical.

Something Haretian.

Sol nudged me forward, his strong hands grasping my hips and lifting me above Jack. I didn't need any further encouragement, and I slid down Jack's thick cock to the hilt in one smooth motion. He hissed in pleasure and began to move instantly. His thighs were far enough down on the edge of the table that I might have been in danger of falling backward if it hadn't been for Sol still pressed against my back.

I leaned forward and placed my palms on Jack's chest, giving myself the leverage I needed to fuck my dragon right. My body was ravenous, though, and I soon wanted more than one cock.

"Sol?" I asked, as his tongue traced the shell of my ear. "I want you next - now," I added on a gasp as Jack's fingers began to play with my clit.

My lion growled in my ear, his rumble vibrating deliciously through my chest. Killian slid in to hold me and steal a few kisses, while I heard the sound of clothing dropping to the floor behind me. Then Sol was back, nuzzling along my neck and down my spine.

"Try a bit of this, lion."

I turned heavy-lidded eyes on Dair, who was offering Sol a snuffed candle. The melted wax on top carried a sweet, musky scent and the sheen of oil.

Sol dipped his fingers into the oil, and I moaned as the liquid was spread across my hips. It was almost too hot at first, but it cooled quickly, leaving behind a silky moisture.

"Vampires always have these around," Dair said with a chuckle. "It's the best oil in Haret - perfect for *massage*."

Sol's slick fingers spread my ass wider, and I bounced harder on Jack's cock, my nails digging into his chest. His hands smoothed up my arms and cupped my cheeks, pulling me just close enough for a lingering kiss before Sol pushed a finger inside my asshole. Pausing my movements, I whimpered into Jack's mouth as Sol readied me.

The stone table was at the perfect blessed height, and I

reveled at the feeling of Sol's hard cock pressing against my ass. His palm spread the oil across my tattoo.

"I'm honored to be a star to your moon, shortcake," he murmured, and I grinned against Jack's lips.

"Cheesy," I said, gasping as he pushed his cock slowly inside of me.

"You love it," he answered, bottoming out and pulling me upright, tight against his chest.

"I fucking do," I agreed. My head fell back on his shoulder as Jack began to move again. Sol groaned, and I tried to manage my breathing for a whole new reason. My body was filled to the brim, balancing on a knife-edge of pleasure.

And I still wanted more.

"Dair," I growled. "I know you're shy around other swords, but I need you next."

He leaned a hip against the table, watching the three of us move. There was a hunger in his eyes, but it was only for me. Sol and Jack didn't exist for him, except to be useful in bringing me pleasure.

I reached a hand out to him, fisting a handful of his shirt and pulling him close. His mouth crashed into mine, and suddenly the dam of desperation broke in him, too. He stopped being calm and controlled and flipped to my demanding mage.

"You only have one hole left, Cariño. Do you want me to fill it?"

"Yes," I panted as Sol and Jack hit a punishing rhythm. "Please," I added.

He hopped up onto the table, towering above me. He stepped over Jack's chest and unbuckled his pants. I would have snickered at how he was managing to stay clothed around the other guys, but then his ready cock was prodding my lips. I licked away the bead of pre-cum, then opened wide. My hands clenched on his pants, and I pulled him deep. He wove his fingers into my hair, keeping me where he wanted me most, and his hips began to move.

I didn't have to ask Killian to join in - I felt his mouth on my breasts, nipping and licking. His fingers slid down to my clit and took over, pinpointing my pleasure and tossing me over the edge a second time.

My body shook with bliss as they filled me with their bodies, their love, and their magic. Dair pulled out of my mouth and bent to kiss me sweetly, his lips a tender contrast to everything else.

Jack shouted his release, and I felt a burst of garnet magic light up my heart. My skin rippled with shiny dragon scales before they settled into sheer armor over my hips and ribs.

Somehow, while I was lost in ecstasy, Jack and Killian had managed to switch places. I cried out as I sank down on Killian's wide cock, but he was slick with oil, and my body took him in like the greedy Qilin I knew I was.

He hit new places inside of me and stoked my inner fire to incineration levels.

Sol had begun to pant and shake behind me, and I knew he was close. I twisted my head around and kissed him hard, fisting Dair's cock in both hands.

"Fuck me, lion," I whispered against his lips. "Fuck me hard while I ride Killian's cock."

He groaned and shuddered. "Shortcake," he said, his eyes squeezing closed as his muscles tensed. He pumped deep in my ass a few more times, and I felt my eyes roll back in my head as he pinned my sensitive body against Killian's cock. He panted my name over and over as he thrust, and then he came with a roar, his arms wrapping around my body in the sexiest hug I'd ever gotten.

Warm orange magic spread through me like a summer afternoon, and I almost sank into laziness.

"Get the rest of your sugar, shortcake," he murmured, pulling gently out of me. I moaned at the loss, and my back felt suddenly cold.

Then Dair's hands were on my face. "Where's my good girl?" he murmured, his navy eyes boring into mine.

"I'm here," I whispered, caught like a mouse in a cat's gaze. He gathered my hair into one hand, tugging my head back.

"Do you want to cum, good girl?" he asked. I tried to nod, but his grip tightened on my hair.

"Yes," I breathed.

His eyes flicked to the side. "Jack, a little help?"

Jack seemed to know what Dair had in mind because he moved to my back with the candle in hand. I leaned into the sensation of the hot oil being massaged across my shoulders, slowly dripping down my spine.

Killian's pace had slowed as well. He was still moving inside me, but it was as lazy as Sol's summery scent. Like we had all the time in the world.

Jack's fingers found my asshole, and although I should have been spent and sore, my body welcomed him. Pleasure began to spread through me again, wrapping around my hips and sparking down my thighs.

Dair tugged at my hair again, his other hand sliding down my throat and gripping my neck from the back. He slid his cock between my lips and began to thrust deep in my throat. Sol leaned on the table, and he began to tug at my nipples, in time with Dair's movements. Killian did the same with my clit as he rocked inside of me.

"Good girls wait," Dair reminded me, his voice rough with desire. I moaned around the fullness of his cock. I couldn't possibly wait if the others kept up what they were doing. I tried so hard, though, knowing that the effort required to hold back my orgasm would make it that much stronger.

Finally, I felt Dair's cock swell and pulse in my mouth, and his hot cum slid across my tongue. I swallowed, and he bent to kiss me, all teeth and tongue and fierce yellow magic.

"Cum for me, Cariño," he ordered, and my body exploded in pleasure as his hands gripped my jaw, focusing my scattered attention on him alone. After a final, closed-mouth kiss that seemed to seal his work, he climbed off the table and leaned against the wall, arranging his clothes again.

He smirked at me, and I realized I must look like a used mess. I grinned, not caring a goddamn bit. I still had one more mate to claim.

Swinging a leg over Killian's chest, I surprised him by rotating on his cock, so he had a nice view of my ass.

"Fuck it like you're driving it," I said, throwing him a wicked grin over my shoulder. His golden eyes blazed with challenge, and he sat up, wrapping one tattooed arm around my waist and scooting forward just enough to touch his feet to the ground.

Sol stepped up, offering his chest for me to lean against, and Killian began to thrust deep and hard inside me.

I moaned as he sped up, going at a pace only a fae could manage. The joke I'd once made about him fucking like he drove was quickly becoming my favorite taunt.

"Mine," he growled, his hand sliding lower to cup the front of my pussy. He began to make frantic circles on my clit, and I grew dizzy with pleasure.

"No matter what," I gasped, just before spiraling out of control. My muscles trembled as my body soaked up the green magic he offered, and I was riding as high as the clouds when he finally came inside me.

Someone helped me lay back on the table, and Killian gathered me close, pressing a kiss to my forehead. I was too weak to even return it, boneless from so many orgasms I'd lost count.

"I think I like Haret," I murmured, as my eyes slid closed. Another warm body joined us on the table, and someone began to massage my calves, working out the cramps from our magical claiming session. I felt fingers begin to comb through my tangled hair, and I sighed.

"What more could a Qilin want?" I asked.

"How about some sugar?" Jai's voice reached me through my haze of sleepy bliss, and I popped open an eye to watch him saunter back in the room with a tray of food.

"And I have coffee," Toro added, bounding in right behind.

"Fuck, I love you guys," I said, grinning so hard. Sure, we had a metric fuck ton of evil to contend with, and a whole new world to explore and save, but if this was what a girl had to look forward to? So worth it.

LAUREL CHASE

WANT MORE?

Find Laurel and the Piece of Fae fans in the Facebook
reader group LOVERS OF HARET.
https://www.facebook.com/groups/676410892715276/

Join Laurel's newsletter for new release information, sales,
and special, sexy bonus content.
https://laurelchaseauthor.com/newsletter/

REVIEWS

Please consider leaving an honest review on your favorite
reading and retail sites.
Lots of readers depend on reviews and recommendations
to find their next read.

Love, Laurel

LaurelChaseAuthor.com

ACKNOWLEDGEMENTS

All the thanks to all the Lovers! I get so much motivation and inspiration from my readers, so you guys get top billing this time around – mwah!

Alisha, thanks for checking in with me when I felt too busy to chat. I need a shove sometimes! Beta girls, I appreciate the time it takes to leave comments. Helen, Jesika, Keri, Laura, Leanne, Heather, and Cecily: Your feedback keeps me working, laughing, and loving every bit.

I have a fantastic ARC Team - thank you so incredibly much for reading and reviewing so fast, and super thanks for being too sexy to pirate books.

To my busy editor, I work harder for you than anyone else, and I love it, too.

Christian Bentulan, your covers are simply gorgeous, and I'm lucky to stay on your schedule.

Finally, thank you to my wonderful husband and children, who let me escape to Haret a couple of times a week. Even Mama needs some time to play with her imaginary friends.

Stay sexy and sweet, Lovers! See you next book.

ABOUT THE AUTHOR

Laurel Chase lives in the state that boasts of fast horses,
fast cars, and fast women.
She writes steamy romance and lives in her head more and
more each day – hey, the scenery is great in there.
She never sleeps enough, and she drinks too much coffee,
but she'd never replace any of that with sensible stuff.

Find her hanging out on social media,
usually in the Lovers of Haret readers' group!

Made in United States
Orlando, FL
26 June 2022

19166422R00170